The

Medium

AN EMILY CHAMBERS SPIRIT MEDIUM NOVEL

C.J. ARCHER

Other books by C.J. Archer:

The Medium (Emily Chambers Spirit Medium #1)

Possession (Emily Chambers Spirit Medium #2)

Evermore (Emily Chambers Spirit Medium #3)

Her Secret Desire (Lord Hawkesbury's Players #1)

Scandal's Mistress (Lord Hawkesbury's Players #2)

To Tempt The Devil (Lord Hawkesbury's Players #3)

Honor Bound (The Witchblade Chronicles #1)

Kiss Of Ash (The Witchblade Chronicles #2)

Redemption

Surrender

The Mercenary's Price

FOR

Samantha and Declan

Words cannot express how much
I love you both.

CHAPTER 1

London, Spring 1880

Whoever said dead men don't tell lies had never met Barnaby Wiggam's ghost. The fat, bulbous-nosed spirit fading in and out beside me like a faulty gas lamp clearly thought he was dealing with a fool. I may only be seventeen but I'm not naïve. I know when someone is lying—being dead didn't alter the tell-tale signs. Mr. Wiggam didn't quite meet my eyes, or those of his widow and her guests—none of whom could see him anyway—and he fidgeted with his crisp white silk necktie as if it strangled him. It hadn't—he'd died of an apoplexy.

"Go on, young lady." He thrust his triple chins at me, making them wobble. "Tell her. I have no hidden fortune."

I swallowed and glanced at the little circle of women holding hands around the card table in Mrs. Wiggam's drawing room, their wide gazes locked on the Ouija board in the center as if Barnaby Wiggam stood there and not beside me. I too stood, behind my sister and opposite the Widow Wiggam who looked just as well-fed as her dead husband in her black crepe dress and mourning cap. However, where his face was covered with a network of angry red veins, hers was so white it glowed like a moon in the dimly lit room.

"Are you sure?" I asked him. If he knew I suspected him of lying, he didn't show it. Or perhaps he simply didn't care.

"Sure?" Mrs. Wiggam suddenly let go of her neighbor's hands. My sister, Celia, clicked her tongue and Mrs. Wiggam quickly took up the lady's hand again. It's not as if anyone needed to hold hands at all during our séances but my sister insisted upon it, along with having candles rather than lamps, a tambourine and an Ouija board even though she rarely used either. She liked things to be done in a way that added to the atmosphere and the enjoyment of the customers, as she put it. I'm not convinced anyone actually *enjoyed* our séances, but they were effective nevertheless and she was right—people expect certain theatrics from spirit mediums, so if we must put on a performance then so be it.

Celia had taken it one step further this time by wearing a large brass star-shaped amulet on a strap around her neck. The recent purchase was as unnecessary as the hand-holding but she thought it gave us authenticity amidst a city filled with fake mediums. I had to admit it looked wonderfully gothic.

"Sure about what?" Mrs. Wiggam asked again, leaning forward. Her large bosom rested on the damask tablecloth and rose and fell with her labored breathing. "What does he want you to say, Miss Chambers?"

I glanced at Mr. Wiggam's ghost. He crossed his arms and raised his fluffy white eyebrows as if daring me to repeat his lie. "He, er, he said..." Oh lord, if I repeated the lie then I would be contributing to his fate. He could not cross over to the Otherworld until he was at peace, and he would not be at peace until he let go of his anger towards his wife. Lying to her wasn't helping.

On the other hand, it was his choice.

"Emily," Celia said with the false sing-song voice she employed for our séances. "Emily, do tell us what Mr. Wiggam is communicating to you. Give his poor dear widow," she paused and smiled beatifically at Mrs. Wiggam, "some solace in her time of mourning."

"Mourning!" Barnaby Wiggam barked out a laugh that caused the edges of his fuzzy self to briefly sharpen into focus. For a moment he appeared almost human again. To me at least. "Tell that...that WOMAN who sits there pretending to be my demure wife that there is no fortune."

"He says there's no fortune," I repeated.

A series of gasps echoed around the small drawing room and more than one of the elegant ladies clicked her tongue. Mrs. Wiggam let go of both her neighbors' hands again. "Nonsense!" Her gaze flitted around the room. "Tell that lying, cheating, *scoundrel* of a husband that I know he amassed a fortune before his death." She placed her fists on the table and rose slowly to her considerable height, well above my own. She even dwarfed her ghostly husband. "Where is he? I want to tell him to his face." She reminded me of a great brown bear at the circus Mama had taken me to see as a little girl. The creature had expressed its displeasure at being chained to a bollard by taking a swipe at its handler with an enormous paw. I'd felt sorry for it. I wasn't yet sure if I felt the same emotion towards Mrs. Wiggam.

I must have glanced sideways at her husband because she turned on the spirit beside me even though she couldn't see it. He took a step back and fiddled with his necktie again.

"I *know* there's money somewhere." Her bosom heaved and her lips drew back, revealing crooked teeth. "I *deserve* that money for putting up with you, you wretched little man. Rest assured Barnaby *dearest*, I'll find every last penny of it."

A small, strangled sound escaped Mr. Wiggam's throat and his apparition shimmered. Fool. He was dead—she couldn't do anything to him now. Her four friends shrank from her too.

My sister did not. "Mrs. Wiggam, if you'll please return to your seat," Celia said in her conciliatory church-mouse voice. She ruined the effect by shooting a sharp glance at me. Mrs. Wiggam sat. She did not, however, resume handholding. Celia turned a gracious smile on her. "Now, Mrs. Wiggam, it's time to conclude today's session." My sister must have an internal clock ticking inside her. She always seemed to know when our half hour was over. "Everyone please close your eyes and repeat after me." They all duly closed their eyes, except Mrs. Wiggam who'd taken to glaring at me. As if it were my fault her husband was a liar!

"Return oh spirit from whence you came," Celia chanted.

"Return oh spirit from whence you came," the four guests repeated.

"Go in peace—."

"No!" Mrs. Wiggam slapped her palms down on the table. Everyone jumped, including me, and the tambourine rattled. "I do *not* want him to go in peace. I do *not* want him to go anywhere!" She crossed her arms beneath her bosom and gave me a satisfied sneer.

I'm not your husband! I wanted to shout at her. Why did everyone think I was the embodiment of their loved one? Or in this case, their despised one. I once had a gentleman kiss me when I summoned his deceased fiancée. It had been my first kiss, and hadn't been entirely unpleasant.

"Let him go," Celia said, voice pitching unusually high. She shook her head vigorously, dislodging a brown curl from beneath her hat. "He can't remain here. It's his time to go, to cross over."

"I don't want to cross over," Mr. Wiggam said.

"What?" I blurted out.

"Did he say something?" Celia asked me. I repeated what he'd said. "Good lord," she muttered so quietly I was probably the only one who heard her. Especially since Mrs. Wiggam had started laughing hysterically.

"He wants to stay?" The widow's grin turned smug. "Very well. It'll be just like old times—living with a corpse."

One of the guests snorted a laugh but I couldn't determine which of the ladies had done it. They all covered their mouths with their gloved hands, attempting to hide their snickers. They failed.

"Tell the old crone I'm glad I died," Barnaby Wiggam

said, straightening. "Being dead without her is a far better state than being alive with her."

"No, no this won't do," Celia said, thankfully saving me from repeating the spirit's words. She stood up and placed a hand on Mrs. Wiggam's arm. "Your husband *must* return. We summoned him at your behest to answer your question and now he needs to cross over into the Otherworld."

Actually, he probably wouldn't be crossing over. Not while there was so much lingering anger between himself and his wife. He needed to release the anger before he could go anywhere. Until then he was tied to this world and the Waiting Area. That's why some places remain haunted—their ghosts aren't willing to give up the negative emotion keeping them here. Although Celia knew that as well as I, she couldn't be aware of the extent of Barnaby Wiggam's sour mood. She certainly couldn't have known he deliberately lied to his wife about his fortune.

I sighed. As always, I would have to explain it to her later. *After* we returned the ghost to the Waiting Area. "You have to go back," I urged him. "You shouldn't be here. Tell your widow you're sorry, or that you forgive her or whatever and you can cross over and be at peace." At least that's what I assumed happened. Since I wasn't able to summon anyone from the Otherworld—only the Waiting Area—I couldn't know for sure what occurred in their final destination. For all I knew the Otherworld was like a political meeting. Endless and dull.

From what the spirits had told me, all ghosts ended up in the Waiting Area until they'd been assigned to a section in the Otherworld. Which section depended on how they'd behaved in life. However, none knew the fate awaiting them in their respective sections. It caused many of the ghosts I'd summoned an anxious wait.

"I'm not sorry." Barnaby Wiggam sat in an old leather armchair by the hearth and rubbed his knee as if it gave him pain although it couldn't possibly hurt now. He seemed so at home there, nestled between the enormous rounded arms and deeply cushioned high back, that I wondered if it had been his favorite chair. "I think I'll stay a little longer. I rather fancy haunting the old witch. It'll be a jolly time."

"Jolly!" I spluttered. I appealed to Celia but she simply shrugged. "But you can't do this!" I said to him. "It's...it's illegal!" Nothing like this had happened to us in a year and a half of conducting séances. All our spirits had duly answered the questions their loved ones posed then returned to the Waiting Area, content and ready to cross over. Then again, we'd never summoned anyone who clearly wasn't a loved one.

What had we done?

Mr. Wiggam picked up a journal from a nearby table and flipped open the pages.

A woman screamed, others gasped, and one fainted into the arms of her friend. Only Celia, Mrs. Wiggam and I remained calm. Celia was used to seeing objects move without being touched, and I of course could see the ghostly form holding the journal. I suspect Mrs. Wiggam was simply made of sterner stuff than her companions.

"The *Ladies Pictorial!* Utter trash." Mr. Wiggam threw the journal back onto the table where it collected a porcelain cat figurine and sent it clattering to the floor. The two ears and the tip of the tail broke off. He laughed. "I never liked that thing."

Mrs. Wiggam simply stepped around the pieces and flung open the heavy velvet drapes. Hazy light bathed the drawing room in sepia tones. London's days were not bright but I suspected the Wiggams' drawing room would always be dreary even if the sun dared show its face. The dark burgundy walls and squat, heavy furniture made the space feel small and crowded, particularly with all of us crammed into it. I took a deep breath but the air was smoky, close, and stuck in my throat.

"Let's have some refreshments, shall we?" Mrs. Wiggam said as if she didn't have a care in the world. She tugged the bell-pull then bent over the woman who'd fainted, now reclining in one of the chairs at the card table. She slapped her friend's cheeks then saw to it she was made comfortable with an extra cushion at her back.

I turned to Celia. She frowned at me. "Close your mouth, Emily, you are not a fish."

I duly shut my mouth. Then opened it again to speak. "What are we to do?" I whispered.

Celia huffed out a breath and looked thoughtful as she fingered the large amulet dangling from a strip of leather around her neck. She'd purchased it last Thursday from the peddler woman who sells bits and pieces door-to-door. Considering Celia was a stickler for maintaining the same format for our drawing room séances, I was surprised when she'd produced a new artifact. It was rather a magnificent piece though, made of heavy brass in the shape of a star with delicate filigree between the six points. Etched into the brass were swirls and strange, twisting patterns. It looked like an ancient tribal token I'd once seen in a museum. I could see why she'd accepted it although the fact it cost her nothing was probably a factor. Celia was not so careless with our meager income that she would squander it on trinkets.

"I wonder..." she said.

"Wonder what? Celia—?"

Celia's soft chanting interrupted me. With both hands touching the amulet, she repeated some words over and over in a strange, lyrical language I didn't recognize. Considering I only knew English and possessed a basic knowledge of French, that wasn't saying a great deal.

She finished her chant and let the amulet go. As she did so a blast of wind swept through the drawing room, rustling hair and skirts, dousing candles and flapping the journal's pages. A shadow coalesced above the table, a shapeless blob that pulsed and throbbed. It was like the mud that oozed on the riverbank at low tide, sucking and slurping, threatening to swallow small creatures and boots. But the shadow—I could think of no other word to describe the dark, floating mass—altered of its own volition.

No longer shapeless, it became a hand reaching out. Two or three of the guests screamed and scuttled to the far side of the drawing room. Beside me, my sister tensed and circled her arm around my shoulders, pulling me back. She said something under her breath but the loud thud of my heart deafened me to her words, but not to her fear. I could feel it all around me as I stared at the shadow, which was quickly changing shape again.

It became a foot then the head of a rat then a dog with snapping jaws and hungry eyes. A hound from hell, snarling and slavering and vicious. It stretched its neck toward me and before I could react, Celia jerked me back.

Too late.

The shadow creature's sharp teeth closed around my shoulder. I squeezed my eyes shut and braced myself. Nothing happened. Oh there was screaming coming from everyone else, including Celia, but I heard no tearing of flesh or clothing. I felt no pain, just a cool dampness against my cheek. I opened my eyes. The creature had turned back into a shapeless cloud. For a brief moment it hovered near the door and then with a whoosh it was gone.

A breathless moment passed. Two. Three.

"What was that?" I whispered in the ensuing hush.

Celia looked around at the white faces staring wide-eyed back at us, hoping we could give them answers. We couldn't.

She indicated the armchair. "Is he still here?" Her voice shook and she still gripped my shoulders.

"Still here," both Mr. Wiggam and I said together.

"Did you see that?" he said, staring at the door. He didn't look nearly as frightened as the others, but then what did a dead man have to fear? He went to the door and peered out into the hall. "I wonder what it was."

"It's gone now," I said. My words seemed to reassure the ladies who stood huddled in the corner of the room.

"The air in this city," Mrs. Wiggam said with a click of her tongue and a dismissive wave of her hand. "It gets worse and worse every year." She ushered the ladies to seats, plumped cushions and pooh-poohed any suggestions of a menacing spirit ruining her social event. "It was a trick of the light, that's all," she said. "The tense atmosphere in here has got to you all, stirred your imaginations."

"Stupid woman," Mr. Wiggam muttered. "She can't possibly believe that cloud was natural."

I didn't care what Mrs. Wiggam thought, as long as her guests accepted her explanation. Clearly some of them did, or perhaps they simply *wanted* to believe it and so willingly forgot what they'd seen only moments before. One or two seemed unconvinced and I hoped they would not gossip about it later. If word got out that we'd released something sinister during one of our séances, our business could flounder. Celia and I could ill afford such a disaster becoming public knowledge.

"Well," Celia said, peering down at the amulet hanging from its leather strip. "I thought it a harmless piece."

"Then why use it?" I hissed.

She gathered up the tambourine and Ouija board, packed them into her carpet bag and snapped the clasp shut. "The peddler who gave it to me said I was to say those words three times if I needed to solve something."

A maid entered carrying a large tray with teapot and cups. Two other maids followed her with more trays laden with cakes and sandwiches. Celia's face relaxed at the sight of the refreshments.

"What were the words?" I pressed her.

She waved a hand as she accepted a teacup with the other. Her hands shook so much the cup clattered in the saucer. "Oh, some gibberish. She didn't tell me what they meant, just that I should repeat them if I needed to fix something. Well I did need to fix something." She leaned closer to me and lowered her voice. "The spirit of Mr. Wiggam wouldn't leave."

I wasn't entirely convinced that the ongoing presence of Mr. Wiggam was what the woman had meant. Nor was I convinced that the words were gibberish. I looked at the door then at Mr. Wiggam. He stood with his back to the fireplace as if warming himself against the low flames—although he couldn't feel the cold—and stared at the door, a puzzled expression causing his wild brows to collide.

"The peddler was a mad old thing," Celia muttered around the rim of her teacup. "Completely mad." She sipped.

"At least it's gone, whatever it was, and no one seems affected by it."

No. No one at all.

***

"Tell me about the peddler woman," I asked Celia when we were almost home. We'd decided to walk from Mrs. Wiggam's Kensington house instead of taking the omnibus. It wasn't far and we would save on the fare as well as gain some exercise. Celia is all for exercising in the fresh air, although London's air couldn't be considered fresh by anyone's standards as Mrs. Wiggam had reassuringly pointed out to her guests. It stank of smoke and horse dung, made eyes sting and left skin feeling gritty. It was cool, however, and certainly invigorating as the chilly spring breeze nipped at our noses and ruffled the ribbons on our hats.

Celia sighed as if the task of recollection was a burden. "She looked like any other old crone. As wrinkled as unpressed linen, I do recall that. Gray hair, which she wore long and uncovered." She sniffed to indicate what she thought of that. "Oh and she had an East End accent. I'd never seen her before, she wasn't the usual Thursday peddler. I don't know her name, and I don't know anything else about her except that she was dressed all in black. Now stop fretting, Emily. We'll let Mr. and Mrs. Wiggam sort out their differences then return him to the Waiting Area tomorrow. There's nothing more we can do."

"How can they sort out their differences when she can't see him or speak to him?" A strong breeze whipped up the street, flattening our skirts and petticoats to our legs. We both slapped a hand to our hats to keep them from blowing away. We lived on Druids Way in Chelsea and it's always windier than everywhere else in London. It must have something to do with the length and orientation of the street as well as the height of the houses lining both sides of it. None of them were less than two levels and all showed signs of neglect. Much of Chelsea was still occupied by the reasonably prosperous, but our street seemed to have slipped into obscurity some years ago. Paint flaked off front doors and the brick facades were no longer their original red-brown but had turned almost black thanks to the soot permanently shrouding our city. All one had to do was turn the corner and see streets swept clean and houses tenderly kept but Druids Way was like a spinster past her marrying days—avoided by the fashionable set.

I hazarded a sideways glance at Celia and felt a pang of guilt for my unkind comparison. At thirty-three she was unlikely to find a husband. She seemed to have given up on the idea some years ago, preferring to dress in gowns that flattered neither her slim figure nor her lovely complexion. I'd tried many times to have her dress more appropriately for an unwed woman but she refused, saying she'd prefer to see *me* in the pretty gowns.

"We'll pay a call on Mrs. Wiggam tomorrow," Celia said, bowing her head into the wind. "Perhaps Mr. Wiggam will have tired of his wife and be willing to cross over by then. Will that satisfy you?"

"I suppose so." What else could we do? I couldn't simply let the matter drop. Not only had we failed to return Mr. Wiggam to the Waiting Area, we'd left him with a person who despised him. There was no handbook for spirit mediums when it came to summoning the dead, but I knew deep down that this situation wasn't acceptable. Celia and I had no right to rip souls out of the Waiting Area and reignite emotional wounds in this world. It had never been a problem in the past, so I'd never given it much thought. Besides which, the ghosts we summoned at our drawing room séances had always willingly returned to the Waiting Area afterwards, and they'd done so feeling content that their

11

loved ones could move on too.

Or so I liked to think. The Wiggams' situation had shaken me. Celia and I were fools to think we could control the deceased, or the living for that matter.

I also had the awful feeling we'd released something else in Mrs. Wiggam's drawing room by using that strange incantation. Something sinister. I only wish I knew what.

"Now, what shall we have for supper?" Celia asked.

I stopped with one foot on the stairs leading up to our front door and suppressed a small squeak of surprise. A man stood on the landing, leaning against the door, his arms crossed over his chest. He looked older than me but not by much, tall, with short dark hair and a face that was a little too square of jaw and sharp of cheek to be fashionable. It wasn't a beautiful face in the classical statue sense but it was certainly handsome.

The odd thing about him wasn't that we'd not noticed him earlier—we'd had our heads bent against the wind after all—but the way he was dressed. He wore black trousers, boots and a white shirt but nothing else. No hat, no necktie, jacket or vest and, scandalously, the top buttons of his shirt were undone so that his bare chest was partially visible.

I couldn't take my eyes off the skin there. It looked smooth and inexplicably warm considering the cool air, and—.

"There you are," he said. I dragged my gaze up to his face and was greeted by a pair of blue eyes that had an endlessness to their depths. As if that wasn't unsettling enough, his curious gaze slowly took in every inch of me, twice. To my utter horror, my face heated. He smiled at that, or I should say he half-smiled, which didn't help soothe my complexion in the least. "Your mouth is open," he said.

I shut it. Swallowed. "Uh, Celia?"

"Yes?" Celia dug through her reticule, searching for the front door key.

"You can't see him, can you?"

She glanced up, her hand still buried in her reticule, the

carpet bag at her feet. "See who?"

"That gentleman standing there." I waggled my fingers at him in a wave. He waved back.

She shook her head. "No-o. Are you trying to tell me Mr. Wiggam is here?"

"Not Mr. Wiggam, no."

"But..." She frowned. "Who?"

"Jacob Beaufort," the spirit said without moving from his position. "Pleased to make your acquaintance. I'd shake your sister's hand," he said to me, "but given she can't see me she won't be able to touch me either." *I* could see him, and therefore touch him, but he didn't offer to shake my hand.

Unlike ordinary people, I could touch the ghosts. Celia and the other guests at our séances simply walked through them as if they were mist but I couldn't, which made sense to me. After all, they could haunt a place by tossing objects about, or upturn tables and knock on wood, why wouldn't they have physical form? At least for the person who could see them.

I wondered what he would feel like. He looked remarkably solid. Indeed, he looked very much alive, more so than any ghost I'd ever seen. Usually they faded in and out and had edges like a smudged charcoal sketch, but Jacob Beaufort was as well defined as Celia.

"Er, pleased to meet you too," I said. "I'm Emily Chambers and this is my sister Miss Celia Chambers."

Celia bobbed a curtsy although she wasn't quite facing Mr. Beaufort, then picked up her bag and approached him. Or rather, approached the door. She walked straight through him and inserted the key into the lock.

"I say!" he said and stepped aside.

"She didn't mean any offense," I said quickly.

"Did I do something wrong?" Celia asked as the door swung open.

"You walked through him."

"Oh dear, I am terribly sorry, Mr..."

"Beaufort," I filled in for her.

"As my sister said, I meant no offense, Mr. Beaufort." She spoke to the door. I cleared my throat and pointed at the ghost now standing to one side on the landing. She turned a little and smiled at him. "Why are you haunting our front porch?"

I winced and gave Mr. Beaufort an apologetic shrug. My sister may be all politeness with the living but she'd yet to grasp the art of tactful communication with the deceased.

"Celia," I hissed at her, but she either didn't hear me or chose to ignore me.

"It's all right," Mr. Beaufort said, amused. "May I enter? I won't harm either of you. I simply need to talk to you and I'm sure you'll be more comfortable out of this breeze."

"Of course." How could one refuse such a considerate suggestion? Or such beautiful eyes that twinkled with a hidden smile. I told Celia what he wanted. She hesitated then nodded, as if her permission mattered. If a ghost wanted to come into our house, he could.

He allowed me to enter behind Celia then followed—walking, as ghosts don't float like most people think they do. They get about by walking, just like the living. Oh and sometimes they disappear then reappear in another location, which can be disconcerting.

Bella our maid met us at the door and took our coats and Celia's bag. "Tea, Miss?" she asked.

Celia nodded. "For two thank you." She didn't mention the addition of Mr. Beaufort. Bella was easily frightened and we didn't want to lose another maid. The last three had left our employment after witnessing one of our in-house séances. It was difficult enough to find good help with what little we could afford to pay but it was made even harder thanks to our line of work. Gentlewomen of leisure may find our séances a diversion, but I've found the servants and poor to be far more superstitious.

Bella hung up hats and coats and had retreated down the hall to the stairs. I indicated the first room to our right. "If you wouldn't mind waiting in the drawing room," I said to

Mr. Beaufort. "I need to speak to my sister for a moment."

The ghost bowed and did as I requested. "Celia," I said turning on her when he was no longer visible, "please don't ask him any questions about his death or haunting...or any morbid things."

"Why? We have a right to know more about the people we invite into our home, dead or alive."

"But it's so terribly..." Embarrassing. "...impolite."

"Nonsense. Now, why do you think he's here? To hire us perhaps?"

"I suppose so." I couldn't think of any other explanation.

"Good. Hopefully the other party can afford our fees." She tilted her chin up and plastered a calm smile on her face. "Come along," she said, "let's not keep him waiting."

Jacob Beaufort was studying the two framed daguerreotypes on our mantelpiece when we entered the drawing room. A small frown darkened his brow. "A handsome pair. Your parents?"

"Our mother," I said, "and Celia's father."

"Ah," he said as if that satisfied his curiosity. I could only guess what had piqued his interest. Most likely it was my skin tone, so dusky next to Celia's paleness, and the fact I looked nothing at all like either of the people in the pictures he held.

Celia sighed and sat on the sofa, spreading her skirt to cover as much of the threadbare fabric as possible, as was her habit when we had company. "Really, Emily," she muttered under her breath.

The ghost's gaze darted around the room. "Is there no image of *your* father here?"

"My father?" I said for Celia's benefit. "No."

She narrowed her gaze at me and gave a slight shake of her head as if to say *not now*. It was a well-chewed bone of contention between us. She insisted I call our mother's husband, Celia's father, Papa as she did. She in turn always referred to him as "*Our* father" and even Mama when she was alive had called him "Your Papa" when speaking of him to either one of us.

Despite the fact he'd died over a year before I was born.

I knew he couldn't possibly be my real father but I had long ago accepted he was the closest I'd get to one. Mama had refused to discuss the matter of my paternity despite my repeated questions. Not even Celia cared to talk about it, but I wasn't entirely sure she knew who my father was anyway. She had only been sixteen when I was born, and it was unlikely Mama had confided in her. It must have been terribly scandalous at the time, and explained why we never spoke to any of our relations and had few friends.

Although I accepted I may never know, a part of me still burned to learn the truth. I'd even tried to summon Mama's ghost once after her death to ask, but she'd not appeared.

"Mr. Beaufort," I said, shaking off the melancholy that usually descended upon me when thinking of my father.

"Call me Jacob," he said. "I think we can dispense with formalities considering the circumstances, not to mention my attire."

"Of course." I tried to smile politely but I fear it looked as awkward as I felt. His attire was not something to be dismissed casually. It was what he happened to be wearing when he died. Mr. Wiggam must have died wearing his formal dinner suit but it seemed Mr. Beaufort—Jacob—had been somewhat more casually dressed. It's the reason why I'll never sleep naked.

"What's he saying?" Celia asked, linking her hands on her lap.

"That we're to call him Jacob," I said.

"I see. Jacob, do you think you could hold something so I know where you are? The daguerreotype of our father will do."

I rolled my eyes. There she goes again—*our* father indeed.

"That's better," she said when Jacob obliged by picking up the wooden frame. "Now, please sit." He sat in the armchair which matched the sofa, right down to the faded upholstery. "Who do you wish us to contact?"

"Contact?" Jacob said.

"She means which of your loved ones do you want to communicate with," I said. "We can establish a meeting and you can tell them anything you wish, or ask a question. It'll give you peace," I said when he looked at me askance. "And help you cross over. Into the Otherworld." Good lord, he must be a fresh one. But he didn't look in the least frightened or wary as most newly deceased do.

"For a small fee," Celia added. "To be paid by your loved one of course."

"You have the wrong idea," he said, putting up his free hand. It was broad and long-fingered with scrapes and bruises on the knuckles, which struck me as odd. They looked fresh. He must have got them just before he died. So what was a handsome man with an aristocratic accent doing brawling with his bare knuckles? "I'm not here to contact anyone."

Bella entered at that moment carrying a tray of tea things. I had to lean to one side to see past her rather prominent rear as she bent over to set the tray on the table. I forked my brows at Jacob to prompt him—asking him outright might seem a little odd to Bella, particularly if Celia, the only other person in the room as far as the maid was concerned, failed to answer.

"I'm here because I've been assigned to you," he said.

"What?" I slapped a hand over my mouth.

Bella straightened and followed my line of sight straight to the framed daguerreotype of Celia's father hovering—as she would have seen it—above the armchair. She screamed and collapsed onto the rug in a dead faint.

Celia sighed. "Oh dear. She was such a good maid too."

CHAPTER 2

"I don't think your maid will last long," Jacob said as the drawing room door closed on Celia guiding a trembling Bella down the hall.

I waited until the door was completely shut and Bella's terrified mutterings had faded before I spoke. "I hope she's already prepared supper." It sounded uncaring but I'd been in this situation before and it was very trying. As our only maid, Bella worked long, hard hours. I appreciated that enough to know I didn't want to take on her chores. "Good maids are difficult to find, particularly ones not afraid of the supernatural." Or ones we could afford.

"Have you tried the North London School for Domestic Service in Clerkenwell?" He returned the picture frame to the mantelpiece and remained standing. "They train suitable orphans in all aspects of domestic service and help them find employment by the age of sixteen or so. We've hired many of our servants from there."

"We?"

"Ghosts." I must have had an odd look on my face because he snorted softly which I think was meant to be a laugh. "Joke," he said without even a twitch of his lips. "I meant my family. The one I had before I died."

"Oh." I swallowed. So he came from a family wealthy enough to afford servants, plural. I wanted to ask more about his life but it didn't seem like the right time. It also wasn't the right time to ask about his death, although I'm not sure there ever is an appropriate time to enquire about that. It feels a little like prying into one's private affairs.

Besides, a far more pressing question was why was he standing in my drawing room looking every bit the gentleman of the house as he rested his elbow on the mantelpiece. Perhaps it was the casual attire that made him look like he belonged precisely *there* as if this really was his home. Or perhaps it was the strength of his presence. I think I would have known where he was at all times even with my eyes closed. A remarkable feat for a spirit. "What did you mean by assigned to me? Assigned by whom and for what purpose?"

"Assigned by the Administrators——."

"The Administrators?"

"The officers who control the Waiting Area and the gateway to the Otherworld's sections. They ensure each spirit crosses to their correctly assigned section, as well as keeping the Waiting Area orderly." It all sounded terribly efficient, more so than our own government's departments, notorious for their crippling rules and mountains of paperwork. "Haven't you ever asked the ghosts you've summoned about their experiences there?"

"Of course," I said, reaching for the teapot on the table beside me. "All the time." I poured tea into a cup. "Why wouldn't I?"

"You haven't, have you?"

I stared into the teacup and sighed. "Not really. I'm not sure I want to find out too much. I mean, I know about the Waiting Area and how ghosts need to release all negative emotions associated with this world in order to cross over but...I don't want to know anything more."

"You mean before your time."

I nodded. Hopefully I had many years to wait.

I glanced at Jacob over the rim of my cup and caught him watching me with a steely intensity that made my skin tingle. I blushed and sipped then risked another look. This time his attention seemed to be diverted by the tea service. I would have offered him a cup but there was no point since he didn't require sustenance. Perhaps I should have offered out of politeness anyway. I wasn't entirely sure of the etiquette for when ghosts came calling.

He really was undeniably handsome though. The more I looked at him, the more I liked his features. None were remarkable on their own—except for the vivid blue of his eyes—but together they made his face extraordinary. What a shame he was dead. Even more so because he'd come from a wealthy family—Celia would be particularly disappointed by the waste. The number of eligible gentlemen we knew could be counted on a butcher's hand—five less a few missing digits and fingertips. Perhaps it wasn't a complete loss however. Jacob might have a living relative or friend he wanted us to contact while he was here. Preferably one of Celia's age or a little older.

"So these Administrators," I said, "why have they sent you here? Is it something to do with Barnaby Wiggam? Because if it is, I should explain that it was his own choice not to return to the Waiting Area. We tried to convince him—."

"It's nothing to do with Wiggam." He drew his attention from the tea tray and gave it all to me. There was heat in his gaze, an undeniable flare of desire that tugged at me, drew me into those blue eyes and held me there. I couldn't look away but I could blush and I did, although hopefully the darkish shade of my skin hid the worst of it. I hated being the center of attention, which made being a legitimate spirit medium a rather difficult occupation at times. As our reputation grew so did the stares and the whispers. But I'd never been the center of this sort of attention. No man had ever looked at me like that.

"Whether Wiggam's ghost wants to stay and haunt his

wife or return to the Waiting Area is entirely up to him," he finally said, breaking the spell. "The Administrators allow spirits to make up their own minds. No, Emily, what you've done is something much more serious."

"Oh." My stomach dropped. I lowered the teacup to my lap and wished the sofa would swallow me up. "You're talking about that...that horrid shadow, aren't you?"

He nodded. "That shadow is a shape-shifting demon."

"What!" The cup rattled and I put my hand over it to still it. I stared at him and he simply stared back, waiting for me to ask the questions. I had many questions but all I said was, "I'm sorry" in a whisper.

He didn't say "You should be" or "You're a stupid girl" but simply "I know" in that rumbling voice that seemed to come from the depths of his chest.

"What is it? What does a shape-shifting demon do?"

"When it first emerges into this world it holds no shape. Its first instinct is survival, safety, until it can gather its strength. Once it has, it takes on the form of someone or something else almost perfectly." He paused and his lips formed a grim line. "And then it needs to satisfy its hunger."

From the way he couldn't meet my gaze, I suspected that hunger wouldn't be satisfied by buying fish from the markets. It would eat whatever it could kill. Rats, dogs. People.

I cleared my throat. "It was summoned quite by accident. I didn't mean to do it." Celia had better thank me later for taking the blame. It was entirely her fault that we'd released a demon with that new amulet. Not that I would tell Jacob. She was the only family member I had left and although we didn't always see eye to eye, we were all the other had and I wouldn't toss her into the lion's den, so to speak, even if the lion appeared relatively tame. I needed to find out more about Jacob and what the Administrators would extract for her folly first. I was better equipped than Celia to cope with the supernatural.

"Tell me how it happened," he said, sitting beside me on

the sofa, not at the other end but close so that I could touch him if I moved a little to the right. I felt very alert and aware of him, but I could not meet that gaze. "I want to know exactly what was said, how it was said, and what object was used to summon it."

I stood, reluctantly, and fetched the amulet from Celia's bag. When I sat down again, I made sure I was sitting exactly where I had before, not an inch further away. I wanted to sit closer but I didn't dare even though Celia would never know because she couldn't see him.

"A peddler gave it to my sister."

"Gave it? She didn't buy it?"

"Apparently not."

He ran his thumb over the amulet's points.

"The woman said to repeat an incantation three times if we ever needed to solve something."

His hand stilled. "What was it?"

"We couldn't understand the words."

"But you repeated it nevertheless?"

I chewed the inside of my lower lip and shrugged one shoulder.

"Bloody hell, Emily, do you know what you've done?" He stood and paced across the rug to the hearth and back. He completed the short distance in two strides. "Shape-shifting demons are dangerous. They roam at night, searching for food. And I'm not referring to the pies and boiled potatoes variety. I mean living flesh and blood."

I gulped down the bile rising up my throat. "Oh God," I whispered. I pressed a hand to my stomach to settle it, but to no avail. It continued roiling beneath my corset. *What had we done?*

He suddenly stopped pacing and blinked at me. "Sorry," he said softly, "I shouldn't have gone into detail." He crouched in front of me and went to touch my hands, still holding my stomach, but drew back before making contact. "Are you all right? You've gone pale."

"That's quite a feat considering my skin tone," I said,

attempting to smile. I reached out to press his arm in reassurance but he stood suddenly. All the softness in his eyes vanished and I bristled in response to the coldness in them. Obviously physical contact was not something he wanted.

I wondered when he'd last touched a live person. Unless he'd stumbled across someone else who could see spirits— and therefore touch him—it would have been before he died.

"If that incantation is what released the demon," I said, "then it's not a very fool proof system your Administrators have to keep them in check." I couldn't help the sarcasm dripping off the words like rain drops off leaves. His sudden changes of mood had me confused and bothered which in turn threw up my own defenses. I couldn't tell if he was friend or foe yet.

"I think we've already demonstrated that," he said.

I shot him a withering look. "They ought to have better mechanisms for controlling their demons."

"It's not just a matter of repeating the incantation. It must be done when the portals between this world and the Waiting Area are opened as they are during your séances." He held up the amulet. "And while touching a cursed object."

"Cursed? Someone has *cursed* that?"

He nodded.

"It really shouldn't have been given away then."

"Very observant of you."

Another withering look would have been excessive but I gave him one anyway.

He shot me a small smile in return which I found most disconcerting. But then the smile vanished and he was all seriousness again. "The amulet acts as a talisman," he said, "linking the wearer to the demon."

He dangled the amulet from its leather strap and dropped it into my palm. "We need to find the person who gave it to your sister. When does the peddler return?"

"Not until Thursday."

He rubbed his hand over his chin. "Damnation." He glanced at me and bowed his head. "Sorry for my language, it was inappropriate." Despite the bow, he didn't seem sorry at all. There wasn't a hint of regret on his face, just that smile again, as if he was amused at shocking me. Not that I was shocked. I'd heard worse at the markets.

"But you must understand," he went on, "that we need to locate this peddler as soon as possible."

"*We* need to?"

"*You* are the one who released the demon so it's only fair you bear some of the responsibility for returning it."

I bristled and bit the inside of my lip to stop myself telling him what had really happened. Celia had better appreciate my covering for her.

My sister took that moment to enter the drawing room and promptly sat on the sofa and poured herself a cup of tea. She seemed completely oblivious to the tension in the room, even though it was so dense I felt like I couldn't breathe.

"Is the ghost gone?" she asked me.

"No."

"Well Bella is. Packed her bags and almost ran out the door. I couldn't get a sensible word out of her." She lifted her teacup to her lips then lowered it without taking a sip. "I'd no idea she was such a flighty girl. The next one should have a sturdier constitution. Have you still got a copy of the last advertisement we used, Em? No need to write it all out again."

"Jacob suggested we try a school in Clerkenwell. The children learn the art of domestic service there."

Celia scoffed into her teacup. "Hardly an art, my dear, if Bella's efforts at cooking were anything to go by. Very well, I shall go in the morning." She nodded at the framed daguerreotype of her father now back on the mantelpiece. "I see you've put the portrait of Father down." Her voice rose a little, the way it always did when she spoke directly to a spirit. As if it was hard of hearing. Not that she spoke to them very often. She usually left that part of the séance to me. It's why I was the one who received the strange looks from the guests. That way Celia managed to avoid the worst of the Freak label. "Do you mind very much picking it up again so I can see where you are?" she asked him.

Jacob crossed his arms over his chest. "Rather demanding, isn't she?"

I took two steps toward him, bringing me within arm's distance. "You may be ethereal but you are still a guest in our home, Mr. Beaufort, and I would suggest you behave as a gentleman would and do as my sister requests." His eyes grew wider with every word. I squared up to him, and although I was much shorter than he, I felt like I had the upper hand in the exchange. "Or have you forgotten how a gentleman should behave?"

He couldn't have stiffened any more if someone had dripped ice cold water down his spine.

"It is only polite after all to allow Celia to know your general location," I went on, "since you have the advantage of being able to see her."

He lowered his arms to his sides and nodded once. "Point taken." He edged around the furniture to the mantelpiece and picked up the other portrait this time, the one of Mama. "Lucky I'm a ghost or those barbs would have really hurt," he said to the daguerreotype.

My irritation flowed out of me at his absurd sense of humor. I controlled my smile as best I could however. It would have undermined my argument.

"I see you two have become further acquainted with each other during my absence," Celia said, eyeing me carefully. She forked one brow and I shook my head. I was in no danger from Jacob. He needed me to find the amulet peddler. And the demon. "Have you discovered what he means by being assigned to you?" she went on.

I explained about the demon we released, emphasizing the *we* and winking at her as I did so. Now that I had let Jacob think I'd been as guilty as Celia, I didn't want him to know I had deliberately misled him. It felt dishonorable somehow.

Apparently Celia didn't agree with me. "No," she said and placed her teacup and saucer carefully on the table. "I cannot let you take the blame, Em. I was the one who bought the amulet and it was I who invoked the demon. It was nothing to do with Emily," she said to Jacob.

He lowered the picture frame and regarded me levelly. "Very noble of you," he muttered. "And now I suppose I owe you an apology."

"Don't trouble yourself," I said more curtly than I intended.

He winced then bowed. "I've behaved despicably, both as a gentleman and as a guest." He spoke quietly and his mouth softened, no longer forming a grim line. "I hope you can forgive me." As apologies went, it seemed genuine. "I would ask the Administrators to assign someone else to you but there is no one else."

"Isn't the Waiting Area filled with thousands of ghosts? That's what several of them had told me and I'd never had any reason to doubt them.

"There is, but few are like me."

"You mean solid, or at least have the appearance of it?"

He nodded. "Without the solidness as you call it, I couldn't follow you wherever you go. Most spirits are limited to a specific location, as you know. I can go anywhere I please."

"Fascinating." I cast my eye over him again. He certainly looked nothing like the other ghosts with their fuzzy centers and fading edges. Indeed he looked healthy, full of life. And so handsome it was all I could do to stop myself from reaching out and caressing the skin at his throat. It would be smooth and butter-soft, I guessed, but cool. I'd only ever touched a ghost once before and she'd been cool despite it being a warm day.

"Really, Emily," Celia scolded.

I snatched my attention away from Jacob but tried my

best to ignore my sister, which wasn't easy considering her annoyance vibrated off her. She didn't need to say anything else. We knew each other well enough to know what the other was thinking. In this case it was my fascination with Jacob. I could almost hear her asking me why a ghost and not the very much alive vicar's son from St. Luke's who always tried to touch my hand or some other part of me after Sunday service.

But how could she understand? She couldn't see Jacob. Couldn't get sucked in by those eyes, so like a dangerous whirlpool, or that classically handsome face. I could, and was, even though my brain told me I was a fool. He was dead.

"Why are you so solid?" I asked him.

He waved a hand and shrugged one shoulder. "It's just the way I am."

I had the feeling there was more to it than that but I didn't want to be rude and pry. Not yet anyway.

"So how do you propose to return this demon to the Otherworld?" Celia asked.

"We must discover who wanted the demon released and why," Jacob said. "We can start by understanding the words you spoke during the séance."

I repeated his answer to Celia and she in turn repeated the incantation. "It means nothing to me," he said, "but I'll ask the souls in the Waiting Area. It might be a more familiar language to one of them."

"Wouldn't the Administrators know?" I asked. "Or if not, can't they just summon the demon back again with an incantation of their own?"

"The Administrators don't have the power to reverse a curse issued in this realm. No one in the Waiting Area does. It can only be done by someone in this realm and only when the demon is near."

I swallowed and looked down at the amulet in my hand. "So much trouble over a piece of cheap jewelry."

"Keep the amulet with you. Whoever speaks the

27

reversing incantation must be wearing it."

"I should be the one to wear it and seek out the peddler," Celia said. She held her head high, her chin up, as if defying us to disagree with her. Despite her stance, I knew she was afraid. The supernatural was my territory. She'd never been as comfortable around the ghosts as me, and demons were another matter altogether. The guilt over releasing one must be great indeed for her to make such a bold offer to rectify the situation.

"No," Jacob and I said together.

"You can't see or talk to Jacob," I said. "And we need his guidance in this."

She lowered her head and nodded. "Very well." She raised her gaze to where he stood, holding the frame. "Is it dangerous, this demon?" she asked, voice barely above a whisper.

"Not terribly," I said and tried to look like I wasn't lying. If she thought it was dangerous, she would not agree to my involvement, no matter how important. I glanced at Jacob but he said nothing, just watched me beneath half-lowered lids. "Don't worry, Sis, we'll send it back before anything happens."

Celia breathed out and settled into the sofa. "That's settled then," she muttered. "Now," she said to Jacob, "tell me *exactly* what you mean when you say you are assigned to my sister? Will you be at her side until the demon is found? Are you tied to her in some invisible way?"

Jacob went very still. "Tell your sister not to worry," he said stiffly. "I'll be the perfect gentleman."

I almost told him he'd mistaken her and she wasn't suggesting he'd do anything untoward, but I couldn't be sure if that assessment was correct. Knowing Celia, it was highly possible she meant exactly that.

As if understanding my hesitation, she added, "Can he protect you against this demon—and don't try to tell me it's harmless because I know it's not. It *is* a demon after all. And can he protect you against the person who cursed the amulet?" Her knuckles had gone white, clasped as they were in her lap. I gently touched her arm. It didn't seem to help—she remained as taut as a stretched rope.

Jacob took a long time to answer and I began to doubt he would when he finally said, "I will do my best." He held up the picture frame. "I can wield Earthly weapons as easily as I can hold this, but I'm afraid weapons from this realm have little effect on demons. They can only be killed with blades forged in the Otherworld. Unfortunately the Administrators don't have access to one which is why I prefer to banish it."

I squeezed Celia's arm again. "He said yes," I lied. "Don't worry, Sis, he looks very capable."

She stared straight ahead at the picture frame held by Jacob and gave a small nod. "Very well," she said in a tired voice. "You may accompany my sister to find this demon and return it. But if anything should happen to her," she coughed to cover her cracking voice but I heard it nevertheless, "I'll find someone who can make sure your soul never crosses over."

I stared at her open-mouthed. My sister, making threats to a ghost? Remarkable. I loved her for it.

She released her grip on the sofa and picked up her teacup. "It would seem nothing can be done before Thursday, anyway, when the peddler returns. The day after tomorrow. Until then, Mr. Beaufort." She nodded and sipped her tea. Dismissed.

He looked like he would argue but thought better of it and returned the daguerreotype to the mantelpiece. "Don't worry, I can see myself out." He bowed to us then vanished like a bubble that's been popped. There one moment, gone the next.

I flopped back in the sofa in a most unladylike fashion. "Oh Celia, I think we've bitten off more than we can chew."

She handed me my teacup. "We'll conquer this demon, don't fret, my dear."

I hadn't been referring to the demon.

CHAPTER 3

It took me a long time to fall asleep. It was bad enough knowing there was a demon out there hiding in the many shadowy lanes of London searching out something—or someone—to eat, but it was thoughts of Jacob Beaufort that occupied my mind more. Whenever I closed my eyes I could see his bright blue ones staring back at me with unnerving intensity. Now that I was alone I could think of a thousand questions I should have asked him, each one circling my head like a carousel. Finally, when the longcase clock in the entrance hall downstairs struck three, I'd had enough. I got up and threw my shawl around my shoulders then lit a candle and padded barefoot to my writing desk. I sat and pulled a piece of paper and the inkstand closer and wrote every question down, one after the other. Except one. I re-read my list and tried to tell myself it wasn't important, I didn't need to know the answer to it.

I wasn't very good at lying, even to myself. So I gave up and wrote the question at the bottom:

Did he meet Mama in the Waiting Area?

If he answered yes to that then there were so many other follow-up questions but I put the quill down without writing them. It was enough for now.

I fell asleep quickly after that.

Much later, I awoke to the sound of the brass knocker on

our front door banging. It was daytime because light edged the curtains. It wasn't bright but then the days never were in London thanks to either the smog or rain or both.

I heard Celia's voice and listened for another but no one else spoke. Perhaps I'd imagined the knocking and she was simply reciting poetry in the kitchen.

But that was as absurd as it sounded. Celia regarded poetry as a useless form of literature read only by deluded romantics.

Then I heard footsteps running up the stairs. Only one set. "Emily! Emily, are you decent?" Celia shouted. "I think he's here."

"She means me," came Jacob's voice from just outside my bedroom door.

Jacob! Good lord, I was still in my nightgown! What was he doing here so early? It couldn't be much past eight o'clock. What was he doing here at all when we'd agreed nothing could be done until the following day?

"She'll be out in a few minutes," I heard Celia say in a loud voice. The door opened a crack and she slipped inside. She was dressed but her hair looked like it had been hastily shoved under her cap. "My sister is not yet ready to receive callers," she said as she shut the door.

I heard Jacob's chuckle and I pictured his handsome features softening with his smile. "It's nice to know the rules of propriety still apply to the dead," he called out.

Celia leaned against the door as if barricading it. "He hasn't zapped his way in here, has he?"

"No. Help me dress," I said, climbing out of bed. "How did you know it was him?"

She passed me a clean chemise from the wardrobe, which I put on over my head after I shucked off my nightgown. "When I answered the knock there was no one there so I closed the door. But then I heard a knock on the hallway wall and I realized someone was inside, alerting me to their presence. The only ghost I know who has turned up here without being summoned is that Beaufort boy."

Hardly a boy. I made up my mind to ask him his age. Or his age at the time of his death. It was the first question on my list, still sitting on my desk.

"I told him I'd fetch you," she said, helping me into my corset. "But as I walked up the stairs I felt a coolness sweep past me and I knew he was going on ahead."

"At least he still possesses a sense of honor and hasn't entered." I gasped as she pulled hard on the corset's laces. "Careful, Sis, I might need to breathe at some point."

"Why bother breathing if you look fat?" We both knew she was being ridiculous—I was washboard flat in stomach and, alas, in chest—but she was in an odd temper so I let her comment go. "The green gown, I think."

"Really? What's the occasion?" The green dress was my newest and favorite. The color complemented my complexion and dark brown eyes. The bodice was shaped in the latest cuirass style, which hugged my frame all the way down to my thighs, emphasizing my small waist and the curve of my hip. It would have looked better on a taller girl, as did all dresses, but with heeled boots it looked quite good on me too. Although the satin had been recycled from one of Mama's old gowns, it nevertheless cost a great deal to have made. Celia had insisted on using the last of our savings for it. I suspected it was her weapon of choice in the battle to find me a husband. I supposed I looked quite good in it. Indeed, the dress never failed to turn heads, which was always a pleasant feeling when the heads were turned for the right reasons. Being singled out because I could see ghosts or because I wasn't fashionably pale, however, made me feel like the bearded lady in a sideshow.

So, considering it was a dress Celia made me wear whenever she thought eligible men would see me, it was a little disconcerting that she was making me wear it now when I was only seeing a ghost.

"I think Jacob will take you somewhere today," she said, fastening the hooks and eyes at the back of the dress. "He has a sense of urgency about him. Hopefully he wishes to communicate with his family after all, and if he has a brother or cousin..." She let the sentence drift, full of potential and possibility.

"It's more likely Jacob is concerned about the demon," I said.

She guided me to my dressing table and forced me to sit at the stool. "It can't hurt to be prepared," she said, undoing my braid. "You never know whose path you'll be thrown into."

I couldn't fault her logic although I didn't like to think about eligible gentlemen, or marriage or any of those things. Some girls of my acquaintance may be married by seventeen, but I wasn't sure wedlock was for me. What would happen to Celia? And why would I want to live with a man, by his rules, in his house, when I could live here with my sister and do as I pleased?

Besides, what sort of husband would want a fatherless bastard for a wife? And if my parentage didn't concern him, surely the fact I had conversations with the dead would.

A knock at my bedroom door made me turn around, yanking the hair out of Celia's hands. "Be still," she snapped, "or I'll have to start over."

"I can appreciate that a lady needs time to prepare herself to face the day," Jacob said through the door, "but do you think you could go faster?"

"He wants us to hurry up," I told Celia.

"Hurry!" she scoffed. "A lady cannot rush her morning toilette."

"I won't be long," I called out.

"Good because we need to get going," he said.

"We're definitely going somewhere," I said to my sister's reflection in the dressing table's oval mirror. "And where are we going to?" I shouted to Jacob.

He suddenly appeared in the room at my right shoulder, his back to me. I jumped and Celia tugged my hair. "Be still."

"Sorry," he said, "but I don't like shouting through doors. Can I turn around?"

"Yes," I said and hoped Celia thought I was speaking to her. I didn't want her to know he was in the room. She was already wary of him and for some reason I didn't want to turn that into outright distrust.

"It's like hundreds of little springs," he said in wonder, watching Celia's nimble fingers work my black curls into a manageable style on top of my head.

"Little springs turn into little knots very easily," I said.

Celia paused. "Pardon?"

"I, uh, was just thinking about my hair and how I wish the curls were softer like yours." My gaze met Jacob's in the mirror's reflection.

He quickly glanced away, down at the dressing table, up at the ceiling, at the wall, anywhere but at me. "Just tell her to put it up as best she can," he said.

"He's growing impatient," I told her.

"He's no gentleman, that one," she said and put two hairpins between her lips.

I cringed and caught Jacob's sharp glance in Celia's direction. He seemed...alarmed, and then embarrassed by her off-handed comment.

She removed the pins from her mouth and threaded them through my hair. "I wonder if he ever was one," she said, admiring her handiwork." Perhaps he lost all sense of honor when he died."

"Dying tends to cause one to misplace a great many things," Jacob said, voice dark and distant.

"Can you go out and tell him I'll be there in a moment," I asked Celia.

Her hand hovered near the hair above my temple as if she wanted to touch it but didn't want to mess up her work. "Be careful, Em." She kissed my forehead. "You do look lovely. Let's hope it's worth it."

She left and I heard her telling the empty air outside that I'd be there soon. Her footsteps retreated down the stairs and I turned to Jacob.

"You deserved to hear that if you come and go

uninvited," I said.

"I'm not concerned about other people's opinions of me." He gave me a crooked smile. "It's a bad habit carried over from when I was alive."

It was the first time he'd referred to his life and what he'd been like. It wasn't what I'd expected to hear. Instead of giving me a clearer picture of him it just threw up more questions. Why hadn't he cared what people thought? "I'm sure people cared what *you* thought of *them*." I don't know why I said it but it seemed appropriate somehow.

He didn't comment but he was no longer smiling, crookedly or otherwise. Indeed, he'd turned all his attention to my hairbrush sitting on the dressing table as if it was the most interesting object in the world. Its tortoiseshell back and handle certainly weren't worthy of such scrutiny.

I knew an avoidance tactic when I saw one.

"How long ago did you die?" I asked him. He might want to avoid all awkward questions but I certainly wasn't going to shy away from them. If I was to spend time alone with him, I needed to know more about him.

"About nine months ago. I was eighteen." He shook his head, dismissing the topic. "Are you ready?"

So much for my investigative scheme. "Where are we going?"

He strode to the door. I pulled on my boots, quickly laced them and followed at a trot. "The house of someone I went to school with," he said, opening the door. "George Culvert. He lives in the Belgravia area with his mother."

"And why are we visiting this Mr. Culvert?"

He turned around and his gaze dropped to my waist and hips. His mouth fell open and a small, strangled sound escaped. "You're going to wear *that*?"

"Something wrong with it?"

"No," he said thickly. "But can you breathe?"

"Sometimes."

He laughed softly. "I like it. It's very...snug."

"So what were you saying about George Culvert?"

His gaze lifted to mine and a shiver rippled down my spine. His eyes blazed like blue flames but then he blinked rapidly and shifted his focus to something behind my left shoulder. He cleared his throat. "He's a demonologist."

"A what?"

"A demonologist. Someone who studies demons, fallen angels, that sort of thing." He waved a hand casually, as if 'that sort of thing' was like studying for a career in law. "We can't wait until tomorrow to start looking for this demon. We have to start today. Now." He ushered me through the door onto the landing without actually touching me.

"Before it hurts someone?" I asked.

His gaze met mine for a brief second but in that moment I saw genuine worry in his eyes. There was no need for him to answer me. We both knew the demon might have already killed overnight.

"Why didn't it attack us when it was released in Mrs. Wiggam's house?"

"Until it makes contact with the master who set the curse on the amulet and controls it, the demon is weak and relies on instinct. It would have seen it was outnumbered and felt too vulnerable to attack so it fled. Once it felt safe, it would begin to search for nourishment."

I swallowed. "How awful. So tell me more about this Culvert fellow."

"George's father was a demonologist before his death and George has an interest in the field too."

"Demonology," I said. "What an odd thing to study."

"Not really. You'd be surprised at how many people are interested in the paranormal. Although I doubt there's much money in it. Not sure how his father could have sent George to Eton. He must have had another source of income."

"You went to Eton?" The boy's school was the most exclusive in all of England. Money wasn't enough to get accepted into the school, it required wealth *and* privilege. It would seem Jacob's family had both. Another piece to the puzzle that was Jacob Beaufort fell into place.

He shrugged and it would seem the question was dismissed, just like that. As if it were nothing. As if my curiosity could be swept away without consideration. It was most frustrating.

"I'll meet you there," he said. "I need to speak to more spirits in the Waiting Area."

"About the meaning of the words spoken in the incantation?"

He nodded. "The language must be an obscure one as none of the spirits I've asked so far knew its meaning. And anyway, someone might have heard of another demonologist who can aid us. That's how I learned Culvert's name."

"I thought you went to school with him."

"I did but we didn't socialize. Different friends, you understand."

I didn't. Not really. My formal schooling had finished at age thirteen, as it did for most girls, and I'd known every pupil at the small school. After I left, Mama had continued to tutor me and then Celia had tried after Mama's death, but much of my understanding of the world had come from reading books left behind in Celia's father's study. He'd been a lawyer and a great reader apparently. His study was still in tact and the bookshelves covered two entire walls, but most of the books were dry texts with only a few novels squeezed in between. Not a single one touched on the supernatural.

"So what shall I tell this George Culvert when I meet him?" I asked. "I can't very well ask him about shape-shifting demons straight away. He'll think it odd."

He paused then said, "Tell him you have a general interest in demonology and you'd like to look at his books." He shrugged. "We'll make it up as we go."

"Very well." I couldn't see any other way that didn't involve telling George Culvert everything. And that wasn't an option. Not yet. Not until I'd decided if I cared whether he thought I was mad for speaking to ghosts. "Give me Mr. Culvert's address and I'll meet you there after breakfast."

"Fifty-two Wilton Crescent in Belgravia." He gave me

one more appraisal—a lingering one—from head to toe then vanished. But not before I saw the same heated flare in his eyes that had been there when he first noticed me in the dress. It would seem the gown hadn't lost any of its power.

Celia had a simple breakfast of toast and boiled eggs waiting for me in the dining room when I arrived.

"I thought we'd eat in the kitchen since we have no maid," I said picking up a plate.

"Just because there's no one here to see us doesn't mean we can let ourselves go. We have standards."

Celia had standards. I had a growling stomach and didn't care where I ate. I buttered a piece of toast and took two eggs from the sideboard and joined her at the table.

"What did he want?" she asked.

I filled her in and her interest piqued at the mention of George Culvert. "I wonder what he's like," she said more to herself than me.

"He went to Eton," I said, rapping the knife on the eggshell. "With Jacob."

I'd thought it impossible for her eyes to light up even more but they did. "Oh! He must be a gentleman then. I'm so glad you're wearing that dress, it's perfect. But you can't go alone. I'll accompany you."

"I'll be all right."

"Emily," she said on a sigh.

"Please, Celia, I'm old enough." Because our lives were so thoroughly interconnected, my sister and I usually went everywhere together. We just had no need to be separate. But of late I found I wanted to go out more and more without her. It would be nice to have people deal with *me* as an individual and a woman rather than as Celia's little sister. The visit to George Culvert was a perfect opportunity to do so and I wasn't going to let it pass me by.

She paused with her fork in the air, a piece of buttered toast only inches from her mouth.

"Jacob will be with me," I added before she could protest. "That's all the protection I need. Besides, you've got to go to the Clerkenwell school and hire another maid."

She seemed to struggle between the two options. "It's not seemly for a young lady to pay calls on a young gentleman alone. You know that."

"His mother will probably be in at this early hour," I said hopefully. "And besides, I could be there all day studying his books." Celia's eyes went blank at the thought, just as I'd hoped. My sister had never been a great reader. Whereas I'd devoured all of her father's books, even the dull ones, she'd not been in his study for a long time. "Besides, if you don't find another maid today *you'll* have to cook supper. I'm sure I won't be home in time. And of course there's all the cleaning..."

Celia sighed. "You're right."

I ate the toast and one of the eggs and left the other. It was too dry. When we'd finished, Celia collected our plates. "You'd better go or Jacob will be back demanding to know why you haven't left yet."

She didn't need to tell me a second time. I'd avoided both the cooking and the cleaning so far but I wasn't about to test my luck by staying home any longer.

"Wear the hat that matches the dress," she said as I left. "But don't take a parasol. We don't have one in the right shade of green."

Five minutes later, I walked out the door feeling like a perfectly matching green peacock. A few pairs of eyes followed me down Druids Way and I can't deny that it felt good to be noticed for all the right reasons. It made a pleasant change to the suspicious glances usually cast my way by those neighbors and shopkeepers who knew I could speak to ghosts. The stares were something I'd not yet grown used to, even though we'd been in business for over a year. I wondered if there ever would be a day when I'd enjoy the attention.

Oh dear. It sounded like I resented being a medium and wished I didn't have the gift. Sometimes I did, true, but on the other hand I liked being able to reconnect people with their deceased loved ones. I just wished those same people wouldn't treat me with such wariness.

I had to hold onto my hat until I turned off Druids Way and the strong wind eased to a gentle breeze. The sun came out from behind the clouds, briefly, but did little to brighten the day, covered as it was by London's smoky haze. I knew how to get to Wilton Crescent so my thoughts were left to wander. And they didn't wander to the demon or the dangers it posed but to Jacob. The way he'd noticed me in the dress, and how he watched me with such intensity when he thought I wasn't looking.

But there was something troubling him too, something that had nothing to do with the demon. Despite telling me he didn't care what people thought of him, he seemed to bristle at Celia's assessment of his ungentlemanly conduct. And he avoided all questions about his life and what it had been like.

Was he ashamed of it? Or was there something else, something he was hiding?

Whatever it was, his behavior was very confusing, but then he was a ghost so I suppose he could do what he wanted.

I wished he'd accompanied me on the walk. The twenty minutes it took to reach Wilton Crescent would have given me ample opportunity to find out more about him. But then I would have drawn many unwanted stares by seemingly conversing with myself. The mere thought made me cringe and I lowered my head, not wishing to encounter any ghosts that happened to haunt the streets. I'd seen only two over the years who'd met with a road accident and had not progressed to the Waiting Area, having chosen to maintain the negative emotion tying them to this world. I never understood why anyone would choose to linger where they couldn't be seen or heard. Perhaps I would think differently if I were dead.

I turned into Wilton Crescent and strolled along the elegant curved street until I reached number fifty-two. It looked like the other grand houses in the crescent-shaped terrace with its cream stucco façade and colonnaded porch. The main difference I could see was the brass knocker on the door. It was shaped like a large paw.

A footman answered my knock and showed me into a spacious drawing room on the first floor crammed with furniture and knick-knacks. Aside from the usual piano, sofa and chairs, there were tables. Many, many small tables—a console table, a sofa table, at least three occasional tables and a sideboard. Scattered on top of them all were framed daguerreotypes, figurines, vases, busts, decorative jars, boxes and other little objects that seemed to have no use whatsoever except to occupy a surface.

I was admiring an elaborate display of shells arranged into the shape of a flower bouquet when a tall young man entered, smiling in greeting. He was handsome but not in the masculine, classical sense like Jacob but more angelic, prettier although not feminine. Definitely not. Blond hair sprang off his head in soft curls and his pale skin stretched taut over high, sharp cheeks. He wore small, round spectacles through which gray eyes danced. He looked younger than Jacob and if I hadn't known they went to school together and were about the same age, I'd have thought him my own age or younger.

"Miss Chambers?" He glanced around the room, perhaps looking for a chaperone. Eventually his gaze settled back on me, or rather my hips, before sweeping up to my face. His cheeks colored slightly. "The footman said you wished to see me and not my mother?" It was a question not a statement. Mr. Culvert was probably unused to visits from unchaperoned girls.

I cleared my throat then held out my hand for him to shake. He looked at it like he didn't know what to do with it then took my fingers and gave them a gentle squeeze. "I'm definitely here to see you if you are Mr. George Culvert."

His face lit up. "Indeed I am." He squeezed again. His own hand was smooth, soft. It made me think of the split skin and bruises on Jacob's knuckles and again I wondered why a gentleman had hands more suited to a laborer or a pugilist.

Jacob chose that moment to appear beside me and I jumped in surprise. "Tell him you knew me before my death," he said, crossing his arms over his chest as he studied Mr. Culvert, "and that I told you about his interest in demonology. Pretend you also have an interest too and decided it was time you met. That should suffice."

But before I could say anything, Mr. Culvert said, "Do you have a supernatural matter to discuss with me?"

I choked on air and tried to cover it with a cough.

"Are you all right, Miss Chambers?" he said, frowning. "Tea is on its way but if there's anything else I can get you?" He took my hand again and patted it.

Jacob scowled at him.

I managed to stop coughing long enough to say, "Thank you, I'm fine."

Jacob, still scowling, approached our host and waved a hand in front of his face. Mr. Culvert didn't blink. "He definitely can't see me," Jacob said. "It must have been a guess—an uncannily good one."

"You're right," I said. "I do have a supernatural question. That's very intuitive of you, Mr. Culvert."

"Not really." He smiled sheepishly and dipped his head. "I happen to be aware of your work as a medium. I've wanted to meet you for some time." A faint blush crept across his cheeks. It was rather charming. Until I caught Jacob watching me out of the corner of my eye. No, he wasn't watching, he was *glaring* and his eyes had turned the color of a stormy sea. I tried not to look at him. I needed all my wits about me if I was to lie to George Culvert convincingly.

"So you believe I can really talk to spirits?" I said to Mr. Culvert.

"Yes of course. Why wouldn't I?"

"Many people do not."

"Many people don't know what I know about the supernatural." He indicated I should sit on the blood-red velvet sofa.

The footman re-entered carrying a tea tray stacked with tea things and a plate of butter biscuits, freshly baked going by their delicious smell. It was early for refreshments, early for making calls for that matter, but Mr. Culvert didn't seem to mind. Indeed, he seemed quite eager to chat. He sat in the chair opposite and leaned forward as the footman poured the tea.

I took my teacup and wondered where Mrs. Culvert was in the vast house. When the footman left I hazarded a glance at Jacob. He stood beside the mantelpiece, its height perfect for resting his elbow, and watched the proceedings with a closed expression. I thought he'd be impatient for me to ask questions but he said nothing, simply waited.

I decided to follow our original plan. "I heard about you through a mutual friend of ours," I said to Mr. Culvert. "Jacob Beaufort. I believe you went to Eton with him."

George Culvert's brows shot up into his snowy blond curls. "You knew him?"

I nodded and sipped my tea in an effort to disguise my lie. I had one of those faces that was easy to read so the better I hid it, the better I could lie. "His sudden death must have shocked everyone at the school."

"It must have, but I wouldn't know." He too took a sip of his tea but watched me the entire time over the rim of his cup. "He died after we'd both left Eton. Jacob had gone on to Oxford I believe."

My ghost had failed to mention that fact. Jacob shifted his weight. "It was so long ago," I said lightly. "I find it hard to recall the dates."

Mr. Culvert lowered his cup and locked his gaze with mine. "And he wasn't my friend."

Oh dear. This was going to be more difficult than I imagined. "He, uh, mentioned you though. Frequently."

Jacob groaned. "Tell him we were in the same debating

team once."

"You were on the debating team together," I said.

"No, that was my cousin, another Culvert," Mr. Culvert said.

"Oh."

Jacob shrugged. "I thought it was him." He frowned, shook his head. "I just can't seem to recall him. The uncle I spoke to in the Waiting Area was adamant his nephew George went to Eton in my year level. Why can't I remember him?"

"It must have been some other team then," I offered. "Cricket?"

"I didn't play sports unless I had to," Mr. Culvert said. "And Jacob and I were never on the same team. He was always in the firsts—cricket, rugby *et cetera*. I was...not. So you see, I'd be very surprised if he noticed me at all."

Jacob sighed. "He's right. It's a large school and our paths probably never crossed."

"He was like that," Mr. Culvert went on.

"Like what?" I finally had a chance to find out more about my ghost and unfortunately he had to be listening. Perhaps I should have stopped Mr. Culvert before he said something Jacob ought not to hear.

Or perhaps not. I might not get another opportunity to discover more. If Jacob didn't want to listen he could simply vanish and return later.

Jacob, however, did not disappear. He'd gone very rigid and that steely glare was back. "Emily, don't," he said.

He was right. It wasn't fair. I sighed. "Nevermind," I said.

"I don't mind," said Mr. Culvert cheerily. He passed me the plate of biscuits and I took one. "But surely you would know what he was like, being his friend."

"Emily," Jacob warned.

"Uh..." With my mouth full of biscuit I couldn't say anything else without spraying crumbs in my lap and over the floor. The thick Oriental rug was so lovely and I really didn't want to embarrass myself in front of my host...

"He was quite oblivious to those around him, wouldn't you say?" Mr. Culvert said, somewhat oblivious himself to my plight.

Jacob stepped between us and I could practically see steam rising from his ears. "Emily, stop this line of questioning. Now." His fingers curled into fists at his sides. "Please." The plea, uttered so quietly I barely heard it, caught me off guard and I inhaled sharply.

It was the wrong thing to do. A clump of half-chewed biscuit lodged in my throat and a fit of coughs gripped me. Mr. Culvert handed me my teacup, stretching straight through Jacob to do so. I dared a glance at the ghost's face as I sipped. It was dark and threatening but there was something else there, something...vulnerable. I wanted to reach out to him but I dared not. Instead I held on tightly to the cup as I moved a little to the left along the sofa to see around him.

"Yes, oblivious," Mr. Culvert said, not looking at me now. He seemed lost in memories from his Etonian days. "And self-absorbed."

"Self-absorbed?" Jacob spun round. "I was not!"

"He had his circle of friends and anyone who fell outside that circle simply didn't get...seen." Culvert shrugged and I didn't get the feeling he was bitter, just observant. I suspect George Culvert was very good at observing people. There was something quiet and watchful about him. Whereas Jacob was all contained energy simmering beneath the surface, Culvert seemed gentle to the core. I could imagine him watching people from a corner of a room through his spectacles, determining their strengths and faults, seeing how they interacted with others. Jacob on the other hand, was a man of action.

And the action I suspected he was about to perform could end in someone getting hurt and himself being exposed.

"Tell him I am not self-absorbed," Jacob snapped.

I gulped and tried not to look at him. "That's a shame," I

said quickly. "Because you're both nice people. I'm sure you would have got along."

"Not everyone would think that way," Culvert said.

"Oh but you seem very nice to me."

He blushed again and bowed his head. "I was referring to Beaufort. He was well liked by most at school," he said, "adored even. But certainly not everyone put him up on a pedestal. I'm sure some would have preferred to drag him off it."

"I wasn't on any bloody pedestal," Jacob said, drawing himself up to his full height.

I found that hard to believe. I'd spent much of the previous night picturing him on one, made of white marble and carved in the Roman style.

Jacob edged toward Culvert, looking like he wanted to make his presence known in the most dramatic way a ghost can. It was time to steer the conversation away from the subject of Jacob before Culvert found the rug pulled out from under him, quite literally.

"Perhaps it wasn't Jacob who told me about your father's collection of books on demonology, perhaps it was someone else." I hoped I sounded convincing but I suspect I came across like a flighty female. "The fact of the matter is, I have an interest in demons and I'm hoping you'll be kind enough to allow me to make use of your library to further my studies."

Culvert pushed his spectacles up his nose. *"You're* interested in demons?"

"Yes. It's a natural extension from my other activities, don't you think?"

His mouth twisted in thought. "I suppose so. Is there any demon in particular you want to study?"

"Shape-shifting demons."

He paused. "Well that's a coincidence."

"Why?"

"A book on shape-shifting demons was stolen from my library just last week."

CHAPTER 4

Jacob and I exchanged glances. The coincidence was too close for my liking. One week a book on demonology is stolen and the next a shape-shifting demon just happens to be summoned from the Otherworld? Unlikely.

"Stolen!" I said to Mr. Culvert. "By whom?"

George Culvert drummed his fingers on his knee, sighed, drummed some more then finally answered me. "I'm sad to say that it must have been one of the servants. I can see no other explanation. No one enters during the day without Greggs the footman letting them in and the house is locked up at night. It must have been someone who lives here and since Mother and I do not need to steal it..." He sank back into the chair, his shoulders slumped, his head bowed. He looked like a deflated balloon. I knew what it was like to have a trusted servant steal from you. Bella's predecessor had taken the payment from one of our séances before we'd had a chance to put it away. Celia and I had been devastated when we saw the money fall out of her apron pocket.

"Perhaps it wasn't a servant. The book could have been missing for some time," I said. "Months even. If it's an obscure one and your library is large, you wouldn't have noticed it. You probably had any number of people come into the house in that time."

"Good point," Jacob said with admiration.

Mr. Culvert shook his head. "The missing book is large with a beautiful red leather spine. It made quite a hole in my shelves and I noticed it missing immediately. I questioned the servants of course, but none owned up to the theft. However I'm quite certain it was one particular maid. She has been with us for only a month, and as the newest member in the house, I'm afraid suspicion naturally fell on her. Besides, the girl was very nervous when I questioned her."

"She's still with you?" I asked.

He nodded. "I couldn't dismiss her without evidence and I never found the book despite having the housekeeper search the room the girl shares with two other maids."

"We'll speak to her later," Jacob said.

I'd been thinking the same thing but wasn't sure if involving George Culvert any more than he already was would be a good idea. On the other hand, the more we spoke to him, the more I liked him and thought he could be trusted with all the information we knew. He might even prove helpful.

And I had a feeling he wouldn't think I was mad for talking to a ghost.

Before I could think further on the matter, he stood and offered me his hand. "Would you like to come with me to the library, Miss Chambers? We might as well get started on your research topic."

I took his hand and heard a grunt from Jacob. I casually raised my brows in his direction, challenging him to tell me what bothered him so much about the courteous action, but he merely grunted again and turned away. We both followed Culvert down to an enormous room on the ground floor filled to bursting with books. The library took up two entire levels and every spare space of wall was covered in shelves crammed with books of all shapes and sizes. Each wall had a ladder to reach the higher volumes, and two big arched windows framed with heavy crimson drapes allowed light into even the furthest corners. For night, cast iron gas lamps topped with crouching angels were bolted to the vertical sides of the shelves and were also positioned on pedestals beside most of the chairs. The mahogany furniture looked heavy with solid, stumpy legs ending in clawed feet, so unlike the spindly pieces in the drawing room. There were two leather-inlaid desks, one small and one large, and deep reading chairs upholstered in red leather that looked soft enough to curl up in. A small fire burned low in the enormous hearth to keep the chill away and the thick rug covering most of the floor gave the room a warm, welcoming feel. It was my idea of heaven.

"You like it." Mr. Culvert seemed genuinely pleased.

"It's wonderful," I said on a breath. "Are they all works dedicated to demonology?"

"Not all. Only half of that wall there." He indicated the wall opposite the door, the only one where the shelves weren't interrupted by windows or the fireplace. "The rest are volumes on other supernatural phenomena, and there's a few novels and medical texts too. My father's tastes were eclectic."

Even Jacob looked impressed. He went straight to the demonology books and scanned the shelves. "This might be a good one to start with, Emily."

I came up beside him and extracted the book he indicated. "*An Introduction to Demonic Phenomena.*"

Culvert pulled out a chair at the large central table. "Would you like to sit while you read?"

"Thank you, Mr. Culvert."

"Please, call me George."

I smiled at him. "And you shall call me Emily."

"That's a little informal on such short acquaintance, don't you think?" Jacob said, suddenly standing behind me.

I wanted to retort that he and I had dispensed with formalities on an equally short acquaintance but I couldn't alert George to his presence. Not yet. And I suspected Jacob would tell me the normal rules didn't apply to him anyway because he was a ghost.

I sat in the chair—I was right, the leather was soft and welcoming—and flipped to the table of contents. Jacob returned to browsing the shelves while George closed some books he had open on the other side of the large desk and tidied his notes.

"George!" came a shrill voice from outside the room. "George, do you have your nose buried in a blasted book again?" A striking woman dressed in a burgundy satin gown with excessively puffed sleeves and a cascade of ruffles on the skirt strode into the library. She stopped abruptly when she saw me and fixed me with a glare that could have frozen the Thames in summer. "Oh. You have a guest." She didn't sound pleased although she seemed surprised.

I lifted my chin and gave her a sweet smile in return. It was a tactic I'd seen Celia use at our séances. Whenever she was faced with a skeptical audience member, she would charm them. It worked most of the time. "Emily Chambers," I said, rising. "Pleased to—."

"I wasn't addressing you."

I plopped back down in the chair. So much for charm.

I felt rather than saw Jacob move up beside me. "Would you like me to pull the pins out of that ridiculous hair style and poke them one by one into her ear?"

I laughed then tried to stifle it but only ended up making a horrid snorting sound. Mrs. Culvert's glare—for I'd guessed it to be her—turned even frostier. I could not, however, quaver anymore, not after Jacob's offer. She did indeed have a rather ridiculous hairstyle, scraped back so tightly it made her eyes slant. The ridiculousness was amplified by her tiny hat with the very tall feathers shooting straight up from the crown in a V-shape. I'd not seen anything like it.

George placed a book on the table and gave me an apologetic grimace. "Mother, this is Miss Emily Chambers. She was a friend of Jacob Beaufort."

"Beaufort!" Mrs. Culvert's eyes widened and she suddenly smiled. It was dazzling and changed her face from one of severity to friendliness. The transformation was remarkable, if insincere, and I could see she must have been a beautiful woman in her youth. She had the same well-defined cheekbones as her son and a luscious, wide mouth with perfect teeth. *"Such* an illustrious family, and *such* a lovely boy was poor Jacob. So handsome and charming. Clever too. Cleverer even than you, George." This she said with a satisfactory gleam in her eye. George merely shrugged.

"Maybe she's not so bad after all," Jacob said.

"Shame he died," Mrs. Culvert continued with a sigh. "And in terribly mysterious circumstances too. I hear his poor mother hasn't quite got over it."

I glanced up at Jacob. A muscle pulsed high in his jaw and his fingers dug into the leather backrest of my chair. The indentations would have been noticeable to anyone who cared to look. I went to touch his hand to obscure the marks and calm him but he vanished. He reappeared near one of the long windows overlooking Wilton Crescent, his straight back to me.

"My dear Miss Chambers," Mrs. Culvert said, coming up beside me and standing in the exact place Jacob had vacated. She continued to smile but I now thought it stretched, almost gruesome. "How well do you know the family? Could you introduce me to Lady Preston I wonder?"

Lady Preston? Who on earth was she?

"Mother," George warned.

"I believe they throw the most lavish parties," she went on. "Or they used to. There haven't been any parties there since poor Jacob died." She stopped smiling for all of a second then the beam returned, harder than ever. "Perhaps a party is exactly what they need to take their mind off their loss. What do you think, Miss Chambers? We can have one here. I'll send the Prestons an invitation but if Lady Preston refuses you simply *must* speak to her and insist. Tell Lord and Lady Preston their daughter needs to enjoy herself again. It's not wholesome to keep a young lady of spirit away from Society. She should be enjoying herself, attending balls and teas and meeting young men." Her gaze flicked to George, then back to me again. "She must be about your own age, hmmm?"

If I was following the conversation correctly—and that was an If with a capital I—then the Prestons were Jacob's parents and Jacob was nobility!

Good lord, and I'd been addressing him by his first name all this time. I turned to him but he'd disappeared again. Thank goodness. Apart from the awkwardness of knowing he was so far above me on the social ladder that we might as well have been on different ladders entirely, I was also beginning to feel sick on his behalf having to listen to the awful Mrs. Culvert prattle on about his family in such a heartless way.

"Mother," George said again but to no avail. She was completely ignoring him now. It was as if he wasn't even in the room.

"Thank you for the invitation," I said although I wasn't sure *I* was actually invited without the Beauforts or Prestons or whoever they were. "However I must decline. I'm otherwise engaged that evening."

Her smile wilted like a lily in the hot sun as my snub hit home. She hadn't given me a date.

Her cold stare turned on George and I felt sorry for him. To his credit, he didn't flinch. He was probably used to her. "I'm going out for the rest of the day." She strode to the door, her broad skirts rippling like waves in time to her vigorous walk.

"Sorry," George said when she was gone. He glanced around the room. "Is he terribly mad now?"

All the blood drained from my face and plunged to my toes. "Uh...who?" I felt like a fool for even asking. He knew about Jacob. Of course he did. He was a clever man and I was hopeless at lying and keeping secrets. "He's gone," I said, answering my own question.

"Tell me when he returns so I can apologize."

"I didn't realize it was that obvious. How did you work out he was here?"

He smiled. "You are *the* pre-eminent spirit medium in London, you used his name as an introduction to me and you kept looking at certain spots about the room as if you were listening to someone speak. Oh, and you picked out the most useful book on demonology without even browsing the spines first."

I bit my lip and the blood returned to my cheeks with a vengeance. Now I knew why I was a terrible liar—because being caught out gave me such an awful feeling that I preferred not to risk it, hence the lack of practice. "I'm awfully sorry, Mr. Culvert. It was very wrong of me to mislead you."

"You agreed to call me George."

"George, as I said, I'm very sorry. Can you forgive me?"

He grinned and he had the same beautiful smile as his mother, although his was by far the more spectacular because of its sincerity. "Of course, although I'm not sure there's anything to forgive. Not telling me about Beaufort's ghost was understandable. I imagine not everyone is so...believing in your abilities."

"Not everyone, no. Not even all of the people who pay us to perform séances in their drawing rooms. I'm afraid we are still very much seen as a novelty act. A harmless entertainment for ladies."

"You're not entirely thought of in that light, let me assure you. Some are beginning to take you seriously. I'd heard about you and your sister at one of my Society for Supernatural Activity meetings. One of the members had witnessed a séance you conducted and was convinced you were genuine. I wanted to see for myself and tried to convince Mother to have you perform here for her friends while I watched on but she'd have none of the paranormal. She said she'd had enough of that nonsense when Father was alive."

"Then I'm glad we finally get to meet in this way." I indicated the bookshelves, the luxurious furniture. "This is a far more interesting setting. Perhaps one day, after this is all over, I can come back and summon a spirit for you."

"Thank you! That would be fascinating." He frowned. "But what do you mean, after all this is over? Does it have something to do with shape-shifting demons and why you want to study them?"

I nodded and finally told him the story about the demon's release. "Dear God," he murmured when I'd finished. He removed his glasses and rubbed the bridge of his nose. "This isn't good. Not good at all."

"Jacob told me it's very dangerous."

He nodded and put his glasses back on. "It is. But...didn't he tell you everything about them? Why do you need to read books?"

"It seems he's not privy to some details. How is it directed, for instance? Is there another way to return it to the Otherworld? Which cultures know of its existence? That sort of thing. We hoped you might be able to help us while we wait for the amulet peddler to return tomorrow."

"Of course, I'd be happy to. My own knowledge of the shape-shifting variety is somewhat lacking but I'll tell you what I know and then we'll search the books."

"Excellent. Let's see...ah yes. Jacob thinks it can only be killed by a weapon that has come from the Otherworld. But what kind of weapon?"

"It must be a blade of some kind—sword, dagger, axe, that sort of thing. Oh, and the demon's head must be severed from its neck by the blade."

Ugh. "Next question, how does it harm people?"

"Through good old fashioned physical violence, but of course its capabilities are dependent on the form it takes. In other words, if it changes into a snail, it cannot claw someone's heart out. No claws on snails you see."

"Perhaps it could slime them to death."

He laughed, loudly. "Very amusing." He continued to

laugh much too vigorously. I hadn't thought it *that* amusing, particularly considering the gruesome nature of the conversation but I didn't say so. He seemed to suddenly notice I didn't share his enthusiasm for my own joke and his laughter died. He cleared his throat and said, "Did you know it could kill ghosts too?"

"Kill ghosts? That doesn't seem entirely logical. Ghosts are already dead."

"What I meant was a demon can extract a ghost's soul." He tapped his chest. "From here. The soul can be quite literally pulled out. Not by us of course."

Why didn't I know this? Why hadn't Jacob told me? "And what happens if a ghost's soul is removed?"

"You don't know?" I shook my head and he pushed his glasses up his nose. "Well it ceases to exist at all, in any realm," he said. "It has no energy, no cognitive abilities. It becomes...nothing."

Oh. No. To become nothing would be, well, a fate worse than death to use a cliché.

"So your friend Jacob must be careful," he added.

"Yes," I said weakly. "Extremely." This information put Jacob's involvement into an entirely different context—this assignment could destroy him.

"Now, that's all I know. Shall we each find a book and begin?"

We spent the next three hours looking through books, making notes and cross-checking facts. Jacob didn't return but I didn't mind. I suspect I would have found it difficult to concentrate with him in the room. He was rather distracting. George and I worked quietly until a footman interrupted us with lunch, which George had requested to be served in the library.

"What's he like?" George asked, in between bites of warm ham. "Jacob Beaufort's ghost, I mean."

I paused, the fork half way to my mouth. Jacob was handsome, magnificent, intriguing and compelling. I found it hard not to look at him when he was in my presence, and hard not to think about him when he wasn't. "He seems nice," was all I said. Gushing about a ghost, particularly to a man, seemed foolish. It was times like this I wish I had a female friend of my own age to talk to. Celia wasn't quite the understanding type when it came to discussing men, dead or alive, unless it was with a view to matrimony and even then she would want me to temper my descriptions. "I was surprised when you said Jacob didn't really notice people at school though," I said. "He seems very aware of others." He'd definitely noticed me. My face still burned just thinking about his intense stares.

George shrugged. "Perhaps he's changed since his death. I hardly knew him but I do know that his awareness of others did not extend to those outside his circle. How did he die, by the way?"

"I was hoping you could tell me. We haven't discussed it and I don't want to ask...just in case." I put my fork down, no longer hungry. It had just struck me that I'd hit on the reason why Jacob was so solid, so real to me—perhaps he'd taken his own life. I'd never met a ghost who had, so maybe solidness was a characteristic of those spirits. I swallowed past the lump lodged in my throat. The thought was so awful I didn't want to think about it let alone voice it.

"You think he...?" George shook his head so vigorously I worried it would roll off his neck. "Even from my limited knowledge of him I can tell you Beaufort wasn't the sort. I've never met anyone so full of life, so content with his lot. Not to mention he had so much to live for."

Relief made me feel momentarily light-headed so I picked up my fork and began to eat again to give myself something to focus on.

"I didn't speak out of turn in the drawing room earlier," George went on. "Beaufort *was* good at everything. Sport, school, politics. Everyone loved him—students, teachers even the servants." He chuckled as he poked a potato with his fork. "And the girls too."

"Girls! Oh." Of course there would be girls. Jacob

Beaufort was definitely the sort to attract females.

Had he ever looked at any of them the way he looked at me?

"Sorry," George said, "I forgot for a moment there was a lady present."

I pushed my plate away, my hunger gone for good. "So you know nothing about his death?"

More head shaking from George. "He simply vanished from his Oxford rooms one night apparently. His body was never found."

"Never found! Good lord, how awful." Perhaps *that* was why Jacob was so solid and could wander where he pleased. His earthly body had not found a final resting place where his family could honor and remember him properly. It made quite a bit of sense to me.

"Terrible," George agreed. "My mother may be a lot of things, but she is certainly a voracious collector of gossip. If she says Lady Preston is still grieving, then most likely she is. And for Lady Preston to show her emotions in public, she must be very distressed indeed."

Tears pricked the backs of my eyes. Losing a child must be the worst thing that could happen to a mother, but to not have found his body, to be left wondering if he was alive somewhere but unable to contact his family...it was too awful to contemplate.

I forced the tears away. There was no point in getting upset for Lady Preston because I alone knew Jacob was not going to be found safe and sound. He was most definitely dead.

"Tell me about his family," I said. "His father is a lord?"

George nodded. "Viscount. Beaufort is the family name, Preston the title. I don't know them well. As I said, Jacob and I went to Eton together but our families have never mixed socially even though they only live around the corner in Belgrave Square. My father was considered a bit of an eccentric, you see, much to Mother's disappointment. Despite her attempts to further our standing in Society, we were never really accepted, particularly by a family like Jacob's."

"Oh? Are they terribly upright?"

"Very. The family is old, has buckets of money and owns a great deal of land in Essex. They spend most of their time there except when Parliament is open in spring and summer and they come to London together. Lord Preston has a lot of political influence in the House of Lords but he's a Tory—very conservative. Could you imagine a man who doesn't want to give farmers the right to vote associating with a demonologist?"

He laughed and I laughed too. But I couldn't imagine it. I wondered what Lord Preston would think of his dead son communicating with a spirit medium.

"What's so funny?" asked Jacob, suddenly appearing beside me.

I put a hand to my rapidly pounding heart. "You scared me."

"My apologies. If there was another way to come and go without alarming you I'd employ it." He gave me that smile I'd become so used to, the crooked one that made his lips curve in just the right way. It would seem he was no longer upset by what Mrs. Culvert had said.

"Is he here?" George asked, glancing around the room.

"He is," I said.

"Oh. Good." He cleared his throat. "Hello, Beaufort, how are you?"

Jacob sighed and shook his head in disbelief at the polite but inappropriate question. "I see you told him about me. Was that wise?"

"He guessed." To George I said, "He's well thank you, and asks how are you?"

"Very well," George said. "Fit as a fiddle." He pushed his glasses up his nose and grinned at me. He was enjoying this. I suppose he'd never had a conversation with a ghost before. Although to be technically accurate, he wasn't having one now, I was.

"Since he knows about me, I want to ask him something," Jacob said.

"He wants to ask you something," I said to George. "He's standing right beside me."

George's gaze settled on my right.

Jacob, on my left side, sighed again and picked up a book. George's gaze shifted. "Ask him to introduce us to the maid he suspects of stealing the book."

***

The girl, known by her surname of Finch, said she was sixteen but she looked older. Dark circles underscored eyes that drooped at the corners as if they were too tired to open properly. Red blotches on her cheeks and chin marked her otherwise sallow skin and she seemed to have far more teeth than could fit in her small mouth.

"Finch," George said, towering over the girl, "this lady wants to ask you some questions." He spoke to her with his hands clasped behind him and a deeper voice than he used when addressing me. I suppose he was fulfilling his role as master of the house by asserting his authority over her but, like most men, he didn't realize the best way to get answers was with kindness, not by frightening the poor girl.

"My name is Emily Chambers," I said to her. "And you are?"

"Finch," she said, eyes downcast.

George looked at me as if I had a memory like a sieve. Jacob, however, nodded his approval. He at least seemed to know what I was doing.

"Your first name?" I persisted.

"Maree, miss." Her hands, reddened and chapped, twisted and stretched her apron to the point where I thought she might tear it.

"Well then, Maree, Mr. Culvert tells me you started working here only a month ago."

"On the twenty-fifth, miss." Still she did not look at me.

"Ask her if she stole the book," Jacob said.

I refrained from rolling my eyes. Just. "Do you know the

book Mr. Culvert claims was stolen from this library, Maree?" I asked instead.

Maree's gaze flicked up to mine then lowered again. "I don't know nothin' 'bout no books, miss. I can't read." Her hands twisted faster and faster and she shifted her weight from foot to foot as if she would bolt at any moment.

"Don't fret, Maree," I said, touching her shoulder. "No one's going to hurt you. You're not in trouble. I believe you."

She looked at me, her eyes not quite trusting. "You do?"

"I do." I smiled at her. "You must not have any need for books or the time to learn to read them."

"I don't, miss. Them words and stuff all looked funny to me. And the pictures in that book scared me, they did. I wanted nothin' to do wiv it."

George shook his head. "And yet—"

"Of course you didn't," I said, cutting him off.

George cleared his throat and thrust out his chin. Jacob chuckled beside me. "He thinks your methods aren't getting results."

I had a feeling George wasn't the only one. I gave Jacob a pointed glare. If he had a better way of doing this, then he was welcome to feed me questions to ask the maid.

"So if you wanted nothing to do with the book," I said to her, "who did you give it to?"

Maree's gaze remained downcast. After a moment her shoulders slumped and began to shake. She was crying. Oh dear, I was going about this all wrong. I put my arm around her but she stepped away and I let my arm fall to my side.

George frowned at the girl. "Answer Miss Chambers, Finch. Who did you give the book to?"

"No one." She wiped away her tears with her apron but still they came. And still she kept looking at the rug. If she'd only meet my gaze I might believe her.

"She's lying," Jacob said.

"I know," I said on a sigh.

"Answer me, Finch," George said. I was struck by the change in him. When it had been just the two of us, he'd been gentle and kind, but now there was a commanding note in his tone that would make an army general proud. I wouldn't want to be in Finch's shoes. "Have you fallen in with a bad lot, is that it?" George asked. "I was told by the school's administrators that your brother was thrown out for thievery. Is he behind this?"

"No! It's nothin' to do wiv 'im, sir! Please, sir."

"Was it one of your friends from that school? Have they put you up to this?"

"Sir, please, sir, can I go? It weren't my fault! I don't know nothin' 'bout no book! Please, sir."

I caught George's gaze and nodded. He dismissed the maid and she ran from the room. Her footsteps and sobs finally grew distant and I sat down, defeated.

"Good try," Jacob said, perching on the desk near me. He gave me a sad smile. "Are you all right?"

I blew out a breath. "That was awful." I rubbed my temples where a headache threatened.

"But you see what I mean when I say she was lying," George said.

I nodded. "I know she was lying, but I wonder if we could have handled that interview better. It's likely she stole the book for someone else."

"Perhaps she had no choice in the matter," Jacob said.

"You think someone threatened her and if she refused to take the book then..." I couldn't finish the sentence. It was too horrible to contemplate the things that could befall a poor girl like Maree if she fell into the clutches of an unscrupulous player.

"I suppose," George said. He pursed his lips together in thought then shrugged one shoulder. "But she's not likely to tell us anything now."

"Probably not. George, you mentioned a school to Maree just now. Are you referring to the North London School for Domestic Service?"

He nodded. "Many of our junior staff come from there. Why?"

"No particular reason. My sister is going there to find a maid today, that's all."

"It has a good reputation and we've never had a problem with any of the servants from there. Until now," he added with a grunt of disgust.

Jacob narrowed his eyes at George. "Emily, what's say you and I continue the interview without our friend here?"

My thoughts exactly. "I think it's time we leave," I said to George. "I have another séance to conduct this afternoon with my sister." It was the truth. Celia and I did have an appointment to keep, but not for another hour if my pocket watch was anything to go by.

George rang for his footman who showed me out. Jacob disappeared then reappeared when I reached the street corner.

"I'll watch the main door while you go down to the basement," he said. There was a lightness about his step that hadn't been there before, and although he wasn't smiling, I suspected he was controlling it.

"You're enjoying this, aren't you?"

"George Culvert deserves us going behind his back to speak to his servants."

"That's not fair, Jacob. I quite like him. Most of the time." Although a gentleman couldn't be expected to treat his servants the way he treated his guests, it had come as something of a shock to see him turn from meek to master when the interrogation began. I'd not have expected it from him. Jacob on the other hand seemed like exactly the sort to order people about, no matter their station.

Jacob regarded me with a raised eyebrow. "You can't possibly like him. He's strange. Who chooses to study demonology for pity's sake?"

"Who chooses to see ghosts?"

Two finely dressed women I hadn't seen approaching quickened their steps as they passed by and lowered their parasols to avoid making eye contact. They must have heard me speaking to Jacob, or rather, to myself. At least they were too scared to give me odd looks.

I checked that no one else was within earshot then muttered, "Let's go. And don't say anything to me unless it's vitally important to my conversation with Maree. You're very off-putting at times."

"I am?" He grinned. Dazzled by his beautiful smile, my irritation disappeared and I grinned back.

We walked side by side to the Culvert house once more. Jacob took the steps up to the main door then vanished. I suppose he'd reappeared on the other side where he could keep a closer watch. I descended the other stairs that led down to the basement entrance used by the servants, not the Culverts themselves. I knocked on the door and a maid answered.

"Hello, I went to the North London School for Domestic Service with Maree Finch. Is she here? I need to speak to her."

It was a bold lie and the maid, a middle-aged matronly woman in white cap and apron, looked suspicious. "You friends wiv her?" she asked. I nodded. "Didn't fink the likes o' her had friends."

"Yes, well, can I see her? I'll be brief," I added when she began to shake her head. "It's about...the passing of a favorite teacher."

The maid heaved a sigh and asked me, grudgingly, to wait while she fetched her.

Jacob came in behind me as Maree emerged from one of the rooms off the narrow hallway, her hands buried in her apron again. She took one look at me and burst into tears.

"Leave me be! I dunno nothin'!" she cried. She backed away as I stepped forward.

"It's all right, Maree. I'm not going to hurt you. Please, just tell the truth and everything will be all right. Tell me who made you steal the book."

She shook her head. "No. No." Tears streamed down her face and her nose oozed a thick green sludge. "Leave me be. Go away!"

"Maree—."

"I said go away!" She ran at me, teeth bared, cap falling to once side. A knife in her grasp.

She hadn't been ringing her hands in her apron, she'd been polishing the blade.

I gasped and put my arms up to cover my face.

"Emily!" Jacob's shout sounded strange in my ears, not like him at all. High, strained.

Scared.

CHAPTER 5

Maree's knife was inches from my face. I screamed, or maybe she did, and then I was shoved aside by one of Jacob's big hands. I hit the wall and slid to the floor, landing with a thud on my rear. My hat slid down over my eyes. Jacob removed it and drew me into his arms. He supported my head with one hand and my back with the other and held me against his solid chest. It felt good, safe and...perfect. I closed my eyes and breathed deeply, telling myself I wasn't unnerved by the lack of a pulse or warmth in his body.

I was completely unhurt, of course, apart from a sore shoulder where I'd hit the wall, but Jacob cradled me as if I were an injured kitten.

"Emily? Did she cut you?" He brushed my hair off my forehead. All that violent thrusting about had dislodged not only my hat but my hair from its pins. "Emily, answer me!" His lips were so close I would have been able to feel his breath on my cheek if he could breathe.

Or I could have kissed him.

I wanted to kiss him. Wanted to feel the softness of his lips even though I knew they would be cool, tasteless, and it was a most improper thing for a young lady to do. I didn't care. Blood pounded in my veins, rushed into my head, and I could think of nothing but him. It was madness.

I was mad.

He massaged the back of my neck and the cool strength of his fingers shocked me out of my daze. I looked into his eyes but his gaze darted over my face, assessing, and he didn't notice my scrutiny.

"Emily?" My whispered name seemed to hover on his lips for an eternity.

I remembered I hadn't yet answered him. "I'm well," I whispered.

His Adam's apple bobbed furiously and a muscle high in his cheek throbbed. He nodded once, a small movement that I would have missed if I hadn't been watching him so closely. "Good," he said thickly. "Good, good." His eyes suddenly shuttered. Where before they'd been wide and urgent, now they were distant, cold. "Good," he said again, stronger this time.

He let me go, quite unceremoniously, so that I almost fell to the floor a second time. "Jacob, what's wrong?"

The maid who'd let me in the door suddenly appeared. She put her hands to her cheeks and gasped. "Oh lordy, lordy, lordy. Is you all right, miss?" She helped me to my feet. "It was that girl's fault, weren't it? I knew she was trouble, I did. Told Mrs. Crouch the 'ousekeeper to watch out for her. Gone has she?"

"Uh, yes. Thank you." I watched Jacob climb the stairs up to the street outside. "Please don't tell your master about this," I said to the maid. "Just tell him Maree decided to leave his employment."

"What's all the fuss about down there?" came a woman's voice from the back of the service area. "Who's making all that noise?"

"Mrs. Crouch," the maid said to me.

I hurriedly thanked her again, picked up my hat, and left before the housekeeper arrived. Outside, Jacob was waiting at the top of the stairs.

"Are you all right?" I asked him quietly so as not to alarm

anyone within earshot.

He stared off into the distance. "I think that's my line." When I didn't answer him, he turned to me. "Well? *Are* you all right?"

"Is that a genuine question?" I started walking, wanting to put distance between myself and the Culvert house. "It's difficult to tell considering the way you dropped me in there."

We rounded the corner and a policeman in uniform stepped out of the recessed doorway of a coffee house and into my path, startling me. "Everything all right, miss?" He looked over my head, saw no one, and raised his eyebrows. "Who you speaking to then, eh?"

"Is there a law against talking to myself, constable?" I didn't want to deal with him. I was still mad at Jacob although it struck me how selfish my own feelings were on the matter. He'd rescued me and I should be grateful. I *was* grateful.

The policeman's eyebrows rose further, almost disappearing into his tall helmet. "Er, not that I know of. Good afternoon, miss."

I walked off, Jacob at my side. "I'll take that as meaning you're perfectly well," he said, picking up our conversation.

"A little shaken," I said quietly in case anyone else was lurking in doorways. "But otherwise unscathed. Thanks to you. I owe you my life, Jacob."

His pause weighed heavily between us. I tried to look at him out of the corner of my eye but only saw his profile, staring ahead. "Don't," he finally said.

"Don't what?"

"Don't talk about it. Anyone would have done the same thing."

That may be so, but why did he sound so upset? Not angry, just... I sighed. I couldn't even pinpoint the emotions simmering off him let alone determine their reason. Nor did I think I'd get an answer out of him. His face was closed up tight.

So I started a new thread of conversation, a safer one. "Did you see where Maree went?"

He shook his head. "She was gone by the time I reached the street."

If he'd run after her immediately, he might have seen the direction she took, but he'd stayed with me to see if I was all right. No matter how hard I tried, I couldn't be sorry about that.

"Who do you think she stole the book for?" I asked.

He shrugged. "Who knows? Her brother, a friend, or just because she liked the look of it and thought it would fetch a good price. Whoever it was, there's a good chance they were the ones who cursed the amulet, or will know who did. We have to find them."

I nodded. "I'm not sure if our research can help us there though. George and I learned that the demon was well known to gypsies across Europe. They used to summon it then direct it to destroy their enemies, or the horses of their enemies."

"So we can strike gypsies off our list of suspects."

"Why?"

"Gypsies pass down their customs through the generations by word of mouth. They won't need a book to tell them how to summon a shape-shifting demon."

The street grew busier as we drew closer to the Kings Road precinct so we strolled in silence although my mind was in turmoil. I was still a little shaken by the incident with Maree, and even more shaken by the knowledge that someone was directing a demon based on whatever knowledge they could gain from one book.

But there was something even more troubling. No, not troubling as such, but it occupied my thoughts almost to the exclusion of all else. "George told me about your family," I said to Jacob eventually. We were only a block away from my house and I didn't know when we'd have a chance to speak so openly to one another again. I'd expected Jacob to disappear and let me walk home alone but he'd remained by my side the entire time. Was he still worried about the incident with Maree? Did he expect me to faint out of fright at any moment?

He said nothing, so I went on. "Not that George knew much, but he did tell me they're very...distressed about your death because your body was never found, you see, so they can't have peace." I was rambling, the words tumbling out of my mouth without me thinking them through first. I was afraid that if I did think about them, I wouldn't say anything, and I desperately wanted to broach the topic with Jacob. It seemed vital somehow, but to whom, I wasn't sure. Him? Or me? Or his family?

"That isn't your concern, Emily," he said, striding ahead. I had to walk fast to keep up with him. His legs were very long.

"Nevertheless, I am concerned. I'd like your permission to speak to them—."

"No!"

"But I can help them move on. They need to know you're dead, Jacob, or they'll be forever wondering."

"Leave it, Emily. You're not..." He heaved a deep sigh. "This is not your concern."

"But—"

"No!" He stopped and rounded on me so that I almost bumped into him.

I ducked into a nearby alley where we could talk without the stares. I was about to argue but then I saw anxiety behind the fierceness in his eyes.

Why? What about his family worried him so? Or perhaps the real question was, what was it about *me* meeting them had him so concerned?

What would I learn?

"Very well. I understand." I couldn't meet his eyes as I spoke. I fully intended to visit them, but not today. Today I had a séance to conduct.

I started walking again and he fell into step beside me. "There's one other question I want to ask you."

He groaned. "I had a feeling there would be."

"Did your death come about due to an accident?"

"Not an accident, no."

My stomach knotted. Even though it was the answer I expected it sickened me to hear him confirm my suspicions. "So someone must have...killed you." The word stuck in my throat. It was simply too horrible. "Who?"

"I don't know."

I stopped. He stopped too and shrugged. "I don't," he said.

I believed him. "How did it happen?"

"I'm not entirely sure."

I waited but he didn't say anything else. "Would you like to elaborate?"

"Not right now."

Good lord it was like pulling out a rotten tooth—painful. "I see. So your body is located...?"

"I don't know."

"Right. So you don't know who killed you, or how, or where or even why. Do you think any of those things is the reason why you can go wherever you please and why you look decidedly real?"

His gaze fixed on something over my shoulder and I thought he wouldn't answer me, but then he said, "I think they have something to do with the way in which I died, yes."

"So...do you want to tell me more?"

He looked at me with those blue, blue eyes and darkly forbidding expression that thrilled me yet unnerved me at the same time. "Perhaps another day," he said.

If he thought a few simmering glances would deter me, he had a lot to learn. "Why not now?"

He started walking again. "Because I think you'll take it upon yourself to find out more if I do. Give a dog a bone and it'll look for a second when that's gone."

I squinted at him. "Are you comparing me to a dog?"

"When your hair tumbles over your eyes like that, you do

look a little like an Old English sheepdog."

I swept my hair off my forehead and tried to shove it under my hat but without the pins to keep it in place, it simply fell out again. He laughed.

"This isn't funny, Jacob. We're discussing your death."

"Which we haven't got time for at the moment, not with a demon on the loose."

I couldn't argue with him since he was right. Despite the lack of time, however, I would still try, even without his help. He might not want to discover who his murderer was, but he or she had to be punished. Jacob's death could not be swept aside as if it didn't matter. It mattered.

More than I wanted to admit.

"I hope you're not mad about the dog comment," Jacob said as we turned into Druids Way. As usual the wind whipped down the street, making an even bigger mess of my hair. "If it makes you feel any better," he said, "the Old English sheepdog is one of my favorite breeds."

"I hate you," I said and he laughed harder.

We reached home and he disappeared as soon as Celia met me at the door. I stared at the spot where he'd been standing until she pulled me inside.

"Goodness me, Em, look at you!" She clicked her tongue as she removed my hat and groaned when the curls spilled over my face. "We have to be at Mrs. Postlethwaite's house in fifteen minutes." She teased and tugged my hair into shape, rearranged my hat on my head, turned me around and pushed me out the door.

Exactly fifteen minutes later, we arrived at Mrs. Postlethwaite's house. The séance went well. We didn't release any demons and the ghost we summoned—Mrs. Postlethwaite's dead husband—was eager to return to the Waiting Area after his widow had finished asking him if he'd had a clandestine relationship with the next door neighbor. He hadn't, or so he said, and Mrs. Postlethwaite was content with his answer although her spinster sister sitting beside her thought it a lie. She also thought I was a fraud and tried to prove it by inspecting the objects the ghost held up as part of our routine to see if we used hidden wires or magnets. She found none of course, which only soured her temper further.

I managed to avoid her afterwards while tea was being served. Indeed, I managed to avoid all of the guests—an easy thing to do since they left me alone. To be fair, they probably didn't know what to say to me. Some might be scared, others just cautious and I didn't make it easy for them, preferring my own company. Celia was the chatty one, handing out cards to the guests and telling them stories, some true, about the ghosts we'd summoned at other séances. It was all good business, she once told me, and she enjoyed the theatre of it immensely. My sister had missed her calling—she would have been a natural on a Covent Garden stage.

My separation from the group allowed me to think as I sipped my tea. After wondering why there was a rush of widows summoning their late husbands at our séances, I couldn't stop thinking about Mr. Postlethwaite's extra-marital relationship. He'd been quite an attractive man for his age, which I put to be at mid-forties, and he certainly kept an eye on the prettier ladies in the room, my sister included and his wife, unfortunately, not.

I wasn't naïve. I knew married men and women had affairs on occasion, and the idea of my existence coming about because of one wasn't new to me. In fact it was the most obvious explanation. For some time I'd thought Mama must have met someone after her husband's death then nine months later I'd been born. But seeing Mr. Postlethwaite sowed a seed of doubt. Just a small one. He had been precisely the sort of person to have a liaison outside of his marriage—handsome in a preening, peacock-ish way, a roaming eye, and a charming manner.

Mama had been none of those things. She was pretty, I suppose, although it seemed to me she'd always been middle-aged, even when I was little. But she wasn't handsome like some women, or gregarious, and she had certainly never looked at men the way Mr. Postlethwaite looked at ladies.

Could Mama possibly have fallen deeply in love with one man so soon after her beloved husband's death? A man who'd not loved her enough in return when he got her with child?

If not, then...what?

I didn't have any answers by the time we left Widow Postlethwaite's house, nor was there any likelihood of getting any. Mama was possibly the only person who knew my real father's name and I'd not been able to summon her ghost at all since her death. She must have crossed over immediately.

I pushed the problem aside, telling myself it didn't matter, that I was loved by my sister and had been by my mother and that's all that mattered. Anyway, now I had other things to occupy my mind. I had the demon. And I had Jacob.

I was eager to return home and speak to him again. Not for any reason, just because I wanted to. Perhaps I could find out more about his death, but if not it didn't matter. I'd enjoy his company regardless of what we talked about.

"How did your information gathering go this morning?" Celia asked on the way home.

"Well enough." I told her everything we'd learned, including the interview with Maree the maid, mentioning the school but leaving out the part where she tried to stab me. My sister's constitution is incredibly strong but still it wouldn't do to alarm her. She might never let me go out alone again.

"I wonder if Lucy knows her," Celia said.

"Who's Lucy?"

"Our new maid. I collected her this morning from that North London School for Domestic Service. We'll ask her when we get home. Now, enough of that." We turned into our street and I glanced up at our house. No Jacob standing on the doorstep. I sighed. "Tell me about this George Culvert fellow," Celia said. "What was he like? Is he handsome? Was the house very large and does he have older brothers?"

"Older brothers? Why, are you interested in meeting them for yourself, Sis?" I looked at her sideways and had to hold onto my hat as the breeze tried to lift it off my head.

"Of course not," she scoffed. "I simply want to know if an older brother will inherit the house, that's all, or if it all goes to this George."

"This George," I said sharply, "is a nice enough gentleman but he doesn't interest me in the way you're implying." I stalked off ahead and ran up the front steps.

"But—."

"Celia, stop trying to marry me off to every eligible gentleman we meet. I'm seventeen. I want to enjoy my freedom before I settle down with a husband."

"Being married does not necessarily mean you'll lose your freedom."

"Then why haven't you settled down with any of the men who've shown interest in you?" Three gentlemen had courted Celia over the years but despite a great deal of speculation on my part, she'd not married any of them.

She fished in her reticule for the door key. "That's none of your concern," she said, snippy. "Now, come inside and meet Lucy. She seems very sweet."

Lucy did indeed seem sweet. She was a little younger than me, plumper, shorter and fairer. She had an English rose complexion, the sort that's permanently pink and blushes easily. I'd often wished to have just such a complexion but with my tendency to feel embarrassed a lot of the time, it's probably just as well that I don't.

"I hope you'll like it here, Lucy," I said to her.

"Th...thank you, m...miss." She bobbed a careful but wobbly curtsy and stared at me as if I had two heads. If her eyes widened any further they'd pop out of her head.

I turned an accusing eye on Celia, one hand on my hip.

"I thought it best we tell her up front," Celia said, setting down her carpet bag. "Get it out in the open, so to speak, to avoid any nasty surprises later on. Particularly since that ghost of yours seems to be coming and going with ill-mannered frequency."

"I don't think your sister likes me," Jacob said, popping up behind me. Was he watching me and trying to arrive at inopportune moments on purpose?

The thought of him keeping an eye on me sent a shiver down my spine, and not entirely in a bad way.

I ignored him and concentrated on Lucy but the poor thing whimpered beneath my gaze. I certainly wouldn't alert her to Jacob's presence. She might faint and then where would we be? Instead, I gave my sister a glare then turned a smile on the maid.

"He's a nice ghost," I assured her.

"Thank you," he said, "although nice is a rather bland word."

"He won't harm you," I went on, doing my best to ignore him. "And he probably won't be here much longer, only until we sort out..." I bit my lip. Finishing the sentence with "our demon issue" probably wasn't a good way to settle her nerves. "Until we sort out a few things."

The thought of Jacob leaving once we'd returned the demon to the Otherworld filled me with a hollowness I didn't want to explore. I'd only known him a day but he'd somehow managed to fill up my life in a way nothing else had.

It was all I could do not to look around and see if the thought had struck him too.

The girl nodded quickly, her eyes still huge and her cheeks paler. I wasn't sure Celia's tactic to tell Lucy about me being a medium was such a good idea. Having someone stare at me like I was a lunatic in my own house wasn't my idea of comfort. Besides, would knowing mean she'd stay around longer, or just leave earlier? At least she was still here—it was a promising start.

"How is dinner coming along?" Celia asked as Lucy accepted her bonnet and hung it up on the stand. "Good, miss. It'll be ready at six like you said. I set the water boiling for the potatoes and the fish is all ready to go on the gridiron, but I couldn't find it—the gridiron, not the fish—so I'll just use one of the pans instead. Mrs. White our teacher told us to make do with what pots and things are already 'vailable and not worry our mistress 'bout that stuff. She's a smart lady, Mrs. White, but she didn't take no fuss from no one."

It was my turn to stare wide-eyed at her. It seemed our maid was quite the chatterer when she wasn't frightened.

I smiled at Celia. Celia smiled at Lucy. "Can you serve tea in the drawing room, please," she said, "I'm parched after that walk."

Lucy curtseyed again, without wobbling. "As you wish, miss. I'm very good at making tea. Mrs. White always said so. Said I was the best tea-maker in the whole school." She turned to go, stopped, turned back to us, curtseyed again, and only then did she make her way down the hallway to the stairs leading to the kitchen basement.

"Aren't you going to ask her about the Culvert maid?" Celia asked me as we entered the drawing room.

"Exactly what I was going to say," Jacob said, following me.

The room was cool so I stoked the smoldering fire with the irons.

"I'll do that," Jacob offered.

I shook my head. I didn't want to alert Celia to his presence—she already thought him ungentlemanly for his ghostly comings and goings—and I definitely didn't want Lucy to see floating fire irons when she entered with the tea.

"I think Lucy needs a few moments to get used to me before I press her about Maree," I said, poking the coals. "Oh and thank you, Sis, for mentioning the whole spirit medium thing to her. I'm sure she'll be inclined to stay *much* longer than the other maids now that she knows"

"Sarcasm will make your face sag," she said.

"I'm simply saying I don't think it was a good idea." I returned the iron poker to the stand and sat beside her on the sofa.

"I disagree," Jacob said from his usual place by the mantelpiece.

"We had to try something," Celia said, taking up her embroidery.

I picked up the book I'd begun the day before and left on the round occasional table. "Why does 'something' always have to involve me being on the receiving end of odd or frightened looks?"

"It's better than being on the end of pitying ones."

I lowered my book to see her better. Was she referring to herself and her spinster state? But she kept embroidering as if she hadn't a care in the world and it had merely been an off-hand comment.

"Both are better than not being noticed at all," Jacob muttered.

My lips parted in a silent "Oh" and I closed my eyes so I didn't have to look at him. What a horrible, selfish fool I was. Jacob's lot was so much worse than anything Celia or I experienced. That would teach me to be so ungrateful.

"I'm sorry," I said. "You're right."

"Your book is upside down," he said.

I shut it and returned it to the table. He was smiling at me and there wasn't a hint of self-pity in his expression. It shouldn't have surprised me. Jacob didn't strike me as the sort to wallow in his disadvantages, even though being dead was a major one.

I was about to relent and tell Celia that Jacob was in the drawing room with us when Lucy entered carrying the tea tray as if it were made of gold and precious jewels. Her slow, careful shuffle didn't stop the cups from clinking against each other. Her tongue darted out as she eyed her destination—the central table in front of the sofa—and lodged in the corner of her mouth like a bookmark. When she finally set the tray down I let out a long breath and heard Celia do the same.

"Could you pour, please," Celia asked.

I wanted to throttle her. The poor girl was nervous enough and now she had to manage the pouring. Despite her shaking hands, Lucy poured the tea and spilled only a little onto the saucers. I reached for my own cup, as did Celia, and thanked her.

Lucy beamed at us both and blushed as bright as a radish. "I was better at it in school. I'm a bit nervous, see, being my first day and all." She turned to go but I called her back. She stopped and bit her lower lip, the smile and blushes gone. "Yes, miss? Something wrong, miss?" Her hands twisted together in front of her and I was reminded of Maree Finch. Thankfully Lucy wasn't holding a knife.

"No, no, the tea is fine. I just wanted to ask you something. I met a girl from the North London School for Domestic Service today," I said, trying to sound like this wasn't important and we were having a casual conversation. I didn't want to unsettle her any more than she already was.

Lucy blinked. "Oh? Who?"

"Maree Finch. She's recently gone into service for the Culverts."

"I remember Maree."

"What was she like?"

She shrugged. "I didn't know her too well. She was nice, I s'pose. Quiet. Don't really remember much more than that. We weren't good friends or nothing."

"She has an older brother, doesn't she?"

She nodded then frowned. "What's his name? Lord, I can't remember. Thomas, Timmy...something like that. He was at the school too for a bit, but got sent away. No good for service, Mrs. White said. A troublemaker. I saw him at school once, after he wasn't s'posed to be there no more."

"Oh? What was he doing?"

"Came to see Maree."

"Ask her if Maree was a thief too," Jacob said.

"Maree's a good girl though, isn't she." I worded it like a statement rather than a question. I didn't want to give Lucy the idea that we were fishing for information. I wanted her to open up to us on her own.

"I think so. Mrs. White never said anything bad about her, just that she was a bit...what's the word?"

"Violent?" Jacob offered.

"Unpredictable?" I said.

"No, something that means she gets talked into doing stuff easily. Stuff that's not always good for her to do, if you know what I mean."

"Impressionable," I said.

"That's it! Impreshun-able." She frowned. "She hasn't stole nothing from her employer, has she?"

Jacob and I exchanged glances. He nodded and I nodded back. If we wanted answers, we'd have to at least tell her part of the truth.

"She might have stolen a book from Mr. Culvert on demonology."

"Demon-what?"

"Demonology. It's the study of demons and angels."

"Oh," she whispered. She glanced at Celia, perhaps because she thought her the normal one of the two of us.

"Rest assured *we* have nothing to do with demons," Celia said. "We only deal with good spirits, happy ones."

Jacob snorted but I admired Celia's ability to lie so convincingly. She was really very good at it. There wasn't a hint of a blush on her fair skin.

"Mr. Culvert would like his book back," I said. "Indeed, it's quite important that he does get it back. You see..." Oh dear, this was the point at which I should tell her about the demon on the loose. But her face looked so innocent with those big hazel eyes and pale, pale skin, that I didn't want to frighten her anymore than she already was. It was hard enough starting a new job and moving in with two strangers, I didn't want to be responsible for her nightmares too.

Celia, however, seemed to have no such qualms. "You see Mr. Culvert fights demons and the book is vital to his work."

"Why doesn't she just tell the girl he's invisible and can

move mountains too?" Jacob said with a shake of his head.

I bit the inside of my cheek to stop myself from laughing. Jacob, seeing my distress, gave me a self-satisfied smirk.

"Vital?" Lucy repeated.

"Yes," Celia said. She set down the embroidery in her lap, all seriousness. Perhaps she even believed her own lie, or part of it. "Unless Mr. Culvert gets the book back, the people of London could be in grave danger from demons. So you see, if you know anything that could help us, we'd very much appreciate it if you would let us know. Your role is terribly important, Lucy. In fact, you could save London."

Jacob groaned and rolled his eyes. Since I was used to Celia's fondness for melodrama, I simply looked on, somewhat stunned because her method seemed to be getting results. Lucy's forehead crinkled, her brows knitted and her mouth twisted to the side. She was thinking hard.

"Well, let me see now," she said. "Maree might have taken the book if her brother asked her to. I told you I saw him, didn't I, after he was s'posed to have left school. He sneaked into the room all us girls shared to talk to Maree. Caused a right stir but no one told Mrs. White. She'd have blamed Maree and it weren't her fault. She can't control her brother any more than I can control the clouds."

Celia and I sat forward. Even Jacob focused all his attention on the girl.

"Do you know what Maree and her brother spoke about?" I asked.

She shook her head. "No. They whispered."

"Would she have confided in anyone afterwards? A friend perhaps?"

"She didn't have any friends. She was so quiet, see, and a bit...you know." She drew little circles at her temple with her finger. "Maree kept to herself and did what she was told mostly. She looked up to Mrs. White I s'pose, we all did. She's a right good teacher is Mrs. White and she cared 'bout us all too. If Mr. Blunt tried to skimp on our meals, she was onto him right away. Told him it was 'gainst school reg'lations and she'd report him to the board. The board's the gentlemen who run the school, see. There's some right toffs on the board, there is. One's a lord and all."

Her chatter had veered a little off the topic but Celia and I let her go. I wanted her to just talk and see what she said in the hope there was something useful among all the gossip. Unfortunately I'd not detected any so far.

"So you can't think of anyone else, other than her brother, who Maree might steal a book for?" Celia asked.

Lucy shook her head.

"Have you ever overheard anyone talking about demons at the school?" I asked.

"No! It's a Christian place, it is. Mr. Blunt sees we always say our prayers before dinner. The devil, now that's diff'rent. Mr. Blunt's always talkin' 'bout the devil comin' to get us in our beds if we don't behave. Course it's never the devil but Mr. Blunt hisself who comes."

"What?" I blurted out before I could reign in my shock. "Into your beds?"

I expected Celia to admonish me for my outburst but she simply stared at Lucy open-mouthed. Lucy had managed to do the impossible and render my sister speechless.

"Bloody hell," Jacob said, rubbing his chin.

"Oh yes," Lucy said, oblivious to the heavy blanket of horror she'd thrown over us. "Mostly only the pretty girls. Tried it once with me, he did, but I was so scared I couldn't move and he said he didn't like that so he never bovvered me again." She said it as if it were an every day part of life, like dressing or eating. Is that how it was in the workhouses and ragged schools? The children simply accepted their plight because they didn't know any better?

I felt sick to my stomach. And then I felt angry. A hot, gut wrenching anger. Lucy was such a sweet girl, how could anyone take advantage of her like this Mr. Blunt had?

But I didn't want to show my anger in front of her. She didn't seem too upset by what had befallen her, so why make her feel degraded? Hadn't she already endured enough?

Fortunately Celia remained silent although she'd gone very white and still. The only movement she made came from her throat as she swallowed.

Since Celia didn't look like she would begin talking any time soon, I dismissed Lucy. "Thank you for your help. You may go. Oh, and make sure you enjoy a cup of tea yourself."

Lucy beamed. "Thank you, Miss Chambers. You're not all that scary really, are you?"

I couldn't help laughing, despite my heavy heart. Lucy left and as if she'd been wound up, Celia moved once more. She reached for her teacup. "Such a sweet girl," she said and sipped, as if she'd not heard a thing Lucy had said about Blunt's late night visits.

I stared at her in disbelief. Did she think if she ignored the situation it would go away? Or was she avoiding the topic for my sake? Sometimes I suspect my sister thinks I know as little about what happens between couples as I did when I was ten. I may be a virgin but I wasn't naïve.

Jacob moved away from the mantelpiece and stood before me. "You shouldn't have heard any of that," he said, his voice sounding like a roll of thunder, deep and low.

"Good lord, not you too," I muttered. Did everyone think I was an innocent in need of protection from the realities of the world?

"Pardon?" Celia asked, cup poised at her lips. "Is that ghost here again?"

Before I could answer her, Jacob said, "I'm going to pay the school a visit. Let's see what Mr. Blunt thinks when the devil appears to him tonight in the shape of one very angry ghost. With luck he'll turn to God instead of the girl's dormitory from now on."

His conviction made me feel marginally better. If anyone could punish Blunt and force him to change his ways it would be Jacob. I'm not sure I'd like to be on the end of his anger. Although he seemed to keep his emotions in check most of the time, I suspect once his temper was unleashed it would be like a terrible storm—destructive and unpredictable and anyone in it's path had better get out of the way or suffer the consequences.

CHAPTER 6

I knew someone was in my room even before I was fully awake. I don't know how I knew—I couldn't hear any movement or smell any scent and it was too dark to see more than shadows.

Then one of those shadows moved. It was man-sized and it was right by my bed. My heart leapt into my throat and I opened my mouth to scream but a hand clamped over it.

"It's me," came Jacob's voice. "If I take my hand away, will you be quiet?"

"Try it and find out," I mumbled into his palm.

He removed his hand, somewhat tentatively. "Sorry I scared you." He sat on the bed beside me, so close his thigh almost touched mine. I could just make out the whiteness of his eyes and the shape of his face in the darkness but little else. My heart, still in my throat, hammered so loudly I was sure he must be able to hear it.

"I could have woken the entire household if I'd screamed!" I hissed at him.

"But you didn't. I was waiting for the moment you registered my presence and opened your mouth."

"You can see in the dark?"

"Better than I could before I died."

I pulled the bedcovers up to my chin. "What if I'd been indecent?"

"It's all right, I checked and you weren't."

"Very amusing."

His low chuckle rippled through the darkness. "I give you my word as a gentleman that I won't ravish you."

Could ghosts ravish? Did his...masculine parts work the same as when he was alive? Now there was a question that had my curiosity piqued. Instead I said, "You're in fine form tonight. Is there a reason or are you just happiest when you're tormenting me?"

"I'm tormenting *you?"* There was a long silence in which I think he was staring at me. It was disconcerting knowing he could see me when I couldn't see him, particularly when my hair probably looked a mess and my eyes must be puffy.

"Yes," I said huffily, "you are. Please light the lamp so I'm no longer at a disadvantage."

He stood and I heard his footsteps cross the room followed by the scrape of a striking match. The single flame threw patterns of light and shadow over his face, highlighting his beautiful contours. He lit the gas lamp and set it down on the dressing table opposite the foot of the bed. He remained there, looking at the items on the table's surface. No, not quite at my things, but at *me,* in the mirror's reflection. His good humor of earlier seemed to have vanished and he was back to being brooding and unreadable, but that could have just been the lack of light cast by the lamp. It wasn't particularly effective in the thick darkness.

"What's brought this behavior on?" I asked, sitting up. I drew my legs up and rested my chin on my knees, making sure the covers still hid most of me. "Yesterday you knocked and turned your back when you entered my room. Tonight you just appeared with no warning."

"I didn't knock because I didn't want to wake anyone."

"You woke me!"

"Anyone else. I don't think your sister would forgive me if I got her out of bed in the middle of the night."

"I'm not sure I'll forgive you either," I said. I do like my sleep. If I get less than eight hours a night I'm generally not the nicest person the next day. Jacob would learn that the hard way if he wasn't careful. "So is this the real Jacob Beaufort I'm seeing now?"

"No, it's the dead one." He crossed his arms and challenged me with that glare of his in the mirror's reflection.

My own glare faltered. I looked away, mortified and at a loss for words. There was no suitable comeback to his response, let alone a witty one.

He sat on the foot of my bed with a sigh. "I didn't want all the fuss and formality of you and your sister meeting me in the drawing room and your new maid serving us tea as if this were a proper social call. There is nothing proper about my visits, Emily. Nothing at all." His voice faded towards the end, as if he wasn't sure he wanted to say it.

"It's just a little disconcerting," I said. "Most of the ghosts I see are ones I've summoned. Occasionally I come across a spirit haunting a building but I've never had one come and go in my house before. Besides which, I'm not used to male company in the drawing room let alone my bedroom."

He leaned back against one of the posts at the foot of my bed. "This is not how I envisaged our talk to go but somehow...somehow our conversations never do seem to head in the direction I want them to." I was trying to decipher his meaning when he tilted his head to the side and looked at me puppy-like, giving me his crooked smile. "I just wanted to speak to you."

Only speak? If he gave me that smile and that look I'd let him do almost anything.

The thought made my insides clench. Oh lord, was I the sort of woman my sister called a wanton?

"What did you want to talk to me about?" If I didn't rein in my wild thoughts I might find myself saying, and doing, something I regretted.

"I went to see Blunt."

"Ah. The master of the North London School for Domestic Service. Did you haunt him?"

"I did." The smile was back but it lacked the sense of fun of earlier.

"And?"

"And sometimes I like being a ghost. I gave him the full spiritual experience—flying objects, knocking, emptying the bedpan, and my personal favorite, writing a note ordering him to cease his visits to the girl's dormitory.

"Do you think he'll comply?"

"The note told him that if he did not, the hauntings will continue. If his begging for mercy is anything to go by, I think he has seen the error of his ways."

I clapped my hands. "On behalf of all the poor children at the school who'll never know what you did for them, thank you, Jacob. You're a true hero."

His fingers plucked at my quilt. "Don't, Emily."

"Why not? What you did tonight was a wonderful, selfless act. It'll bring about a change in Blunt's behavior, I'm sure of it."

He shook his head. "That may be, but don't call me a hero. It's easy to do what's right when there are no consequences like grave injury, a ruined reputation or death."

The sad edge to his voice pierced my heart. I wanted to see his face but his gaze was downcast so I crept out of the covers to the foot of the bed where he sat. I no longer cared if he saw me in my nightgown. It covered me from neck to toe anyway.

His fingers stilled and he glanced up at me without lifting his head. "Don't come any closer," he said.

I ignored him and sat knee to knee with him. He shifted his leg away. "Why not?" I asked.

"Your sister—."

"Forget about Celia. This isn't about her, or me, this is about what's troubling you."

He shook his head. "Just don't come any closer to me. It...disturbs me."

"What about it disturbs you?"

He stood and paced the room, going from one side to the other in five easy strides. My bedroom wasn't large but nor was it small. He had very long legs. "I didn't just come here to discuss Blunt." The conversation was leaping back and forth like a skittish hare. I had no choice but to try and follow.

"Then what else did you want to talk about?"

"There was a death tonight."

I sat back on my haunches. "Who died?"

He stopped pacing and finally looked at me. "A footman on his night off. He'd had a few drinks at The Lion's Head in Holborn and fell into a drunken sleep in a nearby alley. I don't know his name." He started pacing again. "Bloody hell, I should have found out his name!"

I shivered. I knew where this was going. "It was the demon, wasn't it?" I whispered.

He stopped again, nodded, and rubbed a hand over his face. He looked tired, which was absurd given he no longer required sleep. "This is the second victim."

"Second?"

"The first, a woman, didn't die. Yet."

I breathed deeply in an attempt to calm my churning stomach but it did nothing. I still felt like throwing up. "Do you think...?" Oh God, it was too horrible to even say it but I had to. "Do you think someone directed the demon to attack these two people? These two specifically, I mean?"

He shrugged. "I don't know. The Administrators are giving me as much information as they have and so far there seems to be nothing linking the two incidents. The victims aren't known to each other and the attacks occurred in separate parts of the city. The first one, the woman, happened in Whitechapel. She's a prostitute, no family, lived alone in a single room she used for her work."

The poorest of the poor then.

"The footman died in a better part of town. If he had any money on him, it was gone when his body was found the next morning."

"So the attacks were completely random?"

"Possibly. If the demon is out of control then it would attack the easiest target—a woman alone, a man asleep in the alley. Shape-shifting demons may have a large appetite but they don't like to work too hard for their food if they don't have to. But there's more to it that makes me think the second attack at least wasn't random."

"What?"

"The house where the footman worked was burgled soon after his death."

"Burgled! You don't think it's simply a coincidence?"

"There doesn't appear to be any broken windows or doors, no sign of forced entry."

It took a few moments for his words to sink in. Then it hit me like a punch to the chest. "The demon took on the form of the footman it killed and someone unwittingly let it in thinking it was the real servant."

Jacob nodded grimly. "It probably wandered up to the service entrance and was let in by one of the staff."

I shivered and wrapped my arms around myself.

"You're cold." Jacob was beside me in a heartbeat, my shawl in his hands. He came up behind me and placed it around my shoulders but instead of letting go, he kept a hold of the edges. He was very close. I could feel his strength, his essence, pulsing between us, as alive and real to me as my own. Without thinking, I leaned into him. His body was hard, solid, a comfort despite the lack of a heartbeat or warmth. If I turned around, tilted my head, I could kiss him...

He suddenly stood and moved away.

"I shouldn't have come here," he said. And then he was gone. Just like that. No warning, no discussion, just gone.

"No! Jacob, come back!" I scrambled off the bed and stood on the spot where he'd been. "Come back, I want to talk to you. I have something important I need to ask you. Please, Jacob." My voice was a whine but I didn't care. I just wanted him to return. Partly for me—because I selfishly wanted him there—but partly because I suspect he needed to speak about what had happened. Not to the Administrators or anyone else in the Waiting Area but to *me*.

"I know you can hear me," I said, knowing nothing of the sort. "Listen. I want to stop this demon from hurting anyone else. Help me decide what to do next." I waited but he didn't reappear. "Talk to me Jacob. Tell me how to proceed." Still no answer. "Very well, I'll tell you what I think I should do. I'll wait for the peddler to come but I have a suspicion she won't." If she'd been the one to curse the amulet then she'd be a fool to show up again. "So I'll simply have to find out more about the two victims, see if there is indeed no link between them."

"You'll do no such thing," Jacob said, reappearing in front of me, hands on his hips. He looked very big, very powerful, and very dangerous.

I smiled. "Good. Now please stop popping out like that. I find it more disturbing than your sudden appearances."

"You will not go into Whitechapel on your own, and you will not ask questions about either victim." He held up his hands, warding me off. "Let me rephrase that. You will not go into Whitechapel *at all*. Ever. With or without me, and with or without the entire British Army at your disposal. Disregard everything you've ever heard about that place, it's ten times worse. Do you understand?"

I nodded. "Of course."

He eyed me closely. "You won't go venturing into that part of London?"

"I won't."

His eyes narrowed to slits. Clearly he didn't believe me. "You don't strike me as a stupid female."

"Thank you, I think." It was probably unwise to tell him I'd only said I'd follow up on the victims in order to get him to return to my room. I had no intention of investigating on my own. "Now that we've established that, do you think you could stay awhile. Sit." I indicated the stool at my dressing table. "Talk to me."

He crossed his arms and remained standing. "You should go back to sleep. Dawn's still an hour away."

"I won't get any more sleep tonight."

He gave an apologetic grimace. "I shouldn't have woken you and burdened you with the gruesome events of the evening. There's nothing you can do about them."

"I'm glad you did wake me. I'm one link in the chain that led to the demon being summoned and I want to be kept informed of everything it does." I sighed. "At least we now know why the demon was summoned here."

"To kill a servant from a rich household, take their form then burgle the master's house." He scrubbed a hand over his chin. "Unfortunately there are hundreds of houses that could be targeted next and thousands of servants."

Which meant we were no better off than before. We couldn't anticipate where the next attack would be, couldn't alert potential victims.

"Good night, Emily."

"Wait, don't go yet." I searched for something to keep him in my room and said the first thing that popped into my head. It happened to be the most honest thing. "I'm also glad you came here tonight because I...I wanted to see you."

"Why?"

Ah. Well. I *could* tell him I just liked gazing at his handsome face or that I enjoyed his company, but I wasn't a fool. Jacob was used to girls noticing him. George Culvert told me so. Even his mother had admired Jacob. So why would he want yet another girl—and a middle-class oddity of dubious parentage at that—staring at him? I might be the only person who could see him now that he was a ghost but he'd had a lifetime of people staring at him. He must be heartily sick of it. Indeed, that's probably why he'd tuned most people out when he was alive. Too many admirers must make one immune after a while.

So instead of telling him that, I made up something else. "I tried once before to summon my mother's ghost but she never came. I was wondering...if...perhaps you could ask the Administrators in the Waiting Area about her." I had wanted to ask him about Mama ever since he'd arrived in our drawing room, and now seemed like the perfect opportunity. "Perhaps they can tell you if she's already crossed. I've tried to summon her but...she hasn't answered."

He reached out and I thought he was going to touch my face or my hair but instead he fingered the fringe of my shawl. "I'm sorry. She's gone. I already asked the Administrators after I met you the first time and they told me your mother had crossed quickly into her assigned section of the Otherworld."

"But that means she had nothing to tie her here." No outstanding business, nothing to say to anyone. Nothing to say to *me*. How could she not want to tell me about my father when she knew how important it was to me?

"There is an aunt in the Waiting Area though. Do you want to summon her?"

"An aunt? You mean *my* aunt?"

He smiled. "Yes, your aunt. Your mother's sister, a Mrs. Catherine Sloane. She died about a month ago and hasn't yet crossed."

"I have an aunt? Had," I corrected myself. Catherine Sloane was dead.

He nodded. "She might know...something about your mother." He was too much of a gentleman to mention the unmentionable—the question of my father's identity. "Do you want to summon her?"

I caught his fingers and squeezed. He stared at our linked hands, a look of alarm on his face. Then he squeezed back. "Yes," I said. "Yes I do."

He separated our hands. "Then I'll leave you alone to talk."

"No! I want you to stay." At his puzzled expression, I added, "Unless you've got something better to do."

He barked a short, harsh laugh. "Not really." He stood by the mantelpiece and held out his hand in a go-on gesture.

I drew in a deep breath and let it out slowly. "I summon Catherine Sloane from the Waiting Area. Do you hear me, Catherine Sloane? Someone in this realm needs to talk to you." To call a ghost to this world, a medium simply needs to phrase the request and use the ghost's name. The portal to the Waiting Area is always opened for us—or for me. As far as I knew, I was the only legitimate medium in the world.

A woman of about sixty appeared between Jacob and I. She faded in and out two or three times until she finally maintained a presence, albeit a flimsy one. I'd seen gauze curtains with more strength than her.

She was a taller version of my mother. Mama had been short like me with soft brown hair and curves. Aunt Catherine had the same nose, same mouth, same eyes as her older sister but they were somehow more masculine. The nose was a little longer, the eyes set deeper, the mouth firmer. She wore an ankle-length nightgown and her long gray hair hung loose.

Aunt Catherine stared at me for a long time, her gaze assessing. If her lack of a smile was any indication, she didn't approve of what she saw.

"Aunt Catherine?" I asked, just to be sure.

She inclined her head. "I suppose I must be if you are Miss Emily Chambers."

"I am."

"And who is he? Why do you have a dead boy in your bedroom?"

"Jacob Beaufort," Jacob said, bowing slightly. He didn't answer the second question and I saw no reason to either. She may be my aunt but she had no authority over me.

Aunt Catherine expelled a *humph*. I suspected it was more than just an expression of her displeasure but I didn't particularly care to find out.

"I summoned you here to ask you about my mother," I said. I had a feeling polite chatter wasn't going to be on the cards with this woman.

"I thought as much. You may ask but I cannot guarantee

you will receive an answer, particularly one to your liking."

Jacob glanced over her head at me. He raised a brow in question. I shrugged. I'd come this far, I might as well continue. Besides, any answer was better than not knowing.

I took a deep breath. "What can you tell me about my father?"

"Nothing."

I waited for her to say more but she didn't elaborate. "My mother never spoke to you about him? About a man other than her husband?"

She tossed her long hair over her shoulder. "No."

"But you knew about my birth?"

"Yes."

Jacob cleared his throat. "This would go a lot faster if you gave more than one word answers," he said.

Aunt Catherine lifted her chin and gave another *humph*. "Very well. I'll tell you what I know but it isn't much. About six months after her husband died, my sister wrote to inform us she was expecting a child. She refused to reveal who the father was but gave no reason for the refusal. She simply stated that she would raise the child on her own. Her late husband left her a small annuity for her to live on for some years, you see. Well, seven months after that, she wrote again and said you'd been born."

It all sounded so impersonal as if she were reading a newspaper account of the facts. "You didn't visit her before or after my birth?"

"Of course not!" She may have been somewhat hazy to look at but her eyes still managed to flash at me. "My husband was—*is*—a very important man in Bristol. We could not afford to have our reputation tarnished by your mother's foolishness."

I stiffened and blood rushed through my veins in a torrent. How dare this dragon speak about my mother like that? "Mama was never a fool, Aunt. As her sister I'd have thought you would know that. But then I'd have thought you'd be more sympathetic too. She was alone in London, without friends, and with one daughter already to care for. You couldn't have found it in your heart to visit her? Send her something? Offer her sympathy at the very least?"

Her nose screwed up the way a dog does just before it snarls. "Your mother never wanted sympathy so I never offered it. As her daughter, *you* should know *that*."

I hated admitting it but she was right. Mama had been a proud, independent woman. She would want neither pity nor charity from anyone.

I might agree with Aunt Catherine on that score but I didn't think we'd find common ground on much else, particularly in the area of sisterly compassion. Nevertheless I bit back my opinions and pressed on. "Do you think it possible she fell in love with someone so soon after her husband's death? Perhaps she was lonely or—."

"Love! Bah! You girls talk about it as if it is the answer to all your woes." She clasped her hands in front of her, looking very much like a severe governess, nightgown not withstanding. "Since you are the daughter of my sister, I'll give you some advice as she seems to have failed to do so before she died. There is no such thing as love, not the kind written by poets that is supposed to last forever. There is lust in the beginning naturally, and perhaps companionship for a few years if one is lucky, but not love. Not the all-consuming sort that silly girls spend so much time thinking about.

"Don't throw yourself away to any man who spouts pretty words in your ear. Even if he believes what he says, he'll soon forget that he ever did. The words will stop, as will his high regard, and he'll spend more and more time at his club. Marry for other things, Emily—money or breeding or comfort—but not because you think he loves you or you love him." She finished her lecture with a glance at Jacob. He simply watched her, his elbow on the mantelpiece, the back of his finger rubbing slowly over his lips. He said nothing.

I too said nothing. What could anyone possibly say after a tirade like that? Perhaps if she'd been alive I might have challenged her theory but there was no point now that she was dead. She was unlikely to change her opinion. Besides, I couldn't think of any long-married couples who were still in love as an example. If the evidence from our séances was any indication, then Aunt Catherine was right. Marriage was an endurance and if any of them had begun with love, it had expired years ago.

"So you know nothing of Mama's feelings towards my father then? My real father?"

"Nothing at all. Your mother may have thought she was in love with him but I do not know. She never told me. She never mentioned a thing about him in her letters." She shrugged and her hair rippled. "It was as if he never even existed." Her gaze roamed over my hair, my face, and her lips pinched tighter and tighter together. "If you want my opinion, I'd say he wasn't an Englishman." She waved a thin finger at me. "You certainly didn't get that dirty skin or that ratty hair from your mother. She had been a beauty as a young girl. Pale as a bowl of cream and hair like honey."

In other words, I was certainly no beauty with my 'dirty skin and ratty hair'.

"Not everyone likes cream and honey," Jacob said. No, not said, *growled*, deep and low in his throat.

Aunt Catherine turned on him. "What are you talking about?"

"Or a bitter tongue."

"You speak out of turn, young man." Her face contorted into an uglier version of itself and suddenly her presence brightened. "Is that the reason you died before your time? Someone found you disrespectful?"

"Aunt Catherine!" I couldn't believe it. My sweet mother and this nasty, vindictive woman had been sisters? No wonder they'd rarely kept in touch. "I think you should go now. I'm very sorry I summoned you."

"Not yet." Jacob came up behind my aunt and gripped her shoulders. She yelped and tried to shake him off but he wouldn't budge. I thought I heard him chuckle but I must have been wrong because there was a dangerous spark in his eyes, and not a hint of humor. "Look at her," he snarled. "Look at Emily." My aunt's gaze flicked to me then away. He shook her. "Look!"

"Let go," she ordered.

"Not until you look properly and tell me what you see."

My aunt's gaze settled once more on me, grudgingly. "I see a girl who has brought shame on her family."

I bit back the welling tears. I would not let them spill. Not in front of her. I did, however, lower my head. I couldn't bear to let her see the effect her words had on me.

Jacob snarled in my aunt's ear. "No. You're not looking properly. I want you to *see* her. See her flawless skin, her dark chocolate eyes and her mouth with its thousand different expressions." I lifted my head and his fierce gaze locked with mine. My heart skidded to a halt in my chest. When Jacob looked at me like that I felt beautiful, not at all abnormal, and I could believe that the stares and cruel words would never hurt me again. "Emily is as unique as every sunrise." He spoke quietly to my aunt but I could just hear him. "She has more beauty in her than you've ever had in your lifetime." He let go of her shoulders. "Leave us."

With a sniff, my aunt vanished.

I sat on the edge of the bed and began to shake. I couldn't stop. It wasn't from the cold, or even from learning that my aunt wasn't the person I'd hoped her to be. I shook because of Jacob and what he'd said. His words were like a soothing balm on burnt skin, a lighthouse beacon in the darkness. And yet...had he truly meant them? Or was it merely a retaliation to put a bleak-hearted woman back in her place?

I opened my mouth to ask but realized he too had left.

With a sigh, I flopped back on the bed and wondered if I really wanted to know the answer anyway.

CHAPTER 7

I'd been wrong about the peddler. She did show up at a little after ten o'clock that morning, except...

"That's not her," Celia said, staring at the woman standing on our doorstep.

"Who am I then?" the woman asked, thrusting out one hip. She was dressed in a gown that could once have been deep red but had faded to a dull rust-brown. The shawl draped over her shoulders looked more like a rag than a garment and the bonnet sitting lopsided on her head had frayed at the edges and lost all of its ribbons, if it ever had any.

She pulled back the cover on her basket to reveal her goods but did not take any out. Usually she began her sales spiel before the door had fully opened but this time she seemed to sense our disinterest in her wares from the start.

"She's the previous peddler," Celia explained. "The one before the one who sold me the amulet." She glanced up and down the street. "Are you alone?"

"Alone as any soul can be in this Godforsaken city." The woman smiled, revealing a top layer of teeth worn almost to the gums.

Celia recoiled. "Yes, quite."

I shifted my sister aside gently and smiled at the peddler. "Who worked your area last week?"

The woman shrugged. Her shawl fell off her shoulder and she didn't bother to pull it back up. "No one."

"Somebody must have," Celia said. "You are not the woman I bought an amulet from on Thursday."

"You like pretty jewelry?" The woman sifted through the pieces of cutlery, trinkets, and rags—some clean—and other odds and ends in her basket.

"I don't want to buy any jewelry," Celia said tartly. "I want to know who took over this area last week."

The woman held out a thin bracelet covered in grime. It was as black as my hair. When Celia didn't move to take it, the peddler shook it, all the while smiling that gummy smile.

"How much?" I asked her.

"Three shillings."

"Three!" Celia clicked her tongue. "What's it made of?"

The woman rubbed it with her shawl. "Could be silver."

"I highly doubt it."

"Wait here." I went inside and retrieved my reticule. I dug out three shillings and placed them palm up in my hand. The peddler reached for them but I closed my fist. "Information first."

"Yes," Celia chimed in, giving me a nod of approval. "Tell us who worked your area last week."

The woman tapped her nose with her finger then pointed it at me. "Smart girl. But I can't tell you who done my area last week 'cause no one did." She held her finger up to stop Celia's protest. "Wait, wait, I didn't say nuffink about this *street*, did I?"

Celia hissed out an impatient breath. "Go on."

"A lady comes up to me last week, she did. Just round the corner there. She gives me twenty shillings to do me job on this here street. Twenty! That's more than what I got in 'ere." She shook the basket. "Course I gave 'er me value-bulls. Why wouldn' I for twenty? Bit later she gave 'em back to me and never asked for her money back neever. Job well done, I say." She laughed and wiped her nose on the back of her dirty glove.

"And you didn't find that suspicious?" Celia asked.

"Course I did but didn't you 'ear me? She gave me twenty shillings!"

"Did she tell you her name?" I asked.

"Nope."

"And you'd never seen her before?" Celia asked.

"Nope. Like I said, she came up to me round that corner and gave me the money. Twenty shillings!" She chuckled so hard it turned into a racking cough.

"Are you all right?" I asked.

She nodded then wiped her mouth on her sleeve. "Twenty shillings! Still can't believe it. Course she could prob'ly 'ford it and more."

"Afford it?" I echoed.

"But she was as poor as dirt," Celia said, waving her hand at the woman as if to say "like you".

The peddler didn't seem to notice the slight. "Maybe. Maybe not."

"But her clothes were a motley collection of rags," Celia persisted. "Nothing matched and most of it had holes in one place or another. Even her boots were odd and worn out."

The woman tapped her nose again. "Aye, but she spoke like you two. A toff, she was, I'll bet ya."

Celia tilted her head to the side. "Nonsense. She dropped her aitches and savaged her vowels. She most certainly was not a toff as you put it. Or like us."

"She most cert'ly was!"

Before the disagreement heated up, I thanked the peddler for her time and gave her the coins. She relinquished the bracelet with a smile.

Celia shut the door on her rasping chuckle. "She doesn't know what she's talking about. The woman who sold me the amulet had the most atrocious East End accent."

"Perhaps it was part of her disguise," I said. "Perhaps she wanted you to think she was from the East End. Or at least didn't want you to know she was a lady."

Lucy entered the hallway from the front drawing room, a rag and bowl of paste in hand for polishing the fireplace. She kept close to the wall, as far away from me as possible. Although she now spoke to me without her voice shaking, she was still wary. Her eyes never left me when we were in the same room, as if she didn't dare look elsewhere in case I summoned a ghost while she wasn't looking.

I held up the bracelet to assess my purchase. It was very thin but the links had a pleasing shape to them, despite the coating of filth. "Would you clean it up for me please, Lucy?"

"Yes, Miss Chambers." She stretched out her hand as far as she could reach but leaned back slightly.

I handed her the bracelet without getting too close. "You may keep it if you like."

She gasped. "Oh, Miss Chambers!" Her fingers closed around the chain and she clasped it to her breast. "Really?"

I nodded. "Think of it as a welcoming gift."

Lucy thanked me, twice, then trotted down the hallway to the basement stairs.

"Do you intend to bribe her into not being afraid of you?" Celia asked when she was out of earshot.

I sighed. "Do you think it might work?"

"Yes, but only after several more gifts." She squeezed my hand. "And we cannot afford such extravagances. We can't really afford that bracelet but if it helps us send the demon back then I don' begrudge its expense. So now what do we do about the amulet woman?"

I sighed. "I don't know."

"But you're supposed to be a 'smart girl'," she teased, echoing the peddler.

"Stop it. I don't know what to do. I could ask Jacob."

She let go of my hand and her mouth tightened. "If you must."

"You don't want him here do you?"

She made her way into the front drawing room and

beckoned me to follow. "I don't *mind* him," she said carefully. "I just worry about him coming and going so freely. None of the other ghosts have ever done so before."

"He's harmless, Sis, I guarantee it." If he'd wanted to harm me he would have had ample opportunity before now. He could have done anything to me this morning while I was asleep. Instead he just sat there, watching.

"I'm sure he is." She sighed and perched on the edge of the sofa. "It's just that...there's something unsettling about ghosts." She picked up her embroidery and began stitching. "Now understand, this is entirely from the point of view of someone who cannot see them, but...they have nothing to lose. Nothing to fear. The Bible tells us that we are judged in the Afterlife by our actions when we're alive. If that's true then what is to stop ghosts from doing wrong now they are dead?"

In a way it was what Jacob had said to me that morning. He and ghosts like him no longer had any fear of losing their lives or their reputations, and they didn't feel physical pain. So what was to stop them from doing everything they'd wanted to do during their lifetime but hadn't for fear of punishment either in this world or the next?

"A good upbringing is what stops them," I said to her. "And a good heart. Most of us don't need the threat of punishment hanging over us to do what we know to be the right thing." But as I said it, I wasn't entirely convinced by own argument. Could people change so much after their death? Could they forget or dismiss the code of behavior they'd learned during their life?

She smiled at me but it was weak and unconvincing.

I sat beside her and picked up my own embroidery. I wasn't very fond of the activity, preferring to read, but sometimes the repetitious task helped me to think. "Celia, what do you know of Mama's family? She had a sister, didn't she?"

"Aunt Catherine, yes." She pulled a face. "Horrible woman. Mama and she didn't get on at all well. I met her once when I was about ten. She and Uncle Freddie came for a visit. She used to rap my knuckles whenever she caught me fidgeting and I could never eat, sit, speak or breathe in the right way. Horrible woman," she said again. "As I recall they left after only two days. Papa couldn't stand them and insisted they leave before they drove Mama to distraction with their endless demands. Why?"

I lowered my cloth. "She died last month. I spoke to her ghost this morning."

"You what?"

"I wanted to ask about Mama and...my father."

"Oh, Em, how could you!"

"I just needed to know if she knew him, that's all. I had to try, Celia, since *you* won't tell me anything."

She resumed her embroidery but stabbed her finger on the first stitch. "Ow!" She sucked off the blood. "Now see what you've done. I'm all flustered."

I took her hand and inspected the wound. It had already stopped bleeding. "If it makes you feel any better I didn't learn anything from Aunt Catherine, except to confirm what you just told me about her. Horrible doesn't even begin to describe her."

Celia turned her hand over in mine and clasped my fingers. "I can only imagine what she thought of you," she said quietly. Her eyes shone with sympathy and understanding.

I was grateful that no tears came at the memory of my aunt's cruel words. I didn't want to upset Celia over something she couldn't control. *She* could not summon Aunt Catherine's ghost and chastise her. "She can't hurt me," I said. Not with Jacob around to counter everything she said with his beautiful words. "She's only a ghost."

Celia smiled. "I should be sorry that she's dead, but I'm not."

I had nothing to say to that so I resumed my needlepoint and we both worked in silence. After a while Celia announced she would pay Mrs. Wiggam a visit to see if her husband had departed yet. "Will you come?" she asked.

"Only if you need me. I think I'll go to George Culvert's house again. I have more questions about the demon that need answering."

It was only partly true. I did want to see George again, but not to look at his books.

***

I headed out after luncheon, dressed in a plain blue-gray dress with a matching jacket for warmth. Celia had wanted me to wear something prettier with more ruches and flounces and preferably in a brighter color, but I didn't want to stand out any more than I already did. Not where I was going. I also wanted some protection against the cold. The early spring day was overcast and the breeze sharp but once out of windy Druids Way, I could at least feel my cheeks again. Unfortunately I could also feel the smuts from the city's countless chimneys settling on my skin. That was one good thing about my street, the wind kept the air cleaner than most.

I expected Jacob to appear to ask where I was going but I made it all the way to George's house on my own. It would seem he didn't spend all of his time in the Waiting Area watching me and waiting to join me. I wasn't sure whether to be relieved by that or not.

The footman showed me into the Culvert's drawing room where George met me a few minutes later. He rushed in, all friendly smiles, his hands outstretched. "What a delightful surprise," he said, taking my hands in his. "Absolutely delightful. I was hoping you would return, Emily."

"Oh?"

He indicated I should sit then followed suit, occupying the chair opposite. "Yes, I, er, wanted to, um, see you again to...find out if you'd made any progress with capturing the demon."

His explanation, with all those hesitations, didn't ring entirely true. Did he want to say something else? I couldn't think what. "It killed someone last night," I said. I saw no point in keeping the information from him.

His face drained of color. "Wh...what?"

"It attacked a drunk servant on his night off." I repeated everything Jacob had told me about the two victims and the subsequent burglary, which amounted to very little.

Although the color returned to George's face as I spoke, his forehead crinkled into a more thorough frown. "How terrible," he murmured. "Utterly despicable. We must do something."

"That's why I'm here. I need your help."

He nodded and shifted forward on the chair. "Of course. I understand. You need a man to accompany you into these areas to investigate further." The way he said 'man', so earnestly, had me smiling. I couldn't imagine George fending off any villains unless they were perhaps children. He might be tall but he was slightly built and his hands didn't look like they'd done much more than turn pages his entire life.

"Not quite what I was thinking." I had promised Jacob that I wouldn't go into Whitechapel after all. "I wanted to speak to your maid, Finch, again."

"Oh." He pushed his glasses up his nose. "That won't be possible. She left yesterday after we spoke to her. Just ran right out the door Mrs. Crouch said."

I had suspected Finch wouldn't return but I didn't want him to know that I knew what had happened, let alone that I was responsible for her leaving. It would seem the other servants hadn't told him either, thankfully.

"I see," I said. "Then it seems I will ask you to accompany me after all, but not to the areas where the victims were found. I'd like to find Maree Finch. Perhaps we could try the school she attended. My own maid said she knew Maree and that the brother, a thief, had returned on a few occasions to speak to her. The last time was right before she came to work for you. We might learn something more about them both from the school."

He beamed. "Excellent idea, Emily. I'll get my coat."

A few minutes later we were skirting Green Park. George had wanted to take his carriage but I didn't think it was a good idea. The wealthier we appeared, the less likely the children would be prepared to speak to us.

"Does Beaufort know you're going to the school with me?" George asked as we entered the poorer part of Clerkenwell nearly an hour later. It was darker in the slum area and not only because the clouds had thickened, extinguishing what little sunshine had managed to seep through the smog. The tall tenements lining both sides of the narrow streets like tired soldiers cast permanent shadows onto the slippery cobbles below. Their walls were almost black with many years worth of the city's grime having settled on the bricks.

"No," I said, dodging a fast-moving child of about nine years.

"Ah."

"Ah?"

"How long will it be before he joins us, do you think?"

Another child raced past followed by a shouting adult. "Thief! Thief!" The man stopped near us and gulped in several deep breaths. "That little rat stole my pocket watch," he spluttered between gasps. "Did you see which way he went?"

George pointed in the direction the boy had run off in. The man thanked him and resumed his pursuit. No one joined in the chase. "I'd help him," George said, looking after the man, "but the thief will be long gone."

Even if the child was only one street away the man probably wouldn't have enough breath in him to catch up going by the way he puffed heavily. "How much further is the school?" I asked, walking on. I sidled closer to George and clutched my reticule tighter.

"Just around the corner." He eyed me carefully. "Are you all right, Emily? I say, that was a nasty business to witness just now. I daresay you're not used to such scenes."

"Not really, no." I'd never thought of the area in which

Celia and I lived as being particularly modern or fashionable but walking through Clerkenwell made me realize how safe it was, and how we were far better off there than anyone living here. Exhausted faces watched us from doorways which appeared to be mostly swept clean, something which surprised me. Even here the folk had some pride in their homes and wanted to offer a welcoming entrance. It was a reminder that this wasn't the worst place in London. Poor certainly, but not the most degraded or depraved. That label surely belonged to Whitechapel where the shape-shifting demon had attacked its first victim. Clerkenwell was mostly working class where men, women and sometimes children squeezed out a living doing whatever work they could find. If the child-thief was any indication, that work wasn't always honest.

We found the North London School for Domestic Service easily enough. Whereas most of the buildings on the street were a motley mixture of timber and brick and barely one room in width, the school was grand in appearance with its solid red brick façade, tall windows and at least three times as wide as its neighbors.

George turned to me before knocking on the door. "If I might be so bold as to suggest I ask the questions." He had the good sense to look sheepish about his suggestion. It didn't stop me from giving him a withering glare.

"I may be *only* a girl but I assure you I am used to dealing with men older than myself." I was used to no such thing but I wasn't going to tell him that. I'd lived in an adult world ever since Mama had died and I was used to speaking and thinking for myself, not have someone else do it for me.

"Yes, of course." He tugged on his necktie and cleared his throat. "But, well, perhaps the master *might* be more inclined to speak to me. It's merely a thought." He pulled so hard on the necktie knot I thought it would unravel. "We'll see, shall we?"

He lifted a hand to knock when Jacob suddenly appeared, leaning against the door, and I gave a little gasp of alarm.

George's fist hesitated. It was inches from the door and Jacob's face. "What is it?" he asked at the same time as Jacob said, "What are you doing here?"

"This is not Whitechapel," I said, answering Jacob.

George dropped his hand. "Pardon?"

"I'm speaking to Jacob."

"It's not exactly Belgrave Square either," Jacob said, referring to the exclusive area where his family kept a house. He jerked his head towards George. "What's your puppy doing here?"

"Protecting me. Aren't you George?"

George puffed out his chest and looked pleased with himself.

"Protecting you?" Jacob snorted and crossed his arms. "From what? The newspapers fluttering down the street? Because that's all he's capable of defending you against." He sounded annoyed. I couldn't think why.

"He's an effective deterrent against a thief thinking of taking advantage of me."

Jacob's nostrils flared. It was the only movement on his otherwise still person. "You're right. A visible deterrent works better than an invisible one."

My heart plunged into my stomach. "That's not what I meant." Stupid girl! It was precisely what I'd meant and now I'd made Jacob feel useless and less...human. "Jacob, I'm sorry."

"Forget it. Come on, knock."

"What's going on?" George asked. "What's he saying?"

"Well, he...uh...he thinks I should have brought some...more protection to walk though these streets. But he seems to be forgetting that this isn't Whitechapel."

Jacob gave me a lazy smile, my slight seemingly forgotten. "If this area is so safe then why do you need to bring him along for protection at all?"

Darn. Foiled by my own logic. "Stop being so...male!"

"Male?" Jacob and George both said.

I lifted a hand and knocked.

Jacob leaned down so that his nose almost touched my cheek. "Well?" he said in a quiet, ominous voice that spread across my skin like warm sunshine.

My face heated. I adore sunshine. "You're being overbearing. It's a very irritating manly habit that...men have." I knocked again. Why wasn't someone answering the door?

"You're such an expert on men, are you?" Jacob asked, straightening. I looked at him out of the corner of my eye but I couldn't determine if he was teasing me or if it was a serious question.

"I know a few. Now, either be quiet so I can concentrate or go away."

"Yes," George said, fiddling with his necktie again. "Let us handle this."

"I'm not leaving you alone in this place," Jacob said. "And I'll not allow you to walk home alone either."

"I am not alone," I muttered although I think George heard me anyway if his wince was any indication.

"You might as well be," Jacob said. He looked skyward as if he'd find some patience there, or some way of convincing me I was being a fool. "Bloody hell, Emily, coming here is dangerous. Do you understand?"

The door opened at that moment and I smiled at the maid in relief. We introduced ourselves and George asked to speak to someone in authority.

"Mr. Blunt the master's gone out," she said, "but Mrs. White'll receive you." She showed us into a room that appeared to be either an office or a drawing room or perhaps acted as both. It had a small, unlit fireplace, a large desk with hard, unpadded chairs on either side of it, a sofa and two armchairs, none of which matched, and a threadbare green rug on the floor. There were no decorative items on the mantelpiece, no paintings on the walls and not even a bookshelf near the desk. On second thought the room couldn't possibly function as an office as there wasn't a scrap of paper in sight and the inkwell appeared empty. It must be entirely for the use of visitors then.

The maid left, leaving George, Jacob and I in awkward silence. Having a three-way conversation when only one of us can speak to the other two is difficult at best. It's absolutely awful when we're quarrelling. George and I seated ourselves on the sofa, a respectable distance between us, while Jacob remained standing by the door, arms crossed, glaring at me. It was most disconcerting. My face felt hot and a thousand things ran through my mind. Of course I voiced none of them. In fact, I tried not to look at him at all. I failed.

Thankfully Mrs. White didn't take long to arrive. She wasn't as old as I expected, only a little older than Celia I'd guess, but more homely. Her soft brown eyes crinkled at the corners and a series of lines bracketed her mouth as she smiled at us. Her dark hair, streaked with gray, was pulled into a loose knot and her black gown could have been worn for mourning a loved one or simply because she liked the color. It did suit her although the large bustle at the back didn't flatter her dumpy figure.

"Now, what may I do for you?" she asked after introducing herself.

"I'm George Culvert," George said before I could answer.

Her eyebrows rose. "Mr. Culvert? You took on one of our girls, didn't you?"

He nodded but didn't explain what had happened to Maree Finch. He indicated me. "This is Miss Emily Chambers."

Mrs. White paled. "Chambers? Miss *Emily* Chambers?"

George's eyes twinkled behind his glasses. "You know her?"

It would seem my reputation as a medium had preceded me. It was happening more and more lately. Over the last month or two, the mere mention of my name was enough to cause strangers to ogle me, or walk quickly in the opposite direction. I suppose it meant Celia and I were garnering a good reputation for our work, which in turn would generate more appointments for our séances. But I couldn't be as happy as her about the increase in our trade, not if it meant more reactions like that of Mrs. White.

"I would say she knows *of* me, is that right, Mrs. White?" I asked, trying to allay any fears she might have with a warm smile.

Her hand fluttered to her chest and she gave a nervous little laugh. "Forgive me, yes, I have heard of you, Miss Chambers. Indeed, only this morning the master of our little school, Mr. Blunt, was telling me he was going to contact you." She pursed her lips. "He was very insistent."

"Oh? He wishes to communicate with the dead?"

"I believe so but you'd have to discuss the particulars with him." She clicked her tongue and sighed. "I don't know what's got into him. He's never been interested in the supernatural before."

I glanced at Jacob. He grinned. It was breathtaking, quite literally—the air *whooshed* out of my lungs and my throat went dry. It was rather a relief to see he'd snapped out of his bad temper too.

I smiled back at him.

"The Misses Chambers have an excellent reputation." George smiled too but I suspect not for the same reasons as us. I hadn't told him about Jacob's haunting of Mr. Blunt. "I highly recommend them. Emily really can communicate with spirits."

Jacob snorted and came to stand beside me. "It seems you have an admirer."

"Indeed, she was just speaking to one outside," George went on. He sounded like a proud older brother. It was rather sweet.

Jacob groaned. "If he tells her my name I might have to throw something."

"Thank you, George," I said quickly. "I'm sure Mrs. White isn't interested."

He opened his mouth to say something but must have

caught my don't-you-dare expression because he shut it again.

Mrs. White didn't appear to notice our exchange, or she was too polite to let us think she had. "Your sister left a calling card when she collected Lucy yesterday, you see," she said. I knew the ones. Celia had a habit of leaving them wherever she went so that it acted as a form of advertising. "Mr. Blunt was going to call on you today. I can't think why there's such an urgency." She shrugged.

"Perhaps he's being haunted," George said.

I choked but managed to turn it into a cough. Jacob patted my back and I continued to cough although the need had gone. I simply liked his touch. A lot.

"Are you all right, Emily?" George asked, shifting along the sofa towards me.

Mrs. White stood. "I'll get some water."

I stopped coughing and Jacob stopped patting. "I'm fine, thank you." I refrained from looking at him for about two seconds then couldn't help myself. Unfortunately he had his back to me, striding towards the door. Avoiding me again. He was making quite a habit of it.

Mrs. White sat down. "How is Lucy getting along?"

"Very well," I said. "I think she's a little perturbed to be working in the house of someone who can see ghosts, but she doesn't seem too afraid." She'd got through the night at least, which was more than I could say for one of our previous maids.

"Good, good. And how is Maree?" she asked George.

"Ah," he said. "She is the reason we've come here. She's disappeared—."

"Disappeared!" Mrs. White shook her head. "No, no, no, not Maree. She's such a good girl. We never had any problems with her here."

"She also stole a book from me."

Mrs. White stifled a gasp with her hand. "Oh dear. Oh dear, oh dear. Are you sure?"

"Quite sure." George told her about our interview with

Maree Finch and the reasons for our suspicions. "The odd thing is," he said in finishing, "is that she can't read. So why steal a book of all things?"

"A very good question," Mrs. White said. She frowned and shook her head slowly. "I simply can't believe Maree would do such a thing. And a book too when she can't read, as you say. What was it about?"

"Demonology," George said before I could deflect the question. I thought it was one we should avoid answering truthfully. I didn't want to alarm the lady.

But Mrs. White didn't seem as disturbed as I thought she would be. I'd expected a vehement denial of Maree's interest in demonology, or a little gasp or some show of distress over the book's subject matter. As it was, she simply paled. It was a considerable paling but nevertheless it wasn't a fierce reaction. "I see. Well, that's an...interesting topic for a young girl."

"Particularly for a young girl who can't read," Jacob said. "It's not the sort of book that will help her learn."

I agreed wholeheartedly. "We think she might have stolen it for someone else," I said.

"For her brother," George added.

"Her brother! You mean Tommy Finch?"

"I suppose we do," he said. "He attended this school for a while, didn't he?"

Mrs. White flicked imaginary fluff off her skirts, her attention on the task and not us. "He was but only briefly and that was some time ago. I don't know why he left. I'm not privileged to everything that occurs with the boy pupils. You'd have to ask Mr. Blunt."

"Has Tommy Finch been back to the school?"

"Certainly not!"

"Right," George said. He cleared his throat. "I think you've told us everything we need to know."

"Don't leave yet," Jacob said. He stood beside George but watched me. "Suggest that Culvert look at another girl to replace Finch."

I wasn't sure what Jacob had in mind but I trusted his judgment. "Then let's move onto the real reason we came here," I said to George with a smile. He gave me a blank look. "A new maid."

He flinched. The hiring of staff so far down the household order probably wasn't something he'd be involved in. That would come under the housekeeper's jurisdiction, or his mother's if the housekeeper wasn't a trusted servant herself. My suggestion that he do it clearly shocked him. "Yes, of course. A new maid."

Bless him, he was going along with the scenario with good grace. I was definitely warming to George. Despite insisting outside that he do most of the talking, he'd not once taken over the conversation. Of course that could have been because Mr. Blunt wasn't there.

A flicker of uncertainty crossed Mrs. White's comfortable features but then she smiled. I suppose it must seem odd, not only that I'd accompanied George to find him a new servant, but also that I was the one keen for him to hire again. Perhaps she assumed he and I were engaged to be married and I was taking an active role in running his household already.

My impish side wondered what Jacob would think of that.

"Suggest he look at some suitable girls with her right now," Jacob said. "Then tell them you wish to remain here because you have a headache."

I did as he said. I was afraid George would protest but his quick glance around the room suggested he knew Jacob was nearby and that we had a plan. George was no fool and he was turning into a wonderful ally.

"An excellent idea," he said, standing. "Shall we, Mrs. White?"

She touched my knee. "Will you be all right, dear? Can I get you some tea while you wait?"

"No, thank you," I said. "I just need some peace and quiet."

"It's best if she's not disturbed for a while," George said. He moved towards the door and before they left, winked at me over his shoulder.

I winked back.

Jacob's face turned dark. He crossed his arms over his chest. "He shouldn't be overly familiar with you. People will think there's something between you."

I waited until the door was closed then I stood and faced him. He turned that dark scowl on me. "He winked at me, Jacob. It's not quite as familiar as coming into my bedroom. For example."

His eyes turned the deep gray of a stormy sky. He took a long time to answer and I had the most disturbing feeling deep in my belly. Like a little flippity, somersaulting.

I suspected—hoped—he was going to kiss me.

CHAPTER 8

Jacob did not kiss me. He spun on his heel and strode to the door. "Let's go," he said. "We don't have much time." Then he disappeared. I stared at the spot where he'd been standing and touched my lips. They tingled from the anticipation, and the disappointment.

Was it so wrong of me to want him to kiss me?

The door opened from the other side and he poked his head through the gap. "It's clear," he said. "Follow me."

It would seem I had little choice. I blew out a steadying breath and walked behind him down the narrow wood-paneled hall, treading on my toes so as not to make a sound. The musty scent of dampness clung to the stale air and it was cooler than the parlor.

I hoped Jacob knew where he was going. While haunting Blunt the previous night, he must have spent some time looking over the school. I wanted to ask him if he had a destination in mind but I dared not speak. I had no idea where Mrs. White and George had gone but I didn't want to risk being overheard.

Jacob seemed content to do all the talking anyway and didn't appear to expect me to answer him. "The rooms along here are classrooms," he said, indicating the closed doors on either side of the corridor. One of the doors was ajar and I paused to listen.

Mrs. White's voice came to me clearly. "The girls are given a grounding in arithmetic to help them learn about portions for cooking, making cleaning pastes and the like," she said.

George responded but I didn't catch his words.

Jacob waited at the end of the corridor. "There are some unsupervised boys down here," he said.

I quickly followed him to a room that stank of shoe polish. Three boys aged about thirteen sat on stools at a long wooden table in the center of the room. Each of them had a fist thrust inside a boot, their other hand holding a blackened polishing cloth. Dozens more boots, some shiny but most covered in dirt, stood in rows on the table, and more again occupied a series of shelves on the opposite wall. It would take a small army to fill them all let alone clean them.

The boys glanced up when I entered. Two of them jumped to their feet, the other took his time to stand. He was the only one of the three who didn't bow a greeting.

"Who are you then?" he asked, his stringy blond hair falling over his forehead in jagged wisps.

One of the other boys hissed something at him but I couldn't hear what. The blonde boy merely shrugged in response.

"My name is Emily Chambers," I said. It was rather a relief not to see recognition on their faces. True anonymity at last.

"Find out what you can from them," Jacob said. "I'll keep watch." But he didn't disappear immediately. Instead he sized up the three boys. Although none of them were tall lads, they were all as tall as me and would undoubtedly continue to grow if their lanky limbs were any indication. The two boys who'd stood quickly didn't quite meet my gaze and shifted uncomfortably as if they couldn't keep still. The other boy, the blond one, not only met my gaze but held it.

"I'm 'Arry Cotton," he said, "and this is Johnny Fife and

Peter Bowker." The one who'd hissed at him was Bowker. He and Fife smiled shyly at me and blushed hard. Harry Cotton seemed to think this was funny and sniggered.

"Call if you need me," Jacob said then disappeared.

"You the replacement?" Harry asked. Of the three boys, he looked to be the oldest, or perhaps it was simply because he had the beginnings of a leaner, harder jaw whereas the other two still had the soft, rounded faces of children. Fife had a set of dimples in either cheek.

"Replacement?" I asked.

"For Mr. Felchurch. 'E up and left yesterday. Got a job as a slave at some toff's 'ouse."

"'Arry," Bowker whispered loudly.

"Slave?" I asked.

"Footman," Fife said, blushing again and still not meeting my gaze.

"Slave," Harry Cotton said and sniffed. "As good as." He threw his cloth down on the boot he'd been polishing then spat on it. He followed up his show of defiance with a raised brow at me. Obviously he lumped me in with those same toffs.

"Ah. No, I'm not Mr. Felchurch's replacement." I stepped closer and lowered my voice. I particularly wanted to capture Harry's interest. I suspect if anyone was going to talk, it would be him. The other two were either too afraid or too good. "I'm the employer of Maree Finch," I said, bending the truth. "Do you remember her?"

"Yeah," said Harry, shrugging one shoulder. "So?"

"So...she's gone missing. I need to find her."

Bowker and Fife exchanged glances but there was nothing guilty in their expressions, just concern. Cotton continued to meet my gaze. He crossed his arms over his chest and thrust his hands up under his armpits. "Why do you need to find 'er?" he asked. "She nick something of yours?"

"No," I lied. I was becoming very good at it with all the recent practice. "I'm simply concerned for her." That at least was the truth. I hated to think where Maree had gone. More than likely she'd joined her brother and was learning how to become a better thief. Of course there were worse occupations for a poor girl to learn on London's streets but I didn't want to contemplate that scenario.

Harry snorted. "And I'm the king of bloody England."

"I am worried about her," I insisted. "I'm worried that she'll end up like that brother of hers. If she's caught she'll be sent to the workhouse or prison."

Fife shuddered and twisted his fingers together.

"Least Tommy Finch ain't got no master but hisself," Harry said.

"Now we both know that's not true." I was going out on a limb but it was a step I had to take, not only to win Harry's trust, but to get him talking. "I *know* Tommy Finch is guided by someone else, someone who wouldn't care if Tommy or Maree got caught." It wasn't unusual for gangs of boys to be ruled by an older man, equally poor and desperate but more experienced in avoiding the police. Those unscrupulous men certainly didn't care about the wellbeing of their charges— London was teeming with boys and girls eager to take their place.

Harry blinked and looked away. The defiance was still printed into his features but I sensed he was wavering.

"Do you know who?" I tried. I was met with silence, which was to be expected. "Then can you tell me where I might find Tommy?"

"What, so you can dob 'im in?"

I glanced at the door. This wasn't going at all well and I didn't have much time. "No, so I can coax his sister back to her job. She was good at it." Why couldn't he see the benefits of reliable, honest work for someone like Maree, someone with little education, no home, no parents and few other choices? Why couldn't he see it for his own sake? "She was cared for there with a roof over her head, food on the table and clothes to keep her warm. What's going to happen to her now?" I hadn't realized I'd been moving closer to him as I spoke so that now I stood right in front of him, my face only inches from his. "Well? Is her brother going to take care of her?"

"Tommy'll see 'er right," Harry said thrusting out his chin. "'E's got integ, integra... 'E takes care of 'is own and I ain't gonna rat 'im out so you can make yerself feel good by thinking you're saving 'is sister. None of us will." This last he said to the other two, an unspoken threat threading through his tone.

Neither Bowker nor Fife disagreed with him. They shuffled their feet and kept their gazes firmly on the table.

I was trying to think what to say next to convince them to help me when Jacob appeared. For once I didn't gasp or squeal in alarm. I was growing used to his sudden appearances.

"You need to leave," he said, pacing. "Now."

I hurriedly thanked the boys and left. Out in the corridor, I could clearly hear Mrs. White's voice. It came from around the corner and she was coming our way.

"In here," Jacob said. He indicated a closed door. "It's a storage room."

I slipped inside, alone, then closed the door. I dared not feel around me in the darkness in case I knocked over a broom so I stood still and waited. The stink of old dampness was stronger than out in the corridor and the underlying scent of shoe polish, tallow and other smells teased my nostrils. I heard the voices of Mrs. White and George in conversation as they passed and wondered if they would enter the room I'd just vacated. Hopefully none of the boys would tell her I'd been there.

The door opened and Jacob drew me out by the hand. His cool fingers soothed my hot skin. "You have to get back to the front room before you're discovered."

"But I haven't learned anything useful yet," I whispered.

"Then we'll just have to think of another way." He glanced up the corridor. "But not now." He put a hand to my back and gently pushed me forward.

"What's the hurry?"

"There are no other classrooms after that one. Mrs. White and George will be returning to collect you soon."

I sighed. "Very well, I suppose—."

A door on my right suddenly opened and a man of giant proportions, with a beard and moustache of equally monstrous size, filled the doorway. He stopped when he saw me, and his two pale, yellow-green eyes narrowed.

"It's Blunt," Jacob said. He drew himself up to his full height and although he wasn't as tall as the schoolmaster, he looked just as impressive and rather more dangerous thanks to an expression that could have been hewn from rock.

"Who are you?" Blunt bellowed. "And what are you doing here?" It was difficult to tell if he was speaking in such a formidable tone simply to terrify me or if that was his normal volume. If it was indeed to scare me, it worked.

"Don't let him see your fear," Jacob said. He stood so close to me our arms brushed. The small contact bolstered my confidence. He was right. I had nothing to fear. I was not one of Blunt's pupils. "I won't let him hurt you."

I do so like having my own ghost for protection. I wasn't sure what Jacob would use as a weapon—he couldn't use his fists on someone who couldn't see him—but I didn't care. His presence alone was enough for me.

I lifted my head and met Blunt's gaze. Jacob shot a small smile my way. "That's it," he said.

"I was looking for Mrs. White and my friend George Culvert," I said to Blunt. "I believe they came this way. I've got a headache you see, so I waited in the drawing room while they looked for a suitable new maid." I pressed my fingers to my temples and feigned discomfort. Blunt's expression didn't change so I couldn't be sure if he believed my little act or not. "Unfortunately I don't feel any better so I was looking for George to ask him to take me home."

Blunt's moustache twitched and two wet lips appeared through all that hair. I think he was smiling at me. Or not. It was hard to tell. "Who were you talking to just now?" He looked over my head down the corridor. "There's no one here."

He'd heard me!

"Tell him your name," Jacob said, "and let him make his own conclusions." He chuckled darkly.

"Forgive me, I haven't introduced myself," I said sweetly. "My name is Emily Chambers and I—."

"Chambers!" Blunt's eyes widened. "The spirit medium?" His gaze quickly flicked past me again, side to side, over his shoulder then back to me once more before going through the routine again.

Perhaps my reputation wasn't such a bad thing after all. I tried to keep my satisfied smile to myself. "The very one," I said.

He shuffled closer then bent almost double to speak to me at my level. He reeked of cigar smoke. "A ghost haunted me last night. You weren't, ahem, talking to it just now by any chance?"

I dropped my voice to match his. "I can't discuss that with you. Professional reasons, you understand."

Jacob tipped his head back and laughed. It was very difficult not to laugh along with him.

"Ah." Blunt nodded and straightened. "Yes, of course, you and your sister have to make a living. No one knows about the necessity of a good business ethic more than me." He puffed out his barrel-sized chest, which pushed out his waistcoat and tightened the pocket watch chain. I kept one eye on it in case it snapped and I had to quickly get out of the way of any flying links. "I called on you both this morning but you were out," he said. "Perhaps you could have your sister contact me to schedule an appointment. I am in great need of your services."

"Of course."

"Tell her it's urgent."

"She's always prompt."

"Good, good. Now to that headache of yours. Can I have someone bring you a draft?"

"No thank you, I'll be fine once I get some rest."

"Tell him you're here because Maree Finch left Culvert's employment after stealing a book and you need another servant," Jacob said. "Mention what the book was about too. I want to see his reaction."

I did and watched Blunt's face. All that facial hair made it nearly impossible to gauge his thoughts but his eyes gave away his sharp interest.

"I see," he said, thoughtful. "Demonology you say. An unusual topic."

"Mr. Culvert and I suspect Maree stole the book for someone else," I said. "Her brother perhaps."

The ragged ends of his beard twitched as his lips pursed. "You ask a lot of questions for a girl."

I wasn't sure if that was a slight on my age or my sex or both. Either way, it rankled. "Professional curiosity," I said.

His eyes widened. "You think Tommy Finch has something to do with the haunting here?"

I put my finger to my lips. "Lower your voice please, Mr. Blunt. We wouldn't want to alert the spirit to our suspicions."

"You're very good at this," Jacob said. "Have you considered performing on the stage?"

It really was difficult to ignore him when he was in such a good mood. Actually, it was difficult to ignore him at any time. He was simply so...obvious. "I need to consider all possibilities," I said to Blunt, "particularly where a book on demonology is concerned."

"Yes, of course." The schoolmaster clasped his hands behind his back and rocked on his heels. He appeared to be thinking hard, deciding whether to say something or not. Finally he spoke. "So you think the stolen book has something to do with the haunting?"

"Perhaps. It is a remarkable coincidence. The book goes missing then Maree goes missing and a disgruntled spirit pays you a visit."

"You are wicked for letting him think there's a link,"

Jacob said with a grin. "I like it."

"So tell me about Tommy Finch," I said. "Has he returned to the school since his departure?"

"Absolutely not." Blunt's beard shook with the vigor of his denial. "We don't allow pupils who've left us to return. Not ones like Tommy Finch. He's no good. A bad seed. I hope his sister hasn't joined him in his illicit pursuits. She was a good girl, reliable and quiet. I like the quiet ones."

Jacob bared his teeth in a snarl, all hint of humanity gone.

"Let's hope she's safe somewhere," I said quickly, keeping one eye on Jacob. I didn't *think* he would hurt Blunt but I couldn't be certain about anything where Jacob was concerned. He was proving to be unpredictable.

"This demonology book," Blunt went on. He stroked his beard and paused for several beats. Eventually he sighed and shook his head. "I'd better tell you. It might be important."

"Yes?" I prompted when he hesitated again. He had my full attention, and Jacob's too. My ghost had finally stopped glaring daggers at the schoolmaster.

"A gentleman from the school's board mentioned demons to me quite recently."

"How does one casually slip demonology into a conversation?" Jacob said.

"In what context?" I asked Blunt.

Blunt waved a hand, dismissive. "We were simply discussing our private interests, away from work you understand, and he said he belongs to the Society for Supernatural Activity and has a particular interest in demons." The organization's name sounded familiar. "Indeed, he mentioned your friend Culvert as also being a member with the same interest."

Of course! George belonged to the same society. So this board member probably knew about George's extensive library on the subject. The coincidence was too close for my liking. "When were you talking to him?" I asked. "Could Maree have possibly overheard the conversation?" Or was there some other tie-in with her brother? Or were neither of them involved at all?

More beard-stroking from Blunt. "I can't recall. It was some weeks ago I think. Whether she heard or not..." He shrugged mountainous shoulders.

"What's his name?"

"Leviticus Price. He's a generous benefactor to the school and takes an active interest in our operations. He has some excellent suggestions for improvement, which I naturally try to instigate where possible. Perhaps your friend Culvert can ask him the questions you just asked me when next he sees him at a Society meeting. I'm sorry I can't help you further."

"I bet he is," Jacob muttered.

Mrs. White and George joined us then. Both looked concerned to see me but probably for different reasons.

"Emily?" George came to my side and gently took my elbow. "You must have been looking for me." I think he said that for everyone's benefit, or perhaps to guide me into an answer. Little did he know I'd already successfully navigated my way through a series of lies.

"Has your headache gone?" Mrs. White asked, her gentle eyes searching my face.

"It's worse," I said, pressing my fingers to my temples. "I was looking for George to ask him to take me home but I encountered Mr. Blunt."

George gently rubbed his thumb on my sleeve. The motion was soothing, his smile even more so. "I'll take you home now."

Jacob folded his arms over his chest. "He does know the headache isn't real, doesn't he?"

I allowed George to lead me down the corridor behind Mrs. White. Blunt didn't join us. Jacob, oddly, disappeared. I thought he'd walk with us but apparently he had better things to do. I tried not to let my disappointment show. I had wanted *him* to walk me home, not George.

Outside, swollen gray clouds plunged the street into further shadowy darkness. Women pulled in washing strung up between buildings and one or two men carried umbrellas, although most didn't. It wasn't the sort of area where the people could afford them. I wished I'd brought mine with me or George had. As it was, we'd likely be drenched before we reached my house.

"Stay close to me," George said. He still held my elbow but his touch had gone from soothing to hard, his thumb digging into my flesh. "And hold on tight to your reticule. We don't want to tempt any thieves."

I did as he suggested and kept my wits about me as I told him all I'd learned from Blunt. He seemed surprised at the mention of Leviticus Price.

"I don't know him well," he hedged, "but...are you sure it was him Blunt mentioned?"

"Leviticus Price is not the sort of name to mishear. Why?"

"It's just that he's—how can I put this?—not someone I thought would take an interest in a school for the poor." He shook his head. "Perhaps I'm doing him an injustice and there's another side to him than what I've seen at Society meetings."

"Blunt did say Price is generous with his advice."

"Well Price does like to give advice away in droves and he's not short of it either."

A small boy scampered past me, very close, but George pulled me aside before we could collide.

"Pickpocket," he mumbled.

"We don't know that for sure."

"It's a common ploy used by children of crime."

"What ploy?"

"Bump into their target and in the ensuing confusion, delve into their pockets. But you're safe, he didn't touch you."

"Who didn't touch you?" Jacob asked, popping up beside me and quickly falling into step with us.

"Hello, Jacob," I said for George's benefit. "No one bumped me."

"Then why's he holding you?"

George wasn't holding me, just my elbow but I didn't think Jacob would appreciate the difference. He seemed annoyed at poor George for some reason.

George was oblivious of course. "Good afternoon, Beaufort," he said, deepening his voice in that self-conscious way that some men do when speaking to other men. "Were you with Emily in there?"

"He was," I said, extricating my elbow from his grip.

His lips formed a pout. "Oh. Right." He cleared his throat. "Good show with Blunt in there, both of you. He didn't suspect a thing."

We turned into a busier street that was no less grubby but far more crowded. There were more ragged children playing in the gutters, more washing hanging over our heads and more hawkers selling goods from carts or baskets. A man dressed in a tall hat and a jacket too large for his slight frame tried to interest George in a meat pudding from his cart but George waved him away without addressing him.

"Where did you go?" I asked Jacob. "Did you stay to listen to Mrs. White and Blunt?"

"I did but they returned to their respective offices without speaking to one another." Considering this disappointment he looked rather pleased about something. "So I paid those three boys a visit. They were quite talkative."

I repeated the conversation so far for George's sake. "Go on," I said to Jacob when I'd finished. "What did the boys say?"

"They were arguing among themselves about whether you were searching for Maree because you were genuinely concerned for her welfare as you claimed, or to have her arrested."

"Arrested! For stealing a book? Goodness, who would do something like that to the poor girl?"

George's step faltered and he almost tripped over his own feet. He pushed his glasses up his nose and gave me a quick, unconvincing smile. "Who would indeed?"

Jacob grunted. "Anyway, opinion was divided with only one of them on your side, the one called Fife. He wanted to know why the boy named Harry didn't tell you about Tommy Finch's last visit to the school only three nights ago."

"Three nights!" I stopped. George halted alongside me and waited patiently while I spoke to Jacob.

"Yes," Jacob said. "*After* Maree stole the book."

I told George what Jacob had said. "Did he say who Tommy saw on his visit?" I asked. "Another pupil? A teacher?" Or Mrs. White or Blunt themselves?

"No but I got the feeling Finch returned to the school regularly and these three boys all knew it."

"I wonder what he wants now that his sister no longer attends," George said.

We were contemplating that when a girl of no more than ten or eleven carrying a basket full of violets came from seemingly nowhere. She was dressed in clothes that looked to be older than her if their dirty, patched-up state was any indication. Her head and hands were bare and she shivered as a breeze whipped around us. "Please, sir," she said to George, "buy my flowers, sir. Buy some lovely violets for the pretty lady." She pulled out a bunch of the purple flowers and tried to shove them into George's hand.

"Go away," he said, batting them aside. "We're not interested." He clicked his tongue and put his hand at my back to steer me around the girl.

She sniffed and wiped her nose on the shoulder of her dress but her long brown hair got in the way and she wiped it on the stringy strands instead. She didn't seem to notice as she blocked our path and thrust the flowers at me. "Please buy a poor girl's flowers, sweet lady." She sniffed again and her big brown eyes blinked up at me. "Buy some pretty violets for your dressing table, miss."

"She's not interested, child," George snapped. "Be off!" He tried to move around her, taking me with him, but I stopped him.

"I'll buy a bunch," I said, opening my reticule. "How much?"

"Emily, you shouldn't encourage her," George said. "If you buy things you don't need from these children their parents will only see it as a sign and send them out more. It's an endless circle."

"I ain't got no parents," the girl said, turning her owlish eyes on George.

He frowned down at her, his face not softening in the slightest. "Nevertheless—."

"I'll buy another bunch for my sister," I said. "How much did you say they were?"

The girl's face lit up, her eyes growing so wide they took up half her face. "A ha'penny each, kind lady." She gave me the two bunches and I gave her the money. It wasn't much and we weren't so poor that we couldn't afford the price. Nevertheless Celia probably wouldn't approve of the unnecessary expense. Hopefully she wouldn't notice my purse was a little lighter than when I'd set out.

The flower girl bobbed me a curtsy, turned her nose up at George and went on her way.

"I'd have bought them for you," Jacob said, walking beside me. "If I had any money."

The thought of a ghost handing money over to the girl was so ludicrous I laughed out loud. But Jacob apparently didn't get the joke. His face hardened then he blinked and looked away. Was he embarrassed? Had I offended him?

Oh dear. I was about to apologize when George, who I thought had been sulking, spoke. "Sorry you were forced into that," he said. "I would have got rid of her if you'd only allowed me."

"George," I said, putting as much sternness into his name as I could, "if I want to get rid of someone I will do it on my own. She was just a child and her flowers weren't expensive. I wanted to buy them."

He sighed. "You're too kind for your own good, Emily. I suppose that's part of your charm."

"Charm?" I almost burst out laughing again but I'd already offended one man so instead I said, "Thank you."

He smiled at me. "I'll walk you home."

"No," Jacob growled, "I will."

"You both can," I said and I think George understood Jacob had offered too if his "Oh" was anything to go by.

"No," Jacob said. "I want to speak to you alone."

"But he can't hear you."

"It doesn't matter. You're——." He stopped talking and walking and heaved a heavy sigh. I stopped too and George had no choice but to wait. "I just want to be alone with you," Jacob said. "To talk," he added. "It's easier without him hovering at your elbow hoping you'll trip over so he can catch you."

I was about to tell him he'd summed up the situation between George and I incorrectly but I didn't want George to hear me. I wasn't so certain Jacob had got it wrong anyway.

"Do you mind if Jacob accompanies me from here?" I asked George. "We're out of the worst streets and I have some private matters to discuss with him."

George's lips twitched and pursed and twitched some more before he finally gave in with a deep sigh. "Very well. If you must." He looked up and down the street, which was wider and filled with fewer shadowy corners and characters than the streets we'd just left behind, although it wasn't any cleaner. London's soot covered these sturdier buildings just as thickly as it did elsewhere. George's gaze finally settled back on mine. "Be careful. And hurry home before it rains. All right, Beaufort?"

Jacob grunted. "This farewell has gone on long enough." He strode off, no doubt expecting me to follow.

"We'll be in touch soon," I assured George. Jacob stopped and waited for me, arms crossed in a picture of impatience. "In the mean time, perhaps if you could speak to Leviticus Price."

He nodded and doffed his hat. "Of course, Emily. Good

day, Beaufort." He watched me go and I was relieved to turn the corner with Jacob and be out of George's sight. I wasn't sure why but having him watch me like that, with such interest, made me feel awkward. On the other hand, having Jacob watch me like that made me feel special but only in a good way.

Unfortunately he wasn't looking at me at all. He was staring straight ahead. Several people walked through him but he didn't seem to care.

"What did you want to ask me?" I whispered trying not to move my mouth and draw attention to myself. It wasn't easy.

"Nothing," he said. "I just wanted to get rid of Culvert. I don't like him."

"Why not?"

His entire answer consisted of a shrug. "What private matters did you want to talk to me about?"

We had to cross the road and I waited for a break in the traffic. Jacob wandered out into the middle of the busy street and a carriage pulled by two horses rolled right through him. No, not through him. He could touch them because they were objects, just like he could touch the picture frame or the mantelpiece. He must be vanishing just as they reach him then reappearing after they'd passed.

It took me longer to safely navigate the traffic and horse dung but I managed it without incident and joined him on the other side in front of a row of shops.

"Well?" he prompted.

"Last night you did something for me," I said. "So now I want to do something for you in return."

He frowned. "Last night? You mean meeting your aunt's ghost? I don't think you should thank me for that. She was a witch. I'm sorry I mentioned her at all."

"No, not for that." I spoke quietly but not just because I didn't want to be overheard. The tears in my throat kept me from speaking any louder. "I wanted to thank you for...for telling her you think I'm pretty. It was very...noble of you."

Before my heart could hammer another beat, he'd pulled me into a dead-end alley. It was empty except for a few crates pushed up against the brick wall of the neighboring chop house and some rotting vegetables piled in a corner. "It had nothing to do with nobility, Emily," he whispered. He bent his head so that we were nose to nose, barely a breath separating us. His eyes burned into mine, their smoldering heat seeping through me, warming me from the inside out.

"Then what was it if not to show me you're still a gentleman?" I had the heavy feeling that his answer would bring us closer to something important, something so big that I knew we could never go back. Never undo it.

Nor would it be something I wanted to undo.

CHAPTER 9

Jacob didn't say anything. He simply touched my cheek with his fingertips. It was the lightest, gentlest of touches as if he was afraid anything more would shatter me.

I was afraid of that too—of the emotions swelling inside me, filling me to overflowing, my body almost unable to contain them.

"My conduct around you has nothing to with nobility, Emily. Nothing to do with once having been a gentleman." Then, as if he liked saying my name, he repeated it in a murmur. "Emily." His lips came closer, closer, his eyes never leaving mine.

My nerve endings sizzled at the intensity in his gaze, the feel of his cool fingers on my skin and the sheer masculine presence of him towering over me. "Then what is it about?" I managed to whisper past the lump lodged in my throat.

His thumb traced the line of my jaw, across my chin and down my neck. I thought perhaps he hadn't heard me over the pounding of my heart but then he said, "I don't know." He watched, absorbed, as a trail of goosebumps formed in the wake of his fingers. "I've never felt so drawn to someone before. Not like this. But I can assure you there's nothing honorable about what I feel."

"Then what...?"

"It's primal. Basic." His mouth curved into a crooked, devilish smile that had me gasping for air. "Savage."

As if the word had flipped a switch inside him, he reeled back and dropped his hands to his sides. His eyes shuttered closed and he breathed deep and hard as if trying to regain his composure.

Savage. The word hung above us like a guillotine, ready to fall at any moment.

"I'm sorry." He opened his eyes and stared at the hand that had touched me, a look of utter horror distorting his handsome features. "I don't know what's happening to me," he whispered.

I didn't know what to say to that so I clasped both bunches of violets in one hand and gently took his hand with my other. I placed the palm against my lips and kissed it.

Slowly, like unpeeling layers, his face relaxed and returned to the perfect proportions I admired. "Talk to me," I said. "Tell me what's wrong."

He shook his head.

"Jacob, if you are to be my spirit guide for the next little while then I need to know what's troubling you. I might be able to help."

"You can't help." He pulled his hand away. "You're the problem."

My heart missed a beat. He hadn't said I was *part* of the problem but I was *the* problem. "Do I...scare you in some way?" I tried to wade through all the possibilities of what he might mean but I could only come up with one. "My unnatural ability to see ghosts can be disconcerting—."

"No. It's not that." He laughed ruefully. "You don't scare me in the least. It's—." He shook his head and started again. "It feels like I'm losing my humanity. Every day I'm with you, every hour, every minute, gets harder and harder to—." He pressed his lips together and closed his eyes.

I waited but he didn't continue. I didn't know whether I should prompt him or if that would only anger him, or upset him. I reached out and caressed his cheek instead. The hard, chiseled line of it gave his face a regal quality, commanding and majestic. Fascinating. The skin was soft, cool, and I sighed, enthralled.

With a matching sigh he opened his eyes. And stepped away. "You shouldn't do that," he said but there was no anger in his voice, or alarm. "We must go."

"But I haven't told you what I wanted to say," I said. He waited, feet apart as if steadying himself on a rocking ship. "I wanted to do something for you in exchange for the service you rendered me."

"I told you, getting your aunt to come was a mistake. You owe me nothing."

The best response to that was to ignore it and move on. "I want to speak to your parents."

"No."

"I want to reassure them—."

"No, Emily." He paced from one side of the narrow alley to the other, hands on hips, head bowed. "I don't think it's a good idea."

"Why?"

"Because it's not."

"Why not?"

"Emily, just leave it be. I don't want to discuss this with you."

He stalked off. I remained in the shadows and waited for him to realize I wasn't following. When he did, he came back, his temper seething if the tightness of his face was anything to go by.

"Don't make me hoist you over my shoulder," he said. He wasn't laughing. Not even close.

"I'm going to see your parents this afternoon," I said. "Unless you can give me a good reason not to."

He scrubbed a hand through his hair and down the back of his neck, kneading it as if it ached. "Very well. You've forced my hand. My concern is that they won't believe you." He said it defiantly and I waited for the "so there" but it never came.

"Few people ever believe me at first," I said.

He shook his head and I waited for further explanation. I had the feeling there was more to it than he was letting on. "My father dabbles in the sciences—biology and psychology mostly. It's a hobby of his. He belongs to various scientific societies and regularly writes papers debunking the supernatural. He thinks all mediums are frauds, and that's putting it kindly."

"Most are."

"It won't matter how much evidence you present him with, he'll find a way to discredit you."

I shrugged. "I'm used to skeptics. Is that your only concern?"

He shook his head again and sighed. "You won't find an ally in my mother either. I'm afraid she won't *want* to believe you."

It took me a few moments to understand what he was saying. "You mean she still hopes you'll be found somewhere, alive?"

He nodded. "I visited them shortly after my death. The Administrators warned me against it and I should have listened to them. They said it can be traumatic for a spirit to know how their loved ones reacted to their death. They were right." He leaned against the brick wall of the chop house and tipped his head back. "It was awful. Mother was adamant that I must be somewhere, lost or kidnapped with no way of getting home. Father either believed it too or simply went along with her because it was easier. They've spent a fortune since my death on investigators who claim they can find anything and anyone. None have even turned up my body let alone any answers to explain my fate."

His shoulders stooped and he sagged against the wall. He was clearly distressed about his parents, despite the matter-of-fact way he spoke.

It made me more determined to see them than ever. "That was some time ago," I said. "Perhaps they've changed since then. Perhaps your mother is ready to move on, if only she knew the truth."

"I doubt it." He pushed off from the wall and leveled his gaze with mine. "So you see that she'll be as skeptical as my father. She'll simply refuse to believe you."

"I can still try. You could feed me some information that only you and they could possibly know."

"They'll think I told someone at school or—"

"Jacob!" I balled my fist. I wanted to punch him in the shoulder to knock some sense into him. "I'm going to try regardless of what you say."

His jaw clenched, causing the muscle high in his cheek to throb. "Emily, listen to me." He caught my shoulders and lowered his head to look directly at me. If he was trying to mesmerize me, it was working—I couldn't look away, couldn't move. I wanted to fall into the deep blue depths of his eyes and wallow in there forever. "They'll be resentful of you trying to convince them I'm dead, and...and I don't want to subject you to that. Do you understand?"

"I understand." It came out breathy. Could it really be that he was worried about *me*? "I'm going anyway."

"Emily!" He let go, pushing me a little as he did so that I rocked back. He strode towards the street but stopped before he exited the alley. "You're so stubborn," he said.

"If your only concern is that I won't be believed then it's not enough to stop me going." I joined him and we walked along the street together, neither speaking. We were almost at Druids Way when the rain came.

Jacob took my free hand—the other still held the bunches of violets—and drew me into the sheltered doorway of a coffee shop. Everyone on the street either scattered to seek cover or continued on their way, heads down, umbrellas up. It provided a certain amount of anonymity for us. Except for the handful of patrons visible through the coffee shop's bay window, we were alone—and *they* couldn't hear me.

"Wait inside," he said. "I'll find you an umbrella."

"And do what?" I tried not to laugh to draw attention to myself. "Bring it back here? A floating umbrella might cause considerable panic."

He sighed and peered up at they endless gray sky. "It won't ease for some time, I think. How about I return to your house and write a note for your sister asking her to bring you an umbrella at this location." He peered inside the shop window. "There's a spare table near the fire for you to wait."

I smiled at him. "You're very kind." It felt nice to be fussed over by such a handsome, masculine gentleman. I wondered if he'd fussed over any girls like this when he was alive or if it was a trait he'd picked up after his death. For me.

He frowned. "I'm only thinking of your comfort."

The pressing, desperate desire to kiss him again swelled within me. "Come on, let's run home." With the hand that held the flowers, I clamped onto my hat to hold it in place, picked up my skirts with the other hand and ran into the rain.

Jacob joined me. I'd not thought that he could get wet, but he was as soaked as me within seconds. It made sense, I suppose. If he could move objects and touch things, why wouldn't he be able to touch the raindrops too?

His pace slowed and instead of running he began to skip and turn around, his arms outstretched. He tilted his face to the sky and closed his eyes and opened his mouth. I watched him, fascinated by his response to the rain pouring over him, not caring that I too was getting drenched.

Then he laughed. He opened his eyes again and caught me round the waist, spinning me around in his arms, catching me easily as I lost my balance. And all the while he laughed and laughed. It was magical and I laughed along with him, not caring that a passerby eyed me warily from beneath his umbrella.

"You're soaked," Jacob said, touching the curls at my temple.

"So are you." My gaze strayed to his chest. The wet shirt, almost transparent thanks to the rain, clung to the contours of his lean muscles. My mouth dried, my tongue felt thick and useless. I ached to touch his broad shoulders and the ripple of muscles across his stomach and chest. My fingers twitched at my side. I licked my lips...

"Even your eyelashes are wet," he said in a faraway voice.

I looked up. He was staring at me with that curious intensity that made my insides do odd flips. I smiled at him tentatively.

He smiled back then laughed again, his attention no longer on my face but in the direction we were heading. "I'm sorry," he said. "But we're thoroughly wet now. Do you still want to run?"

"Walking is fine," I said.

He was still smiling when we reached Druids Way. Occasionally he glanced up at the sky but never at me again.

"You like the rain?" I asked.

His smile widened. "I'd forgotten what it was like. It's good to feel it on my skin after all this time."

"Is it cold?"

"No. I don't feel heat or cold. But it does feel wet. And fantastic!" he shouted. He spun around again, finishing the twirl with a flourish by kicking a puddle.

I giggled all the way to my house. We climbed the steps to the front door and huddled beneath the porch. Not that staying dry mattered anymore. I opened my reticule but didn't search for my key. Jacob would leave as soon as I was inside and I wanted this moment to last just a little longer.

"Will your sister be mad at you for being out in this weather?" he asked.

"Probably. But she's my sister, not my mother and she can scold me all she likes, I don't care."

He smiled but it was wistful, perhaps even sad. "She cares about your health, Emily. As I should have done. Go inside and warm yourself by the fire before you catch your—." His lips clamped together as if he were stopping the next word from falling out: death.

I blinked up at him. "Jacob? Are you all right?"

He shook his head. "Your eyelashes," he murmured.

"What about them?"

"They look even longer when they're wet." He backed up to the steps. "Go inside, Emily." He turned to leave.

"Jacob. Wait. I still plan on visiting your parents this afternoon. Come back at two and we can go together. Or I can meet you there if you prefer." *I* preferred to walk with him. I wanted to spend as much time with him as I could, even if we spent it in awkward silence—a distinct possibility considering he was not meeting my gaze again.

"Don't you have a séance to conduct?"

"Not today."

He stood with one foot on the highest step, the other one step down, dripping wet. He was utterly, thoroughly, breathtakingly handsome.

"I won't come with you," he said. "If that's all right."

"Of course." My heart sank at the notion of going to visit his parents without him but I wouldn't beg him to join me. It would be a very difficult situation for him and it was unfair of me to press him.

"I'll come back at two and tell you some things that will help make them believe you, but..." He shook his head and droplets sprayed off his black hair.

"It won't be enough?" I ventured.

"Probably not."

He disappeared and I stood there a moment, hoping he would reappear but not really expecting him to. Then with a sigh, I retrieved my key from my reticule and opened the door.

***

Jacob had been right. Celia was mad at me. Not even the violets softened her. After she scolded me for being "wet through to the bone" she made me change into dry clothes then sat me down in front of the fireplace while she heaped more coal onto it. Lucy brought in a bowl of steaming soup and I sipped while my bones thawed and my hair dried.

To distract Celia, I asked her about her visit to the Wiggams' house. "Is Mr. Wiggam still there or has he left his wife in peace?"

"He's still there," she said, dusting off her hands. "And still haunting her."

"In what way?"

"He throws objects around the room sometimes, particularly when she has guests, and hides things so she can't find them. Important things like money or her corsets."

"Corsets! That is cruel." But rather ingenious. I couldn't imagine a large woman like Mrs. Wiggam wanting to go out without wearing a corset.

"And he likes to keep her awake at night by knocking on the wall or thumping the floor."

"Oh dear. I probably should try and talk to him again."

"I think that would be a good idea, Em." She lifted a strand of my hair and sighed. I couldn't blame her for her disappointment. It would take some time to remove all the tangles and fix it into a half-decent style. "What were you thinking walking around in the rain like that?"

"I had to get home somehow."

She dropped my hair. "You could have hired a carriage."

"We were only around the corner."

"We?"

"Jacob and I. He escorted me home."

She grunted. "A ghost is not a suitable escort."

I sipped soup off my spoon and said nothing.

"So how was your visit with Mr. Culvert?" she asked.

"Good. We went to the Domestic Service school in Clerkenwell."

"Oh? Lucy said Mr. Blunt came here while we were both out this morning. Did you see him?"

"I did. He wants you to schedule a séance. He's being haunted." It was perhaps best not to tell her that Jacob was the culprit. Somehow I didn't think she'd see the funny side to it. My sister prided herself on her morals and taking money for a séance where the ghost was a friend of mine probably bordered on unethical in her book.

"I'll pay him a call tomorrow, or this afternoon if the weather clears," she said.

"Keep your eyes and ears open for any suspicious characters." At her raised eyebrows, I explained what had happened at the school and everything Jacob had learned afterwards from the boys. She sat on the sofa and listened without interrupting me.

"Oh dear," she muttered when I finished. "Do you think Mr. Blunt knew about the Finch boy's visits?"

"It's hard to say."

Lucy entered with a cup of tea for Celia. "Wait a moment please, Lucy," Celia said, taking the cup and saucer.

Lucy's gaze flicked between Celia and me before finally settling on my sister. "Yes, Miss Chambers? Is everything all right? I've not done wrong, 'ave I?" Her forehead creased and she looked like she might burst into tears. "I've been trying so 'ard to do everything right, I 'ave. I'm so sorry if I ain't done it the way you like but there's so much to remember and—."

"Calm yourself, Lucy." Celia smiled serenely. "You've done a superb job so far. We're lucky to have found you, aren't we, Emily?"

"Oh, yes! Very lucky." I smiled too. Lucy seemed to relax a little.

"We want to ask you a question about the North London School for Domestic Service."

Lucy brightened. "Really? That's all? Oh I can answer anything you want to know then."

"I went there today," I said. "I met Mrs. White and Mr. Blunt."

"She's such a kind lady is Mrs. White, ain't she. So nice to us girls, she was." The omission of Blunt from her praise wasn't lost on me.

"Yesterday you said Tommy Finch visited his sister when she was still a pupil at the school. You said no one told Mrs.

White about it, but I wondered if it's possible another adult there knew of his presence."

Lucy shrugged. "Could've."

"Might Mr. Blunt have known?"

She shrugged again. "Don't know. Maybe."

"But someone must have let him in to the building."

"He's a thief. Don't matter 'ow many locks on the door, they won't stop Tommy Finch. He's the best thief in London." It didn't sound like a boast, just a simple statement of fact.

"Thank you, Lucy," Celia said. "That was very helpful." We watched as the maid bobbed a curtsy then left. "That wasn't helpful at all," my sister said when she'd gone. "So now what do we do?"

I shrugged. "George is going to speak to Leviticus Price. In the mean time, I have business of my own to conduct with Jacob's family. I'm going to tell them he's dead."

My sister's head snapped up. "Is that wise?"

I shrugged one shoulder. "I'm going to do it anyway. They need to move forward and they can't do that until they know he's truly gone."

She nodded. "I understand. It's very kind of you to offer. Will you go in the morning? We have a séance in the afternoon."

"I'm going today."

Her teacup came down on the saucer with such a loud *clank* I wouldn't be surprised if she chipped it. "You'll do no such thing! You need to stay home and keep warm and dry." She emphasized the last word with a pointed glare.

"Celia, I'm going today and that's final. I may not get time tomorrow, depending on what tonight brings." I shuddered at the thought of the shape-shifting demon claiming another victim.

"See!" She poked her finger at me. "You're shivering. You cannot go out so soon after that soaking. It's unhealthy."

"I'll take an umbrella."

143

"That is not the point."

"No. You're right." I stood and tossed my hair over my shoulder. It was almost dry. "I am going and that's final."

She stood too. "You'll do as I say, Emily. You are not going out again today."

"Celia," I said on a sigh, "you know I will so let's not argue about it. Red is really not a becoming color on your face."

"Emily!" She stomped her foot. My sister! Stomped her foot! I don't think she's ever done anything so childish in her life. "I am trying to do what's best for you."

"But you're not!" How could she not see that helping Jacob was what was best for me? "You're being selfish and, and...interfering!"

"I am—."

"You are *not* my mother and I will *not* do as you say." I was so angry my voice shook.

She thrust her hands on her hips. "You're being unreasonable, Emily."

"You're the one who's being unreasonable. I am as healthy as I've ever been and going out this afternoon will not change that." I stormed towards the door and jerked it open. "I'm going to my room and I don't wish to be disturbed."

I ran up the stairs to my bedroom and locked the door then leaned back against it. I breathed deeply to regain my composure but it didn't help. My veins pumped with my rushing blood and my heart pounded. I couldn't remember the last time I'd argued with Celia on such a scale. Our disagreements were usually petty affairs—who was going to wear the crimson bonnet or whether the grocer's son would be completely bald by the age of twenty-five (I said yes, she thought not). We rarely needed to raise our voices.

I checked my small pocket watch that I'd left on the dressing table after changing clothes. It was half past one. Only half an hour until Jacob arrived. Fortunately I hadn't told Celia about his pending visit. This way I could speak to him alone, in peace, in my room.

Thirty minutes suddenly seemed like a long time.

CHAPTER 10

"You look upset," Jacob said when he finally winked into existence. "Is it my fault?"

"No," I said from the chair beside the fireplace where I'd read the same page of my book five times. I still had no idea what it was about. I'd sat there after fixing my hair, a task which had taken considerable time as I hadn't requested Lucy's help. I didn't want to place her in the awkward position of aiding me in my escape. "Why would it be your fault?"

"It never hurts to check." He sat on the foot of my bed and stretched out his long legs, crossing his ankles. He looked so perfect, so handsome and real with his too-blue eyes regarding me closely. His hair and clothes were dry and I wondered how long it took for that to happen in the Waiting Area. Perhaps it was instant. "So what's wrong?" he asked.

"I had a disagreement with my sister." I waved my hand. "Nothing of consequence."

His eyes narrowed and I thought he'd detected my lie but he let it go with a nod. "So you didn't catch a chill?"

I rolled my eyes. "It would seem not."

"Good. Good."

"It was fun, wasn't it?" I said. "Dancing in the rain."

He breathed deeply and squeezed his eyes shut. "It was irresponsible. You should have waited in the coffee house."

"You're beginning to sound like Celia. It was simply a little rain—."

His eyes flew open and I stilled at the flare of anger I saw in them. "There are many spirits in the Waiting Area who are there because of *a little rain*."

I bristled and formed a defense in my head but bit my tongue before I could let it free. Nothing I could say would sound appropriate after his outburst because he was right. Sometimes people died from a chill. Usually the old or very young or the weak, but not always. So I blew out a calming breath and thanked him instead.

"What for?" He looked surprised, as if my failure to argue with him had caught him off guard. Almost as if he'd wanted me to disagree.

"Well," I began but stopped. I stood and set my book down on the writing desk then sat beside him on the bed. He lowered his gaze to our hands, inches apart on the bedcover.

And then something happened. His fingers moved ever so slightly towards mine. My breath caught in my chest and I watched, waiting for his fingers to move again, but they did not. Nevertheless, they *had* moved. Jacob was still looking down at them.

Silence enveloped us but it didn't feel awkward or heavy. More...charged, thick with unspoken words and a thousand jumbled emotions.

All of a sudden I wanted to touch him. I wanted to feel his skin against mine, explore the bruises of his knuckles, the smoothness of his fingernails. I inched my fingers closer and his moved too, towards mine, as if we were two magnets drawn to each other. Finally we touched, just our pinkies, but it felt like a spark jolted through me on contact.

"Emily," he whispered. My name had never sounded so good, like the hush of a gentle breeze across a grassy meadow. "Tell me what you'd been about to say." His voice was buttery soft.

"What?"

"Why are you thanking me?"

"Oh. For caring about my health of course."

His fingers recoiled and curled into a fist as if I'd slapped them away. I felt the abrupt loss of his touch so keenly it hurt. "Don't," he said, desolate.

"Don't what?"

He stood and dragged a hand through his hair and took one step towards the fireplace, backtracked, then changed his mind again and stalked across the room. He picked up the coal scuttle and poured more coal onto the dwindling fire. "Let's discuss what you're going to say to convince my parents I'm dead." He set down the scuttle and, still crouching, watched the fire blaze to life. The dancing flames brightened his face and eyes but did nothing to brighten the dark mood that seemed to have descended upon him.

"Yes, er, very well." I tried to concentrate on the task at hand but it wasn't easy. My mind was still scrambled from when we'd touched and his rapid change of mood.

We spent the next little while going through some events from his childhood that only he and his parents could have known. I'd hoped to use our time together to learn more about him but he recounted the memories with little emotion and no invitation to discuss them in detail. He simply imparted the facts and ended the conversation abruptly.

"Whatever my parents say, don't take it to heart," he said on finishing. He stood by the fireplace, one elbow on the mantelpiece, having not sat down the entire time. I'd remained seated on the bed.

"What could they say that would have an affect on me?"

He studied the fire. "Just promise me you won't."

It seemed like an odd thing to warn me about but I shrugged instead of pressing him. "I promise."

"Good." He nodded and suddenly looked over at me. His gaze caught and held mine. "Take an umbrella with you this time." And then he was gone.

I sighed and stood. I picked up my heavy woolen shawl from the bottom drawer of the wardrobe and slung it around my shoulders. Hopefully the extra thick one would appease both my sister and my spirit. Not that I planned on telling Celia I was leaving.

Fortunately I didn't have to. I slipped downstairs, tiptoed past the drawing room, plucked an umbrella from the stand near the door and left without her noticing.

***

The drawing room of the Belgrave Square house belonging to Lord and Lady Preston was larger than one entire floor of my home. The value of the paintings, vases, sculptures and other artworks—all with a touch of gold— was probably higher than the whole contents of my house too. It was difficult to appear sophisticated and worldly in the presence of such wealth and exquisite taste, particularly as I was ensconced in an enormous armchair that seemed bent on swallowing me whole. I felt like a small child again.

Lady Preston sat with regal elegance on the sofa beside her daughter, her exact replica only younger. Both had hair the color of honey, coifed in an intricate style atop their heads, and both had eyes of the same vibrant blue as Jacob. Whereas his face was all masculine angles, theirs—while no less perfect—were softer and rounder as if the sculptor had lovingly polished instead of chipped. Against the gold tones of the room, they looked like royalty.

As if their fair beauty wasn't intimidating enough, their shrewd gazes studied every inch of me. Although I was wearing the green gown with the tight cuirass bodice again, it looked almost drab against their silks. Whereas Lady Preston's expression remained bland and unreadable, her daughter Adelaide's was more open and friendly. She even attempted a smile. I smiled back but it faded when Lady Preston's lips flattened in disapproval.

"You say you knew my son, Miss Chambers?" she prompted.

I had introduced myself to the butler who'd let me in only after I told him I needed to see Lord and Lady Preston about Jacob. Since the viscount was taking lunch at his club, the servant had shown me into the drawing room where I'd waited for Lady Preston to join me. She'd arrived within a minute, her daughter on her heels.

"Actually, that's not quite correct," I said. "You see..." I shifted in my seat but that only made me sink further into the massive armchair. All the bravado I'd felt when talking to Jacob about this meeting had vanished. Part of me wished I was curled up on the threadbare sofa at home reading a book in front of the fire. "You see, I *know* Jacob."

Lady Preston's face finally formed an expression. Shock. She clasped her long fingers in her lap and lifted her chin, revealing her slender white throat. She swallowed. "Know?" she whispered. The cool, bland woman changed before my eyes. Small, thin lines striped across her forehead and everything about her seemed to slacken, loosen, as if she'd had enough of holding herself together.

"Dear lord," Adelaide said on a gasp. She was about my age but seemed older. Perhaps it was because she was so tall and willowy or perhaps because she looked sophisticated perched as she was on the sofa, her soft pink skirts spread daintily around her. "You mean he's alive?"

"No, no, you misunderstand," I said quickly. Oh dear, I'd gone about this all wrong.

The two beautiful faces crumbled. "Then what...?" Adelaide pressed. Her mother straightened again and her expression tightened once more. She sat like an automaton waiting to be wound up, serene but lifeless.

"I'm a spirit medium," I said to Adelaide. I couldn't look at her mother. Something about her unnerved me. She was so still, so empty...it was unnatural. "Jacob's ghost visits me regularly."

Adelaide's jaw dropped. "Ghost," she whispered. She bit her lower lip and blinked rapidly.

There was an awful moment when no one spoke. Then,

"Get out," Lady Preston snapped.

"Pardon?" I spluttered.

"Get out of my house." The venom in her voice was matched by the hatred in her eyes. At that moment, I think she genuinely despised me.

"But—."

"Mother," Adelaide said, placing her hand over both of her mother's, "I think we should listen to what Miss Chambers has to say."

"She's a fraud." Her face contorted into a sneer. I think I preferred the blandness. "She wants to make money from our loss but I'll have none of it."

"No, I've heard of her." The knuckles of Adelaide's hand went white. "I wondered why her name sounded familiar and now I recall. She and her sister hold séances to communicate with the dead. They're very popular."

"That doesn't mean she's not a fraud."

"I am not a fraud," I said. "And I can prove it to you."

Adelaide shifted forward on the sofa without letting go of her mother's hands. "Please do," she whispered.

"She must be a fraud," Lady Preston said again as if neither I, nor her daughter, had spoken. "Because Jacob is not dead."

Shadows of pain passed over Adelaide's face. She momentarily closed her eyes, breathed deeply, then opened them again. "Mother, we've been through this. We don't know for sure—."

"*I* know. He's my son and he is not dead until *I* say he is." She shot to her feet and strode to the window, keeping her back to us. From the slight shake of her shoulders, I knew she was crying.

For the first time since my arrival, I began to doubt my reasons for coming. Would proving to Lady Preston that her son really was dead help her move on, or simply send her over the edge she so precariously clung to?

I looked to Adelaide for an answer but she wiped a tear from her cheek and shook her head at me.

Just as I thought about leaving, a tall man with steel-gray hair and a bushy moustache strolled into the drawing room. He took in the scene but instead of going to his wife, he lifted a thick brow at Adelaide.

"Father," she said, "this is Miss Emily Chambers. Miss Chambers, this is——."

"Chambers!" He snorted. "I know that name."

"She's a spirit medium," Adelaide said.

"She's a fraud," he said, with much more authority but less malice than his wife. "What's she doing here?"

Adelaide glanced at her mother then back to her father. Her gaze didn't falter beneath his cold one. But it wasn't directed at her. It was directed at me. "She's been telling us that Jacob truly is...dead." She looked to her mother again but Lady Preston didn't move. She stood completely still, staring out the window.

Lord Preston stepped closer and regarded me down his long nose. He appeared to be a good twenty years older than his wife but was strongly built nevertheless. He was as tall as Jacob but his features were bolder, heavier, not refined and handsome like his son's. In some ways he reminded me of the sketches I'd seen of cavemen—big-limbed and thick-browed, but not nearly as ugly. He was handsome in his way, but intimidating, particularly when he stood so close.

I tried not to shrink away. "Good afternoon, Lord Preston." I held out my hand in an attempt to maintain some semblance of civility.

He ignored it. "I've been looking into you and your operation."

"He belongs to the London Association of Skeptical Scientists," Adelaide explained.

"Ah. Jacob told me he was a scientist."

There was a moment's silence then, "Bah!" The sound came from deep within Lord Preston's chest. "I'll not listen to another word of your nonsense. You're a trickster, Miss Chambers, just like the rest. And if you think you'll get any money from us——."

"I don't want your money, Lord Preston. I don't want anything from you."

That stopped him momentarily. "Why are you here?" he asked after a long pause in which he watched me through narrowed eyes.

"To give you all some peace. He wants me to tell you that he is dead and that he's happy—."

"Happy! How can he be happy if he's dead as you claim?" Lord Preston had a way of bellowing rather than talking. It was quite deafening. "Get out of my house or I'll have you thrown out."

I gritted my teeth. I couldn't afford to ruin this one chance. "I am not a fraud, Lord Preston. And I would appreciate it if you'd refrain from judging me until you've heard what I've come to say."

He bristled, straightening to his full height. "I do not like your tone, young lady. Your boldness does you no credit. No son of mine would *ever* communicate with the likes of you, whether he was alive or dead."

"The likes of me? As I said, I am not a fraud and I'll—."

"I wasn't referring to your so-called occupation."

I felt the impact of his words like a slap to the face. He was referring to my un-English appearance or my lowly birth or perhaps both. There simply was no argument to either of those facts so I said nothing and glanced at Lady Preston then Adelaide.

The former remained standing at the window, unmoving, but the latter had lowered her gaze to her lap. I couldn't see her expression. It didn't matter. What mattered was that she no longer tried to defend me. I had no allies in that room.

Jacob had been right. It was wrong of me to have come.

Oh Jacob. I'm so sorry I couldn't help them.

I glanced once more at his mother. She was terribly thin. I'd never seen a waist so tiny or a neck so delicate. A big sneeze might snap her. She moved but only to reach out to the window and slide a finger down the glass as if caressing it. What did she see out there? Did she hope to see Jacob strolling past? Would it be so awful if she knew he was dead?

"You used to sing *These Rolling Hills* to him when he was young," I said to her.

She spun round so fast it caught us all by surprise. No one else spoke, not even Lord Preston to chastise me. "How do you know that?"

"He told me."

"Jacob?"

I nodded.

"Enough!" Lord Preston strode to the door and called for the butler. "You'll disrupt this house no more with your lies, Miss Chambers."

But I wasn't watching him anymore, I was looking at his wife. She came towards me, slowly, almost gliding across the floor the way people who can't see ghosts expect them to move. "How do you know that?" she asked.

"She made it up of course," Lord Preston blustered.

"She can't have."

"She must have heard it from someone. Paid a servant, Jacob's old nurse...someone like that. Don't fall for her lies, my dear, she's a fraud."

"A fraud who doesn't want money?" Adelaide scoffed but her flare of defiance dampened beneath her father's glacial glare.

"You stopped singing it to him after he left for school," I went on. "And you never sang it to him when he returned for the holidays even though he wanted you to." I tried my hardest to direct all of my attention onto Lady Preston but it wasn't easy to ignore her husband, looming beside me like a beast ready to pounce. "He wanted you to sing it to him again but you only did once, when he was ill with a fever and you thought he was delirious. But he heard you."

Her own eyes glistened with a kind of fever as she sat down slowly on the sofa, never taking her gaze from mine. Her lips parted and she pressed her thin fingers to them. "No one could possibly know that," she said in a small voice. "No one."

"A servant," her husband said.

"None were there."

"Outside the sick room. Or Jacob mentioned it to this girl before he...disappeared." He nodded, seemingly satisfied with his own explanation.

I ignored him. Both his wife and daughter did too. Their full attention was on me.

"Jacob told you this?" Lady Preston asked. "Please, please don't lie to me, Miss Chambers. If you have any compassion in you...tell me the truth."

Tears sprang to my eyes. How could anyone lie to such a fragile creature about the one thing that could break her entirely? "I would not lie to you. Jacob told me, Lady Preston. At least, his g——."

"Where is he?" She was off the sofa and kneeling beside me in the time it took to blink. "Where is my boy?"

Oh God, she still couldn't see! "He's dead, Lady Preston. His *ghost* speaks to me." My frustration made me speak a little too harshly.

"No!" She clasped my hands. Her grip was surprisingly strong. "He can't be! He doesn't *feel* dead. *You* know where he is, don't you? Tell me!" She shook my hands.

Adelaide came to her mother's side and gently gripped her shoulders. "Come sit down, Mother. And listen to what Miss Chambers is saying."

"I am listening!" she screeched. Tears streamed down her cheeks and dripped off her chin onto the thick Oriental rug. "She knows where my boy is. She knows where to find Jacob."

Adelaide struggled with her but Lady Preston wouldn't budge until Lord Preston took over. He drew his wife up then pressed her face against his chest where she sobbed uncontrollably into his waistcoat.

"Quiet, my dear, the servants will hear," he said, patting her back. To me, he said, "See what you've done! Now get out. You are not welcome here."

I was too dumbstruck to do anything except obey, so I

left without saying another word. The butler waited for me at the door and escorted me out. I wasn't unhappy to leave—the scene had been truly a heart-wrenching one—but I was disappointed. Immensely. That poor woman. I had a feeling she might never find peace, no matter how many years she had left. She truly could not accept that her son was dead.

Tears trickled down my face as I descended the steps to the pavement. It was raining again so I raised my umbrella and began the trudge home.

"Wait!" someone called from the stairs leading down to the basement area where the servants worked. I looked over the iron railing to see Adelaide climbing the steps to the pavement. She was breathing heavily. "Come with me." She glanced up at the main door and took my arm. I tried to hold the umbrella over her head too but because she was so much taller than me, I ended up getting a little wet.

Once around the corner we were able to huddle beneath the umbrella better and use the side wall of the house as a bit of cover. "Miss Beaufort," I said. "What is it?"

"Please, call me Adelaide." She clutched my free hand and gave me a small smile. "Tell me, do you really know my brother? His ghost I mean?"

Did she actually believe me? Was she prepared to give up on the idea that Jacob was alive somewhere when her parents were not?

"Oh, forgive me," she said, "I should apologize first."

"There's no need to apologize. Your parents' grief is affecting their judgment at the moment. Besides, I'm used to not being believed." Although not usually so vehemently.

"It was still a horrible thing to sit through, wasn't it? I am sorry for the things my father said. He didn't really know Jacob, you see. Not very well."

"Oh?" Here was my chance to finally find out more about him. I held my breath and gave her an encouraging nod.

Adelaide glanced back the way we'd come. "Father

doesn't know the sort of people Jacob liked, that's why his comment about you was so terrible and wrong. You are exactly the sort of girl that would have appealed to my brother."

I stared at her. I think I made a small sound in the back of my throat. "Sort of girl?" I croaked.

"Yes. Speaks her mind, is courageous, poised, pretty."

I laughed. "I'll give you the point about speaking my own mind but as to the others, I'm afraid you're wide of the mark."

She waved a hand and glanced over my head again. "There isn't much time. I snuck out while Father took Mother up to her room but he'll be looking for me soon. Tell me, is Jacob really...dead?"

I squeezed her hand. "I'm so sorry but...his ghost visits me often." I decided not to tell her about him being assigned to me because of the demon. It was much too complicated and she had enough to take in already. "He tried to visit you and your parents once a long time ago but it was too traumatic for him." I hoped that went some way to explain why he haunted me and not them.

"I understand. Oh Miss Chambers I'm so pleased you came." Tears filled her eyes but didn't spill. I felt the responding sting behind my own eyes. "Jacob and I were so close, you see, and this wondering...hoping..." She shook her head and pressed her fingers to her nose.

"It's been hard, hasn't it?" My words were almost drowned out by the rain drumming on the umbrella. It came down in heavy sheets, soaking our skirts and forming muddy little streams between the cobblestones. I let go of her hand and pulled my shawl closer then realized Adelaide had come out with nothing for warmth. I stretched one side of it around her shoulders, enclosing us both, and she gave me a grateful smile.

"Mother and Father are both suffering," she said, "but in different ways. Father never speaks of Jacob anymore. Not a single word. He can't bear to hear his name spoken either except when it's to engage the services of an investigator. But Mother talks of nothing else except Jacob. So you see Father can't stand to be home now and Mother needs him more than ever. It's awful. Truly awful." I thought she'd cry but she drew in a shaky breath that seemed to rally her. "If you speak to Jacob's ghost then you must know what happened to him, where his body is. If we could find his body..." Her face contorted as the gruesome nature of what she was saying hit her.

"I'm sorry, Adelaide," I said, "but Jacob doesn't know who killed him or why and he doesn't know where his body is. It's very odd." I wouldn't tell her that the mystery was possibly the reason why he couldn't cross over to the Otherworld. I don't think she was ready to hear it. Besides, I wasn't entirely sure if it was true. "All he's told me is someone tried to kill him."

"Murder?" She gripped my arm so hard I could feel her fingernails through the layers of clothing. "No. No, no, not Jacob." A single tear tracked down her cheek but she swiped it away angrily. "Who would do that to him? He was so well liked. Adored even."

Yes, he would be. Jacob was a very easy person to adore. "Was there anyone in particular who might have turned that adoration into something more sinister if the sentiment wasn't returned? A spurned lover?"

I waited, not wanting to hear the answer but needing to know it nevertheless. The thought of Jacob with another girl was too horrible to contemplate. But then, so was his murder.

"I don't think there was a girl," she said. Then she shook her head. "What I mean is, not one girl in particular."

My insides twisted. There'd been more than one? "Perhaps that was the problem," I said weakly.

"Jealousy?" She thought about that. "It's possible. He was the sort of person to inspire it."

He certainly was. I bit the inside of my cheek and tasted blood. I would not be, *could* not be, jealous over a ghost. It simply wasn't possible, or right.

"But if so then I can't help you," she went on. "I never met any of the girls in his circle and he never spoke to me about them. I think he was rather careful not to so we wouldn't take it as a sign of serious interest. Mother jumped to the wrong conclusion on the one occasion Jacob did mention a girl. He was only seventeen at the time and the girl was the sister of a friend and held no real interest for him. He learned his lesson after that." She grinned at the memory but it soon turned wistful.

"If he never spoke to you about girls, how do you know they were jealous?"

"I wasn't talking about females."

"Then... Oh!" I stared at her so hard my eyes hurt.

She laughed again. "No, not in that way. At least, not for Jacob. I'm talking about boys who were friends. You know what boys are like."

"Not really. I don't have brothers."

"Well, sometimes they worship other boys. Bigger or older boys, clever ones, athletic ones, charmers." She shrugged. "Jacob was all of those so it's understandable some saw him as a hero. They wanted to be his friend, get his attention." She sighed. "And I'm afraid my brother didn't always notice them in return."

George had said the same thing. "Why was that?"

She shrugged. "I truly don't know. He was always kind to people, never cruel the way some boys can be to others, especially to smaller or weaker ones. But..." She sighed again. "But he just didn't *notice* them. I suppose that makes him sound selfish, doesn't it, and that's not really a fitting description either."

I really hoped Jacob wasn't listening to this conversation from the Waiting Area. It wouldn't be fair on either him or his sister. "Self-absorbed?" I offered. "Not interested in other people?" It sounded nothing like the Jacob I knew but I asked anyway. He might have been different when he was alive.

"Oh, he was interested in people. He had a good group of friends who did everything together. He was certainly interested in *them*. But everyone else..." She looked at me and there was sadness in her eyes, and resignation. "You're right. We can call it what we want but he was self-absorbed. Jacob had a power over people. He could charm them into doing anything if he chose to, but he never realized he possessed that power."

I understood completely. I was drawn to Jacob as if he'd put me under a spell, and I could easily imagine other people being drawn to him too. But to then not have Jacob notice me in return... It certainly would be upsetting. I was lucky to be the only person alive who could speak to him or see him now that he was dead, but if I couldn't, if I was just like everyone else, would I be overlooked too?

"He should have realized the effect he had on people," Adelaide went on. "He should have noticed them and not disregarded them simply because they held no interest for him. It was arrogant." Her voice grew quieter, more distant, and she began to cry again.

"No, Adelaide, this is not the way you should remember him. If it was a flaw, it was a small one. We all have them. Mine is vanity." I tugged on a lock of my hair that had come loose from its pins to emphasize my point. "And a willingness to speak my mind, as you saw in there."

She laughed and wiped her eyes. "And one of mine is timidity. I'll allow my brother his one flaw then." She suddenly stopped laughing and blinked at me. "Dear lord, I just thought of something."

"What is it?"

Concern carved out fine lines around her mouth. "It might not be significant. Indeed, it could mean nothing at all."

"Or it could mean something."

She nodded slowly. "A young man came here once, about a month before Jacob died. He said he was a friend of Jacob's from Oxford and wanted to see him. The butler,

Forbes, said Jacob wasn't home and the boy got terribly agitated. I could hear his voice all the way from the library so I came to see what the commotion was about. The boy claimed he wanted to see Jacob and that he didn't believe he was out. He said Jacob cannot possibly always be out whenever he called, and then he accused us of lying to him."

"Lying? Why would he think that?"

"I don't know. But he said he knew Jacob was upstairs, deliberately avoiding him. I tried to assure him he was not, but he would have none of it. He grew terribly upset and his language was truly awful. I grew worried so I called two footmen and they coerced him into leaving. The situation stayed with me for a long time though."

"Who was he, do you know? Did he leave a name?"

"Only a first name, Frederick. I questioned Forbes later and he said the boy had claimed to be a friend of Jacob's from Oxford but I can assure you my brother never mentioned anyone called Frederick and we knew all his friends by sight anyway."

"What did he look like?"

"He was rather plain, not particularly one thing or the other. He had short, light brown hair, was about as tall as me and slightly built. That's really all I can recall. There was nothing very distinguishing about him, I'm afraid."

"So *was* Jacob always out when this Frederick boy called?"

She nodded.

"Is that odd?"

"Not really. Jacob was rarely home in those last few weeks before his death. He came to London from Oxford for the holidays but went out a great deal. I think he was enjoying the sort of freedom that comes to most eighteen year-old boys. He was old enough to go to clubs, taverns, races, that sort of thing. Beforehand he'd always been in Father's shadow but at eighteen he could do as he pleased."

"Did you tell Jacob about Frederick's visit?"

"Yes. He said he had no idea who he was and to make

sure Forbes had at least one footman on hand whenever he answered the door. He was very annoyed and quite concerned. Do you think Jacob was lying to me and that he really knew him?"

"I don't know. I can ask him when I see him."

She smiled at that. "Yes, of course you can. Do you think you could say hello to him for me?"

I couldn't help a bubble of laughter escaping. "I will. I could arrange a meeting between you if you like." Jacob might agree to it if he knew his sister wouldn't be upset by it.

"Could you? How wonderful." But her face fell. "It might not be possible though. Mother is so careful with me ever since Jacob died. Or disappeared, as she thinks. She refuses to let me go anywhere on my own. It's so stifling."

"It must be." I was allowed to go wherever I pleased— well, almost. I couldn't imagine what it must be like for Adelaide always having her mother accompany her. I gave her arm a sympathetic pat then told her my address. "If you think you can get away, send me a message and we'll come and meet you wherever you suggest."

"Thank you, Emily." She leaned down suddenly and kissed my cheek. "I do think we shall be friends."

I smiled. Of course we wouldn't be, but I didn't say so. Our paths were unlikely to cross again unless it was so she could speak to Jacob's ghost. There was nothing about our lives that would cause them to intersect.

"Let me walk you to your door," I said, peering out at the rain still streaming down.

"No, I don't want Father to see you. I'll be all right. It's just a bit of water."

I laughed. It was almost the same words I'd spoken earlier to Celia. I squeezed her arm again, and fought off the melancholy that closed around me. I really would have enjoyed being Adelaide's friend. "One more thing," I said, turning my attention back to Jacob and his demise. "If you could press upon your parents the need to find Jacob's body."

"To learn the cause of his death?"

"Yes," I said, but it wasn't the whole reason. I hoped locating his body would mean Jacob could finally cross over to the Otherworld.

The thought opened up a hollow pit in my stomach. Jacob crossing over would mean he'd be out of my life.

Forever.

CHAPTER 11

For the second time that day, Celia had me change out of my soggy clothes and dry myself in front of a roaring fire. This time she insisted I remain in my room, dressed in my nightgown and a shawl, a hot cup of tea in my hands as I sat up in bed.

"I am not an invalid," I said as she placed another pillow behind my back.

"You could be if you don't warm up."

"I am warm. And dry. I took an umbrella with me."

"And yet you still managed to get wet."

"Only my bottom half. My hair is dry."

She frowned at my hair, splayed over my shoulders like a black, wavy waterfall. "A small miracle."

I sighed. "Celia, the deed is done, there is no need to remain cross with me."

"There is every reason to remain cross! If I do not then you'll not understand the seriousness of your actions."

"My actions? I got a little wet, that's all! Good Lord, Sis, you'd think I'd committed a crime the way you're treating me."

"You are a stubborn, obstinate girl."

"Stubborn and obstinate mean the same thing. Perhaps

you'd like to say out-spoken instead," I said, recalling my earlier conversation with Adelaide. "Oh, and a little vain too." I sipped my tea and watched her over the rim of the cup.

Her face grew redder and redder until I was afraid it might explode. "This is no laughing matter, Emily."

"I'm not laughing."

"You could have been killed."

I snorted. "That is overly dramatic even for you, Celia."

Her lips locked together and tiny white lines ringed her mouth. I'd never seen her so angry. I wouldn't have been surprised to see steam billowing from her nose and ears. "This is all that ghost's fault!"

I choked on my tea. "Jacob?" I spluttered. "Why?"

"His influence over you is obvious."

"His influence?" I shook my head. "No, I truly don't understand you."

"He can walk about and not care if he gets wet. *You* cannot." Her gaze wandered around the room and she leaned closer to me. "He should not be encouraging you to go out in the rain," she added, voice low.

"He is not encouraging me to do anything! I happen to have thoughts of my own, Celia. I am not a puppet with Jacob holding the strings." Of all people, my sister should know I was not easily influenced by anyone. Which was why I was not going to concede the point she was making, even if she was right and I could have caught a chill. There was a different point at stake—she could not order me about. I was seventeen! Other seventeen year-old girls were married, or caring for elderly parents or going to the market on their own. I usually enjoyed the same level of freedom, so why was she getting so upset now?

"Well." Celia strode to the door but didn't open it. She turned back to me and the anger was gone, however the coolness remained. "That is not how it seems. Before he came you and I did everything together, went everywhere together."

Was that the real problem? My sister thought I'd abandoned her? "I didn't think you minded," I said. "Indeed, you seemed quite happy for me to go with Jacob to George Culvert's. I thought you were happy I was meeting new people."

"I was. I am." She shivered and rubbed a hand down her arm. "But I did not expect you to jeopardize your health in the process. It's not like you to be so cavalier about..." She looked down at the door handle and her hand resting upon it.

"Catching a chill?" I offered when she said nothing more.

"About death." She glanced at me and a stab of sympathy pierced my heart. My sister blinked away tears but the fear in her eyes remained. *"That* is the influence I'm talking about."

I climbed out of bed and went to her. "Celia, I am not dying."

"Continue to walk around in the rain on a cool day and you might."

I hugged her. She was as stiff as a plank of wood. "Oh Celia, don't fret. It won't happen again, I promise."

She relaxed a little in my arms then kissed the top of my head. "Good." She opened the door. "Nevertheless, you will dine up here tonight then go to bed early. I'll see you in the morning."

I sighed and watched her go then returned to bed. I read a book until the light faded and Lucy brought up my dinner and lit the lamps. She stoked the fire and added more coal until I asked her to stop. The room was warm enough. She bobbed a curtsy and left.

A moment later, Jacob appeared. "It's not an awkward time, is it?" he asked.

"If it is then it would be too late for you to leave and allow me to retain my modesty."

He chuckled but did not apologize for popping in uninvited. I went to put my tray aside but he stopped me and sat on the bed. "Eat." When I hesitated he picked up the fork and stabbed a slice of beef. He put it to my lips and my stomach growled. I was starving. He gave me a crooked smile as I opened my mouth and bit off the meat. "That's better." He fed me another piece and another. At first he found it amusing but then he grew more serious with each bite.

He watched my mouth as I chewed and my throat as I swallowed as if he'd never seen someone eating before. If it had been anyone else staring at me with such curious intensity I would have felt self-conscious, but not with Jacob. He had a way of making me feel special, not strange.

He reached out to my throat but pulled back without touching me. "May I?" he asked. I nodded. His fingertips lightly grazed down my throat and, as I swallowed, he gently pressed his palm against my skin. Tingles raced across my body as he caressed my throat with his thumb, his hooded eyes riveted to the spot.

"So beautiful," he whispered.

His words startled me. He'd said I was beautiful to Aunt Catherine but part of me assumed that was in defiance and he hadn't really meant it. But here he was using that word to describe me again, and this time he wasn't trying to convince anyone.

I swallowed once more because a lump seemed to have formed in my throat. The movement made him smile, but he pulled away nevertheless. "I'm sorry. That must have been disconcerting."

"Not at all."

"I like to watch you eat."

I'm sure there was a witty response to that if only I thought about it, but my mind wasn't working properly. It seemed to be filled with a fuzziness that made thinking slow. "I like it when you watch me," I said in a voice that sounded breathy and nothing like my own.

"You shouldn't," he said then added, "You shouldn't like me at all." He stood and removed himself to my dressing table stool where he stretched out his long legs, crossed his ankles and crossed his arms over his chest. He regarded me as if I'd been a threat and he was safer because he was further away from me.

I was too confused by his behavior to think clearly. "I'll like who I want to like," I said lamely. "Now stop sounding like my sister and, and..." I waved my hand. There really was nothing in my head worth saying.

He raised an eyebrow. "Your sister?" He grunted. "I see she thinks as I do. That would explain why you're in bed so early."

What in the world was he talking about? "Stop speaking in riddles. You and she are not alike at all, in thoughts or otherwise. *You* would not have confined me to my room after I got a little wet."

That brow forked again. "Wouldn't I? And what do you mean, 'got a little wet'? I told you to take an umbrella with you."

"I did. But it had to cover both myself and your sister at one point so—."

"Adelaide!" In a lightning quick move, he was at my side again. He must have done his vanishing and reappearing trick in order to be that fast. "You spoke to her? Alone?"

"Yes. She followed me out to the street after I left your parents' house."

"How is she?"

"In good health but concerned for them."

He sat down on the bed and took my hand in his although he seemed unaware he'd done so. "And how were they?"

I drew in a deep breath. "Exactly as you said they would be. Your mother doesn't believe you're dead, even after I told her about the song."

He squeezed my hand and gave me a sympathetic smile. "Were they very awful?"

"They were upset, Jacob. That was the awful part."

He lowered his gaze to our linked hands. "Yes, of course. But even when I was alive my father could be...domineering."

"You didn't get along, did you?"

He looked up, startled. "Not really. You learned that from a brief meeting?"

I laughed. "No, Adelaide told me."

He chuckled. "Yes, of course. My sister likes to gossip so I'm not surprised. She never did know when to hold her tongue." He said it without a hint of irritation and I got the feeling he would give anything to hear his sister talk just one more time.

"She wants to meet with you," I said.

"When?"

"When she can get away. It's not easy for her."

He nodded. "What else did she have to say? Tell me everything."

I rubbed his knuckles with my thumb. "We got to talking about your death and how it might have occurred."

His hand shifted in mine but I held it tighter, not letting him go. "I've told you not to concern yourself with my death," he said. "It happened and that fact cannot be altered."

"And I've told you we must learn more. It might be the key to why you can't cross."

He tore his hand from mine and stood up. "What makes you think I want to cross over?"

I stared at him but he was pacing back and forth, not looking at me. "But you must—."

"Why must I?" He stopped pacing and I recoiled at the anger in his eyes. Anger directed at me. "Why do you want me to go?"

My stomach knotted at the thread of pain through his voice. I climbed out of the covers and kneeled up on the bed but did not reach for him like I wanted to. "You think I want you to leave?" I shook my head over and over and fought against the tears threatening to spill. "You are the best thing that has ever happened to me, Jacob. You tell me I'm beautiful, you look at me as if I'm more precious than the stars in the sky, and your very touch leaves me aching for more. I've known you two and a half days and yet it feels like forever. How can you think I want you to leave?"

His breathing came heavy and fast. The muscles in his jaw pulsed rapidly and it took him a long time to speak. "I didn't know," he murmured. "You talk about me crossing over...I didn't know the extent of your feelings." He stepped closer, closer, until there was nothing between us but an inch of air.

I reached up and placed both my hands on either side of his face. "I only want what's best for you," I whispered. "What's right."

"This is right. You are right for me. Emily." He lowered his head and his lips brushed my forehead, the touch as gentle as feathers. "I don't want to cross. I don't want to leave you."

He didn't say "however" but I heard it nevertheless. My heart opened up and began to bleed, or so it seemed. It hurt so much. "Go on," I said, even though I didn't want to know any more. Didn't want to hear the awful words, the ones where he said he had to go because staying was too hard. Watching me grow old when he stayed the same was unnatural.

But instead of speaking, he lowered his lips to mine. His kiss was as light as air as he tasted and teased again and again until finally I could stand it no more and I pressed my hands to the back of his head and pulled him closer, locking him against me. A deep growl rumbled low in his chest and he put his arms around me and held me tight. I melted into him, conscious of nothing but the strength in his body, the tenderness of his mouth on mine, and the desire consuming me.

I don't know how long we explored each other but we became utterly lost as we did so. Eventually, too soon, we parted.

Jacob rested his forehead against mine. "Why is it that something that's so wrong feels so good?" he asked.

"Is it wrong?"

He kissed the end of my nose. "A ghost and a girl as full of life as you?" He nodded sadly. "Very wrong."

I'd not thought my heart could hurt any more than it already did, but it felt like someone was trying to pull it out of my body through the eye of a needle. "Are you going to tell me we must stop this?" It was too hard to keep the hurt from my voice so I didn't try. "Stop feeling what we feel?"

"Can you?"

"No more than I could tear my own arm off."

He smiled sadly. "Me too."

"Then what?"

He let go of my hands and I almost toppled off the bed as I'd been using him for support. He went to the fireplace and watched me from there, as if it were safer with more space between us. I wasn't so sure about that.

"I cannot watch you live half a life, Emily."

I shook my head. "What do you mean?"

"Either you will find another man in time—."

"I won't. There's no one else for me." Stupid, stupid ghost. How could he think that?

"Or you will spend your remaining years waiting to join me. That is not the sort of life you deserve."

I sat back on my haunches. "But if you are here with me, the waiting won't be so terrible." Except that I would grow old and he would not. Of course it would be easier for me, looking at the handsome young man everyday, but for him to see the woman he'd stayed for turn into an old hag...I couldn't imagine how distressing that would be.

"And how long can you wait?" he asked, challenging now. "How many years? You would not have children, not have a family of your own—."

"I would have you."

"Is that enough?" He shook his head and buried his face in his hands.

I went to him and drew his hands away. "Yes. It is." I traced the contours of his cheeks with my fingertip, down to his lips. They were still full and soft from when he'd kissed me.

"I cannot allow you to do it," he said, taking my wrists and gently drawing my hands away. "I cannot allow you to give up on living for me."

"I'm not asking you to allow it."

"You are. And what if..." He turned his face to the side and shook his head.

"What?"

He closed his eyes and the dark lashes cast long shadows on his high cheekbones. "What if I grow weary of watching you wait?"

What did he mean? That he would grow tired of me in years to come? I could never grow tired of him. Never.

And yet *he* was not the one who'd turn gray-haired or wrinkly, his body would not sag and his eyesight or hearing fail him. That would be my fate alone. Of course he wouldn't want to remain here and watch me age. I really couldn't blame him for it either.

And yet it hurt knowing his love for me wasn't strong enough to survive the ravages of time.

I let go of his hands and as if that was a signal, he opened his eyes and faced me.

"I'm not strong enough, Emily."

"Not strong enough?" Didn't he mean not in love with me enough to watch me age?

"It doesn't matter," he said and rubbed both hands through his hair. "I don't want to discuss it. All that matters is that you were right before. I *must* cross over."

"No," I said weakly. "I was wrong. I don't want—."

"Please, don't do this to me! I cannot stay. It'll be...torture."

Hot tears poured down my face. I couldn't stop them any more than I could stop loving him. I began sobbing, the sort where you can't breathe or barely make a noise but when you do your entire body shudders with the effort.

He put his arms around my waist and drew me to him as gently as if I was made of glass. He kissed my tears and caressed my hair. At some point he pulled my head against his chest. I listened for the heartbeat that wasn't there and held him. He rocked me and I stopped crying but the pain inside was so immense I didn't think I would ever feel normal again.

"Please," he said after a long time. He didn't need to say anything else. I knew it was a continuation of the same plea without having to hear the words.

"If it's what you want," I said through my raw throat.

He touched my chin and tilted my face up. His face, while still handsome, was distorted as if he were in pain. "It's not what I want. But it's what has to be. Do you understand the difference?"

I nodded. I understood. He could not stand to see me grow old. Could not look upon an ugly, toothless crone.

"Good." He kissed the top of my head again then held me at arm's length. So that was how it would be from now on—at arm's length.

I returned to the bed where I wanted to curl up and go to sleep then wake up from this nightmare. But it wasn't a nightmare. It was real and Jacob was in earnest now. I sat on the bed and rested my chin on my drawn up knees. I couldn't bear to look at him.

"After we've sent the demon back to the Otherworld," he said, "we'll search for my body. And my killer."

Body. Killer. Oh God, it was all so awful, so hopeless, so horrible.

At that moment I realized with startling clarity that I would do what was best for Jacob, and it was the best thing for him to cross over. It's what spirits are supposed to do. No matter how much I wanted to keep Jacob with me, I could not let the injustice done to him go unpunished. Whoever had taken his life should not be allowed to get away with it. Right then I set my mind on catching his killer. The man I loved deserved nothing less.

"Your sister told me something that might help us," I said.

His fists curled into balls at his sides and those blue eyes, duller than usual, stared unblinking at me for an inordinately long time. I could see he wasn't entirely convinced he wanted to follow through on his new resolution to cross over. We both knew that this was just the first step on what could be a long road, but it was still the first step to an end neither of us really wanted.

"You'd better tell me what it is," he finally said.

"Do you remember a boy called Frederick?"

I could have sworn he paled, something that wasn't possible considering he was dead. "Yes." He recounted the same story that Adelaide had told me about Frederick coming to their Belgravia home and accusing her and the butler of lying about Jacob's whereabouts. "It upset her greatly at the time but I'd thought she would have forgotten about it by now."

"*You* clearly haven't. Which means you thought it was important."

He gave me his crooked smile and I was overjoyed to see the charming Jacob back. No matter how hurt I was by the fact he didn't want to stay with me forever, I couldn't be mad at him for long. "You know me so well already." He sat on the chair near the fireplace and leaned forward, his elbows resting on his knees. His shirt gaped open and I was rewarded with a rather delicious view of his naked chest underneath.

Would I ever get to touch it now?

"Emily, are you listening?"

"What? Yes, of course I am. You said I know you so well."

"And *then* I said I told Adelaide I didn't know anyone called Frederick. But that probably wasn't true."

"Why would you lie to her?"

"I didn't lie deliberately. I thought at the time that I didn't know anyone called Frederick. But now...now I think I must have."

"Why would you say that?"

"Because I now think he had something to do with my death."

I hugged my knees closer to my chest. "Why? No, let's start with who he is. How well did you know him?"

He turned his hands out, palms up, without shifting his position. "I didn't. That's the thing, I don't remember anyone from Oxford named Frederick."

"No one? It's a common enough name."

He looked down at his hands. "I know."

"Adelaide said he was fair haired, slight build, plain features. Can you recall anyone from school matching that description?"

"Not really. I suppose it could describe several of my classmates though."

"None of whom were named Frederick?"

He sighed and slumped back in the chair. "I can't recall. There might have been one or several Fredericks in my year. I just..."

"Can't recall." I sighed too. "It would seem you spent more time with your head in the clouds *before* you died than after."

He cocked his head to the side and gave me a withering look. "Very funny."

Adelaide and George hadn't been exaggerating when they said Jacob never noticed people. I was only now beginning to believe it.

"If I could have my life over again," he said, serious, "I would speak to everyone I ever met. Every single person. I'd stop people in the street and ask them how their day was."

"You would get some very strange looks." I tried to make light of the situation but it was no joke. It was obvious Jacob regretted what he'd been like when he was alive. It made me think about everything I wanted to change about myself. I made a mental note to give Celia a hug in the morning.

"Do you think Frederick killed you because he thought you were avoiding him?" I shook my head at the absurdity. "Not only is it a big leap but it also doesn't make sense. If he wanted to be your friend, then why would he kill you? He could never be your friend then." I drummed my fingers on my knee as another thought occurred to me. "Or perhaps there was some other reason he wanted to see you. Could you have owed him a debt?"

"How could I owe a debt to someone I didn't know? No, my death was certainly related to the fact he thought I was avoiding him."

I frowned at him. He looked away. "How do you know?" I hedged.

He shrugged one shoulder. "I just do."

"Jacob, what aren't you telling me? What do you know?"

"Nothing. Just leave it be. Accept that I'm almost certain Frederick the boy from Oxford is somehow relevant to my death."

"You mean he killed you."

"No. I think he had something to do with my death, but didn't commit the act himself."

I put my hands up, stopping his convoluted riddles. "If you don't know who killed you, how can you discount Frederick from the list of suspects? He sounds like the most likely one to me."

Jacob scratched his head, making his hair stick out at odd angles. "I can't tell you why I know he didn't do it, I just do."

"You *can* tell me, you just don't want to."

That cynical smile again. "Thank you for clarifying."

I climbed off the bed and crouched in front of him, touching his knees. "Jacob, you have to tell me everything. I need to know what you know."

"No!" He gripped my forearms and hoisted me up as he stood too. "There are some things you should not know, Emily. This is one of them."

Anger flared, bright and fierce, behind my eyes. Already tonight *he'd* decided we would not be together and now he was keeping information from me that could help me solve his murder? It was too much. *I* deserved to decide what was important and what wasn't too. "Why shouldn't I know?" I jerked out of his grip. He sat down again, shock rippling across his handsome face. But I wasn't prepared to let my anger evaporate beneath his sudden change. Sometimes anger is a benefit, if channeled correctly. "What could it possibly matter now? You're dead. And I *will* find out who killed you so you might as well tell me everything you know."

He said nothing for a long time, just stared at me, and for one breathless moment I was scared that he found my anger ugly and that he was relieved he'd not committed to spend the rest of my life with me. But I could not regret it any more than I could control it. Something was bothering Jacob deeply and I was determined to get to the bottom of it.

"Very well." He sucked in his top lip and indicated I should sit. I sat on the bed, my stockinged toes just touching the fringe of the rug, my hands at my sides on the quilt. "I suppose it doesn't matter what you think of me now anyway," he said, bleak.

"What I think of you?" I felt like all the air had been knocked out of me along with my anger. I shook my head. I didn't understand.

"It might even be for the best." He rubbed his fists down his trousers and didn't quite meet my gaze. "Now that we've decided I must cross over, having you...despise me will make that easier."

"Despise you?" I got up and went to him but he lifted a single finger, halting me from curling into his lap and kissing him all over. "I could never despise you," I said instead.

He pressed the finger into his eye socket and his thumb into the other. "You haven't heard my story yet."

I sat back down on the bed and tucked my hands beneath my thighs. "Go on."

"I know that boy Frederick didn't kill me because...because I killed him." He waited for me to say something but I didn't. In truth, I couldn't have spoken anyway. I was too shocked by his admission to make any sense. "I was walking home late one night when a boy accosted me. I didn't realize then that it was the same boy that had come to the house. That only came later. Much later, after I died. Anyway, the boy began shouting at me, accusing me of ignoring him and deliberately avoiding him. Of course I had no idea what he was talking about. I tried to calm him down and make sense of what he was saying but he just got angrier and angrier." He rubbed his cheek as if trying to remove a smudge. "He struck me. It wasn't a very strong blow but I hadn't been ready for it and I must have stumbled back. He came at me again but I'd recovered enough to defend myself. In the ensuing struggle I punched him. He fell and...and hit his head on the ground. The pavement was uneven and... The sound..." He closed his eyes and his nostrils flared. "The sound his head made as it hit the ground has stayed with me all this time."

I sat on the bed and waited for him to go on but he didn't. My heart beat hard in my chest and blood pounded in my ears. Jacob had killed someone. Jacob. My Jacob. A murderer.

I sucked in air between my teeth and let it out slowly. No wonder he'd avoided telling me about the circumstances surrounding his own death. I'd suspected outside George's house that he was withholding something vital from me and now I knew what it was, and why. He was racked with guilt and he was afraid I would think badly of him.

"Don't look at me like that," he said upon opening his eyes.

"Like what?"

"Like...like you still love me."

"I do." What a stupid thing for him to say! "Of course I do."

"But...how can you after what I just told you?"

"Because you didn't mean it. It was an accident." I got up and crouched before him again. I took his hands in both of mine. "It was an accident, Jacob, and you don't deserve to carry this guilt, just as you didn't deserve to die." Oh God, is that what he thought? That he deserved death because he'd accidentally killed someone?

He blinked once then looked down at our linked hands. He lifted them to his mouth and skimmed his lips across my knuckles. "Do you really believe that?"

"Yes! Jacob." I caught his face and drew it up so he looked at me. Our gazes met, briefly, then his flitted away to a point over my shoulder. "You are not to blame. Do you understand me?"

He smiled but it was weak and unconvincing. "I am to blame. Just because I didn't mean it, doesn't mean I didn't do it."

"But he attacked you first!"

"And I hit him last. That's what counts."

Men! Why did they have to think like brutes when it suited them? "Your logic is ridiculous, Jacob. No court would convict you."

"Emily." He said my name with great effort, as if he was beyond exhausted. "You don't understand. I hit him. I *wanted* to hit him. I wanted to stop him annoying me so I could go home, and to do that...I knew I would have to hurt him."

I frowned and shook my head. "That doesn't matter. You're a good person and I will not see you so angry with yourself because of something that wasn't your fault."

He drew my hands away from his face. His nostrils flared as his gaze met mine and held it. "You're not afraid of me?"

"No."

"You should be." He shoved my hands away, setting me unceremoniously back on my haunches, and stood up. "I'll stay away from you unless it becomes absolutely necessary." And then he was gone.

CHAPTER 12

I sat on the rug and stared at the chair where Jacob had been sitting. The cushion, embroidered with a vine pattern by my mother, hadn't yet sprung back to its full plump shape. I lowered my head and would have cried—I *wanted* to cry—but the tears wouldn't come. Perhaps I had none left. I felt empty.

After a while I climbed back into bed and pulled the covers up to my chin. But I didn't sleep. I couldn't. Jacob might come back. He might explain the meaning of his final words to me.

You should be.

I should be afraid of him. But I wasn't. Not of Jacob. He was gentle and considerate and protective. He would never hurt me, nor would he harm someone who didn't deserve it, I was certain. Frederick had hit him first and he'd been dogging Jacob for some time if his visits to the Beaufort's house were an indication. Jacob wasn't to blame for his death.

But Frederick was the key to Jacob's.

I knew that as well as I knew my own name. The events leading up to Jacob's murder were too coincidental for it not to be linked to Frederick and the incident in the alley. But if

Jacob had killed Frederick in the fight, who had killed Jacob later?

The answer to that lay in what might have happened after Jacob felled Frederick. I couldn't believe he'd leave the boy lying there, dying. Jacob was no coward. He would have faced up to his actions and I doubt he simply walked away.

So what had happened next?

And who on earth was Frederick?

These questions and a thousand others swirled around my head until, drained, I finally drifted to sleep.

I awoke with a start the next morning to knocking on my door. I jumped out of bed. "Jacob!" I opened the door but Celia stood there alone.

"No," she said with suspicion. "Why would you think I was he?" Her already narrowed eyes became slits. "Has he been visiting you?"

"Occasionally."

Her lips puckered. "Please don't tell me he's been in your room."

If Celia wanted to make it easy for me then she'd just given me the perfect opportunity. "Of course not." *Of course not, I won't tell you.* It wasn't exactly a lie...

"Because if I learn that he has—."

"Celia, stop questioning me." I stood with my hands on my hips blocking the doorway but she still managed to slip past me into my room.

"It's most improper," she said from my wardrobe where she contemplated my gowns.

"I doubt my reputation will be ruined by the irregular visits of a ghost."

She turned to fix me with a withering glare. "Don't be so sure. Anyway, I'm worried about more than your reputation."

More than...? Oh. "Jacob has been the perfect gentleman, Sis, don't worry." I bit the inside of my cheek. He'd kissed me. Perhaps perfect was too strong a word.

"Emily..." She shook her head but I could tell she was

bursting to ask me something. I had a feeling I would regret prompting her but I did anyway.

"Ye-es?"

"Well, do you think ghosts can...you know?"

Oh dear, regret wasn't a strong enough word for how I felt about this conversation. It was heading into very murky waters. "I have no idea what you're talking about and I don't think I want to."

"I know you know what I'm suggesting because we had that little chat only last year."

"Oh, *that*," I said, feigning nonchalance. "You're asking me if ghosts can have marital relations?" It was the phrase Celia had used during our talk on how babies were made. Even though most unwed girls my age were quite ignorant about what happened between men and women, my sister had insisted I be made aware. I'd thought it very progressive of her, particularly since she was essentially a prude. Not even I had seen her without her clothes on. Still, discussing it with her now was no less embarrassing than it had been then.

"Yes," she said. "Well, what do you think? Can they...you know?"

"I don't know. Would you like me to ask Jacob for you?"

"No!" She turned back to the wardrobe and studied the clothes with extra intensity.

I think I won that little battle.

"Why have you been crying?" she asked suddenly.

Oh dear, I was losing the war. I rubbed my eyes and yawned dramatically, putting my arms above my head and twisting my body for effect. "I slept poorly. I've a lot on my mind."

She seemed to believe me this time. She patted my arm and sighed. "So have I. What are you going to do today?"

"About the demon?" I padded across the floor to my dressing table and peered into the mirror. Good lord, I really did look awful. My eyes were rimmed red, my nose had swelled up and the dark shadows made it look like someone had punched me. Not even a strong cup of tea would help me look like myself again. "I think I'll go and see if George has contacted Leviticus Price," I said, frowning at me reflection. Hopefully a dose of cool air would help my complexion.

"Good idea." She laid the dress on the bed and whipped her palm down the skirt to flatten it. Satisfied, she made for the door. "If there's anything I can do, let me know." She left, her back not quite as straight as usual. She must still be blaming herself for letting the demon loose.

What she hadn't asked me was if there'd been another victim and burglary overnight. Of course I didn't know because Jacob had not appeared that morning.

My heart dove violently into my stomach as I realized he may not appear at all, ever again.

***

George was home, as was his mother unfortunately. When Mrs. Culvert saw us together in the drawing room, she turned her nose up at me and said, "You again," as if I was the plague. "George, a word."

"Yes, Mother." But he didn't move.

"In private."

With a loud sigh, he joined his mother outside the drawing room. A few moments later, I heard him say, "This is my house and I can entertain any sort of guest I want. Emily is an outstanding girl and—."

His mother's voice cut him off but I couldn't quite make out what she said. The click-clack of her footsteps retreating on the tiles was a welcome sound to my ears.

"Sorry," George said with a sympathetic smile when he returned. "Mothers."

I smiled too even though I didn't necessarily understand his meaning. My mother had never dictated who I could be friends with, but then I'd had so few friends growing up she'd probably have encouraged me to speak to the poor little girl who sold matches on the street corner.

"Now, where were we?" he said, sitting down opposite

me once more. "Ah yes, Leviticus Price. I sent him a message requesting to see him."

"A message? *Requesting* to see him? George, you are being much too polite."

He looked slightly taken aback at that. "Emily, there is no such thing as too polite."

I refrained from retorting that he might as well live in a prison with all the society rules he and the people of his station had to live by. I suddenly felt an immeasurable amount of freedom, as I had done after speaking to Adelaide Beaufort the day before. My life, while complicated, was at least my own. "Come on, let's pay him a visit now."

I stood. After a moment, George stood too. "I'm not sure this is a good idea," he said slowly. "Price isn't the sort of man who likes insolence, particularly in youngsters."

"You're nineteen!" The urge to click my tongue, roll my eyes and generally make him see how immature he was behaving was very strong.

"You're right. Let's go." He tugged on his coat lapels and stretched his neck. "Greggs!" he called as he strode to the drawing room door. "Send word to the stables for the carriage."

***

Leviticus Price rented a few rooms in a brick terrace house in one of the newer suburbs on London's outskirts where street upon street was lined with identical brick terrace houses. The only distinguishing feature between them seemed to be the color of the door, but even there the palette was limited to blue, white and green.

Price's landlady showed us up to the tiny parlor where a thin man with short white hair and a long white beard sat eating breakfast. *The Times* was open on the table beside him and several books and journals were piled or scattered around the small space. Oddly, the mantelpiece was empty except for a smoking pipe on a wooden stand. The walls too were bare. It was almost as if he'd just unpacked after moving in.

Although it was almost noon, Price didn't seem concerned that he'd been caught eating at such a late hour, or that he'd been caught eating at all. He kept right on shoveling eggs and bacon into his mouth as if it was his first meal in a week. By the thinness of him, it might very well have been.

He greeted George with a nod of his long, horse-y head but hardly acknowledged me at all until George introduced us. My name did, however, catch his attention.

"Emily Chambers," he said, pausing in chewing to look me over properly. "Well, well, well." He had eyes of the palest blue, like a frozen lake, which left me shivering in the wake of his bald scrutiny.

"You've heard of her," George said, sounding pleased.

Price wiped his mouth with the back of his hand, all the while watching me. It was most unnerving. "I have indeed. She's the spirit medium. Quite a good one, I hear."

I did not like the way he spoke about me as if I wasn't there, or as if I was an object without the capability of thought or speech. "Mr. Price, if you would stop staring, I would be most grateful." I gave him a tight smile. "I'm not at my best today you see." It was a light-hearted attempt to cut through the awkwardness I felt in his presence but it was also a grim reminder of why I wasn't looking my best—I'd been up half the night crying over Jacob.

I shoved all thoughts of my ghost away. I needed to concentrate and I couldn't do that if I let sadness consume me.

Price snorted a laugh and sat back in his chair. The move made his smoking jacket gape open, revealing a plain linen shirt underneath. "Sit, sit, both of you." I sat on the only spare chair, a hard-backed, unpadded affair that looked as old as the white-haired man himself. George removed a stack of books from another chair and, not finding anywhere to deposit them, piled them up on the floor near the unlit fireplace. He sat too and offered me a small shrug. Price wouldn't have noticed since he was still staring at me. I felt like an exotic bird at the zoo, a feeling that wasn't entirely foreign but definitely not welcome.

"Can you really see ghosts, Miss Chambers?"

"Yes." I saw no reason to lie to him, or indeed to anyone. Once upon a time I would have been considered a witch but this was an enlightened age. Society had come a long way since the days when my kind was burned at the stake.

Price rested his elbows on the arms of his chair and pressed his steepled fingers to his lips. "Interesting."

Usually at this point people ask me to demonstrate my abilities by summoning a loved one. Sometimes I oblige them but most of the time—because Celia is with me and insists upon it—I agree to come back for a séance. Price didn't ask and I didn't offer, although he undoubtedly was intrigued. He couldn't stop staring.

I tried not to let him see how unsettled his scrutiny made me. It wasn't easy.

"We've come to ask you about a Mr. Blunt from the North London School for Domestic Service," George said. He offered no preliminaries, no how-do-you-do's or idle chatter and I sensed that was the best way to deal with Price. He didn't seem like the sort of man who liked to discuss the weather. George may not be the most socially adept person but he knew enough about Price to keep to the point. Was that because they were so alike in their obsession with the Otherworld?

"Blunt?" Price turned to George and I let out a relieved breath. I'd had enough of being viewed as a museum piece. "I'm on the board of his school. What of it?"

"He told us you and he had a discussion about demons, mentioning myself as an authority on the subject."

"We might have. What of it?" he asked again.

George cleared his throat. "I was burgled recently. *The Complete Handbook of Shape-shifting Demons and Weres* was stolen from my library."

I think Price squeezed his lips together but it was difficult to tell with his untrimmed moustache hanging over his mouth like a hedge in need of pruning. "A good general primer on the subject, suitable for a newcomer to the art of demonology."

Art? Now there was a word I'd not thought to hear in the same sentence as demonology.

"What a shame to lose it from your collection," Price went on, "but I fail to see the connection to myself or Blunt."

"I suspect it was stolen by my new maid who was sent to me from Blunt's school. I wondered if she perhaps overheard your conversation with the schoolmaster before she left. He suggested you might remember when exactly you had the conversation."

"He did, did he?" He appeared to think about this for a moment, then said, "No, sorry, I can't recall. Memory's not what it used to be. Could have been last week, could have been a month ago." Price picked up a piece of bread from his plate but didn't eat it. "What does it matter anyway? I assume the girl's long gone."

"She is but we'd like to find her."

Price frowned. "Does the book really mean that much to you?"

"It's not so much the book." George glanced at me.

"What then?" Price prompted and popped the bread in his mouth. He had not so much as offered us a cup of tea. Not that I would have agreed to one—I didn't want to stay any longer than necessary—but it would have been polite.

"A demon was summoned from the Otherworld during one of my séances," I said. "It was unwittingly done but it appears to have been orchestrated by someone intent on doing harm to others. The only lead we have is the stolen book."

We waited while Price chewed then swallowed. His frown grew deeper and darker as his mouth worked slowly. "You think the girl is using this demon for her own nefarious reasons?" he eventually asked.

"Yes," I said quickly before George could tell him we

suspected she'd been ordered by others to steal the book. Thankfully he didn't counter my answer. "But we wouldn't like to blame her if she's not responsible. So if you could remember when you had that conversation with Mr. Blunt, we would be most grateful. Indeed, if you could remember anything at all...you could be saving lives."

Price rubbed his beard, dislodging a few crumbs, then reached for the newspaper. He flipped it open to a page and pointed to a small article with the headline DOG ATTACKS SERVANT. "Read it only this morning. It says the police think the footman was mauled to death by a stray dog. He sustained terrible injuries that killed him a few hours later. Do you think that's your demon?"

"Probably," I said without reading the article. "So you understand we need to find out as much as we can. The police can't do anything in this situation. It's up to us."

He nodded, stroking his beard again as he re-read the article. Then he suddenly folded the newspaper and placed it back on the tea table. "Sorry, Miss Chambers, but I can't recall the exact date of my conversation with Blunt." His freezing gaze shifted from me to George then back again. "I do, however, remember that he asked some very precise questions about demons."

"What do you mean?" said George.

Price suddenly stood and pressed a hand to his temple. "I don't like to tell you this as it might get the man into trouble."

George and I exchanged glances. "Go on," I urged Price.

He sighed and picked up the pipe from its little stand on the mantelpiece. He put it into his mouth but didn't light it. "Blunt wanted to know how to summon one," he mumbled around the end of the pipe, "how to control them, all the different kinds of demons, that sort of thing."

"You didn't think his questions unusual?" George asked, incredulous.

"Of course I did, boy!" He pulled the pipe out and pointed the end at George. "I told him about you and your library and I said if he wanted to know anything, you were the man to ask." He sighed, and folded his long, thin arms over his chest. "I even told him about that specific book you mentioned. I said it was a good place to begin."

George groaned and I closed my eyes. It was looking more and more like Blunt was involved. But if that was the case, why did he tell us about the conversation with Price at all? He must know Price could turn the suspicion back on him.

"And no one else overheard you?" I asked.

Price shrugged sharp, angular shoulders. "They might have. I don't know, do I?" He strode to the door, reaching it in two giant strides even though he had to avoid George's chair and a pile of books stacked beside it. "Anyway, it's not my problem, I didn't summon the bloody thing." This he directed straight at me, as if it were my fault my sister had accidentally released the demon. I suppose it was, in a way. "Give my regards to Blunt."

George stood but instead of leading the way out, he confronted Price. "I say, you don't seem too perturbed by the fact there's a shape-shifting demon loose in the city and that you might be partially responsible."

"I am not responsible, partially or otherwise." Price grunted and popped his pipe back in his mouth. His gaze flicked to me, cool and assessing once more, then back to George. "The death is a tragedy of course," he said with a nod at the newspaper. "But I don't see how I can help. Demons are your specialty, Culvert. Of course if there's anything I can do to help, I trust you'll let me know."

Dismissed, George and I had no alternative but to leave although George hesitated for a brief moment in the doorway. Once outside, we climbed back into his carriage just as the clouds parted above and let the sun shine through. It didn't last long and the gray clouds had swallowed up the beams by the time we reached the end of the street.

"He's not a particularly nice gentleman," I said. We sat opposite each other, our knees almost touching. Fortunately the bench seats were covered in padded maroon velvet cushions or it would have been a terribly uncomfortable ride. The carriage traveled fast along the wider, emptier outer-suburban roads and we were jostled about like beans in a pot of boiling water.

He sighed. "I'm sorry I subjected you to his rudeness. I should have come alone."

"Nonsense. I found it quite beneficial."

"Oh?" George pushed his glasses up his nose. "In what way?"

"It gave me a chance to form an opinion about him and I now think he had something to do with the release of the demon."

The spectacles slid down his nose again and he peered over the top of them at me. "You've made that assumption on the basis that he's not particularly nice?"

When he put it like that it didn't sound like a very convincing reason. "And because he didn't seem shocked at the damage the demon has caused."

George nodded and once more pushed the glasses up to their rightful position. "True. He was quick to turn the discussion back to Blunt and his possible involvement too. You do think he's involved, don't you?"

"Blunt? Of course he is. It's obvious."

"Yes, yes, obvious." He gave me a grim smile but it vanished when the carriage turned a corner and we both lurched to one side. Righting himself, George banged on the cabin roof. "Slow down, Weston!" To me he said, "Apologies. The driver knows I like to go fast but I don't usually have a passenger of the female persuasion with me."

"It's quite all right, George." I straightened my pillbox hat and hoped my hair had managed to maintain some semblance of control. "And another thing about Price," I said. "Blunt mentioned he was a generous benefactor, but I cannot see how Price would have much money if his housing situation is any indication." I pointed at the buildings through the window but we'd long since left behind the rows and rows of identical houses. They'd been replaced by the statelier, colonnaded, residences of old money and the occasional shop that catered for their exclusive needs. "Price doesn't seem like he can afford to be all that generous with his funds."

George nodded. "I'd not thought of that. Well done, Emily."

"Thank you, George."

He smiled at me. I smiled back.

And then I realized *why* he was smiling. He moved to sit beside me and covered my hand with his own. With a squeak of alarm, I slipped it free and shifted to where he'd been sitting so we were once more opposite each other.

His crestfallen face told me he understood the meaning behind the maneuver. Thank goodness. I thought he might attribute it to female coquettishness or some nonsense. He at least was mature enough to realize I was rejecting him.

That didn't make me feel any less horrible for doing it. "George," I said softly, "I'm so sorry."

He waved a hand and gave me a smile that was much too bright in its eagerness. "That's all right. We're not really very well suited, you and I, are we?"

I wasn't sure how to take that. Was it simply an excuse to cover the fact I'd hurt his feelings, or did he genuinely believe we weren't a very good match? Why he would think we weren't, I couldn't say. Perhaps deep down he agreed with his mother that I wasn't good enough for him. Perhaps I was just *too* odd.

I shoved that line of thought aside. George could think what he liked of me. It was Jacob's opinion that mattered most. "We are still friends, aren't we?" I ventured.

"If you'd like to be." I detected a pout in his voice even though there wasn't one on his lips.

I reached across the space between us and took his hand. "I have so few true friends, but I'd like to count you amongst them."

His face lifted and brightened. "And I you. Let's forget all this, shall we?"

"Gladly." I smiled but something inside me felt hollow, sad. I missed Jacob and it didn't help not knowing when I would see him again. I desperately wanted to speak to him, ask him more questions, and just hold him. But I could not.

How much easier it would be to love a man like George. Dependable, sweet. Alive.

"It's looking more and more likely Blunt and the Finch boy are involved," he said as if the rather embarrassing interlude hadn't occurred. If he wanted to pretend it never happened, then I was more than willing to go along with him. "The big question is whether Price is in it too."

"What I find odd is that Blunt asked Price about demons. If Price is to be believed, Blunt's questions were entirely unprompted and were quite specific. If he was indeed acting with Finch alone, then where did either of them hear about demons? The idea to summon one must have been planted in their minds at some point but by whom?"

"Price," George said. But then he shook his head. "It goes against the code of the Society. None of us would intentionally bring harm upon another by using supernatural means."

I wasn't convinced by the gentlemanly rule of conduct but I didn't say as much. I got the feeling the Society was important to George. It was probably the one place he felt accepted by people with similar interests, and I didn't want to destroy that security.

"There's one other mystery in this too," I said. "Who was the woman who sold Celia the amulet?"

"Mrs. White?"

It was looking more and more likely. I hoped I was wrong. I liked her. Lucy our maid liked her. But if Blunt had orchestrated the demon's release, then she might very well be involved. Drat.

"Shall we go and confront them now?" I asked.

"Perhaps we should contact the police."

"We can't tell the police there's a demon on the loose!

They'll never believe us, and if they do then they're more likely to lock Celia and I up for releasing it, not Blunt."

"You're right." He sighed. "I'll drive you home then I'll go alone to the school."

"Don't be ridiculous. I'm coming."

George had the good sense not to argue with me although he made a great show of scowling his displeasure at the suggestion. "I think Jacob should come along too," he said. "He could scare Blunt a bit if need be. Throw something around or create a disturbance."

I would have loved to have Jacob with us but I wasn't sure he would see the benefit of my presence. I wasn't sure he'd want to see me at all.

"I could do much more than create a disturbance," Jacob said, suddenly appearing on the seat beside me. He sat with his shoulder against the door, as far away from me as possible.

"Jacob's here," I said to George, jerking my head in the brooding ghost's direction. I tried not to let his presence unnerve me in any way, but I failed. My heart tripped merrily over itself at the mere sight of him and I ached to get closer to him.

"We were just talking about you," George said. He sat up straighter and pressed his finger to the bridge of his glasses even though they hadn't slipped down. "Care to visit Blunt with us?"

"You're not going," Jacob said to me, ignoring George.

"I am so," I said. "And you can't stop me."

"It's dangerous."

"Riding in this carriage is dangerous." I crossed my arms but it wasn't because I was making a point, it was to hold myself back from climbing into his lap and kissing him. I didn't think George would appreciate witnessing such a scene. Besides, I was almost certain Jacob would disappear again if I did. His closed expression with the shuttered eyes was a clear indication he didn't want to get into a discussion about last night.

Proving he was full of surprises, he said, "Is this about what happened between us in your room?"

"No, this is about you telling me what to do. You have no right."

He groaned and fixed his gaze on the ceiling. "I'm sorry we parted on such angry terms."

"I wasn't angry."

"You're angry now."

"No, I'm...never mind. Now is neither the time nor the place to discuss it." I risked a glance at George. He was staring out the window a little too hard for me to believe he was interested in the scenery whizzing past at an astonishing rate. "Aren't you going to tell the driver to go to Clerkenwell?" I asked him.

"We'll return to my house first," George said. "I have a pair of old dueling pistols that belonged to my grandfather in the study."

"Pistols! Do you think that's necessary?"

George nodded grimly. Jacob nodded, equally grim. "There was another victim last night," he said.

I gasped and put a gloved hand to my mouth as bile filled it. "Oh God." I told George what Jacob had said. He removed his glasses and squeezed the bridge of his nose.

"Another footman," Jacob said. "Later on, the house where he worked was burgled. There was no sign of forced entry."

I passed the information onto George, all the while trying not to think what a shape-shifting demon could do to a poor, unarmed man.

"This is awful," George said with undisguised horror. "It's looking more and more like the person or persons who summoned the demon are directing it to take on the form of its victim in order to gain access to the house where he worked." He screwed his top lip up and shook his head. "For money," he spat. "Despicable."

We were all silent for some time after that.

"Did you speak to the footman's ghost?" I eventually

asked Jacob.

He nodded. "He couldn't tell me anything useful. He thought a wild dog or a bear had killed him. He said it came out of nowhere, from the shadows. When I explained what happened he decided to stay in the Waiting Area until the demon is returned to the Otherworld."

We remained silent until the carriage stopped outside George's house and he got out. Finally I was alone with Jacob. But after the terrible news, I didn't want to argue with him anymore. I just wanted to hold him and be held by him.

On the other hand I couldn't allow the opportunity to speak pass me by. I might not get another one.

"You failed to finish your story last night," I said.

"I know." He shifted his long legs, cramped in the tight space of the cabin, but still managed to keep them well away from mine. He must not want to risk getting too close. "I owe you an explanation after...everything." He shifted his legs again, putting them back where they were to begin with, under the seat we shared, crossed at the ankles.

"You got to the point where Frederick fell and hit his head," I prompted. "What happened next? Did you check to see if he was thoroughly dead?"

"He wasn't dead at all. He got up and ran away."

"Got up! Not dead! Jacob, that's——."

He held up a hand. "Wait, let me finish. I know what you're going to say—that I didn't kill him."

"Well of course!"

"He was unconscious for only a few seconds during which time I tried to waken him. I was in the middle of feeling for a pulse when he opened his eyes. He took one look at me, screamed, then got up and ran off. He seemed disoriented and I went after him to ensure he didn't fall again but he climbed into a carriage that I hadn't noticed waiting further down the street, and sped off before I could catch up.

"For days I worried if he was all right. I also tried to think who he might have been, but I had no luck. Anyway, about a week after that incident, I was walking home again and was attacked once more. This time it was by someone wearing a hooded cloak. Whoever it was caught me off guard, delivering a blow that made me lose my senses. I woke up some time later with a blanket or cloak over my head. I struggled to free myself but my wrists were tied." He lifted both hands to his face and stared at them. "I was hit again as I struggled and it was then that I realized I was inside a carriage and it was traveling fast. I continued to struggle of course and by this time I was asking my companion, or companions, what they wanted. The only answers I received were more blows and again I became unconscious."

"Oh, lord." I sidled up to him and touched his cheek. How could anyone hurt my Jacob?

He took my hand and pulled it gently away and placed it on his thigh. Tears stung my nose and eyes and burned the back of my throat. He did not want my sympathy, or my love.

"The carriage stopped and I was dragged out. We were in the country, I know that much. I could smell earth and grass."

"Did it have a farm smell?" I screwed up my nose. I'd only been to one farm in my life, when Mama had taken me to see where milk came from as a child. I'd got dung on my boots and straw in my hair and the aroma had stayed with me ever since. I knew after that experience I was a London girl through and through.

He smiled, despite the horrible tale he was telling. "No. Just a pleasant country odor. I could hear an owl but nothing else. It was very quiet. I was dragged further away again and I remember rolling into a ditch."

"And left there to die," I whispered.

"I suppose so. I was in and out of consciousness by this stage. I remember being extremely cold, all the way through, as if my very bones had frozen. I'd lost my coat and hat and the blanket had also disappeared."

I shivered and hugged myself. "How long before you

died, do you think?"

He shrugged. "It could have been minutes or days, I really don't know."

I looked out the window but there was no sign of George, which was good because I hadn't finished questioning Jacob and I wanted to continue to do it alone. I'd discovered years ago that discussing a ghost's death with them could be quite an intimate affair. I suspected Jacob wouldn't want George to know all the harrowing details. I felt privileged that he was confiding in me.

"Did the killer remain with you until you died?"

"No." He blinked rapidly and rubbed a finger across his bottom lip. There was something he wasn't telling me.

"Did your killer say something before he departed?"

He hesitated then his gaze leveled with mine. "Yes. He cursed me for killing his son."

My heart thudded once against my ribs. "Frederick."

Jacob nodded. "He must have died from his injury. The injury *I* gave him. Only not straight away but some time later."

I felt like I'd been punched in the chest. Breathing suddenly became difficult. I didn't understand. There was something wrong, something missing in this puzzle and I couldn't put my finger on it. Perhaps Jacob was still withholding information.

"What exactly did he say?" I asked. "Tell me the curse. We can do some research on it and perhaps find out more about your killer that way."

"I won't tell you the precise wording of the curse since I don't know if it can be activated by words alone." I agreed with an urgent nod. George had just emerged from the front door of his house and was speaking to the driver. "My attacker said if I wanted to live, I must prove I deserve to by sacrificing something important to me." His voice shook slightly. "He likened it to the loss of his only child, the most important thing to *him*. My loss had to match his."

"But prove how? You were dying in a ditch for goodness

sake!" I clutched Jacob's hand. George would be joining us at any moment. There wasn't much time. "What did he think you'd do, get up and walk away to perform this sacrifice he wanted? And if you didn't, was he threatening to...?" I couldn't finish the sentence. It was just too horrible to think about Jacob's murder. Besides, George was opening the door and climbing into the carriage.

He lifted the coat he carried over his arm to reveal a rectangular wooden box about the size of a large book. He placed it on the seat beside him and called out, "Drive on!"

The carriage jerked forward and the horses' hooves clip-clopped a merry tune on the road. I looked to Jacob. If he wanted to speak, he could and it would be like having a private conversation with me. But he did not. He turned away and looked out the window.

His words haunted me the entire journey to Clerkenwell: *if I want to live, I must prove I deserve to by sacrificing something important to me.*

So why hadn't the murderer given Jacob the chance to make the sacrifice before ending his life?

CHAPTER 13

I was still thinking about the curse placed on Jacob when we arrived at the Clerkenwell school. It hadn't taken long by carriage but there was only so much silence three people in close confines can endure before time starts to stretch painfully. George had tried to instigate a conversation with me but I wasn't in the right mood for chatter so he spent the remainder of the journey loading the pistol. Before we climbed out of the carriage, he placed his coat strategically over his arm and hand to hide the weapon.

The school's maid showed us into the drawing room where we waited for Blunt. The giant figure of the schoolmaster soon filled the doorway. "Ah, Mr. Culvert, Miss Chambers, you've returned." His wary gaze flicked around the room. "But where is your sister, Miss Chambers? I'd hoped you had come to organize the séance." He bent down to my level and that's when I noticed the puffy, sagging skin beneath his reddened eyes. "The ghost still haunts me," he whispered.

I raised an eyebrow at Jacob. He gave me a smug smile. "We're not here about the ghost," I said to Blunt. "Mr. Culvert and I have some very serious questions to ask you."

"Yes," said George. He squared up to the much larger

man and I wanted to cheer his bravery but then I remembered he held a loaded pistol. A weapon can make a person twice as courageous but sometimes twice as stupid too. I wasn't sure which camp George fell into. "Do you recall on our last visit we mentioned a book on demonology had been stolen from my library?"

"I do," Blunt hedged.

"We think you used the information within it to summon a shape-shifting demon from the Otherworld."

Oh dear, George had about as much tact as Jacob. Perhaps it was a male thing. His accusation certainly had an affect on Blunt. The schoolmaster bristled and his beard took on a life of its own as he spluttered an objection.

"How dare you accuse me of such a thing! Get out. Get out of my school." He stabbed a finger at the open door.

"Not until we have answers," George said.

Blunt stepped closer to him so that they were chest to chest, or would have been if the height difference weren't so pronounced. George only came up to the other man's armpit. He swallowed and a bead of sweat popped out on his pale brow.

Blunt chuckled, a nasty sound that gurgled up from his throat. "Stupid *boy*. What did you possibly hope to achieve by coming here?"

"The truth," George said without blinking.

Jacob sidled over to them. "You'd better say something before he gets himself clubbed by one of Blunt's paws. Use your charm," he added when I gave him a questioning look.

We were in trouble if we were relying on my charm. "Er, Mr. Blunt," I began, "we've just come from Leviticus Price's house and he claimed you were asking some rather specific questions about demonology."

"Did he?" He turned eyes the color of a stagnant pond on me and I recoiled at the viciousness in them. He wasn't trying to hide it now. "And what makes you think you can believe him, Miss Chambers? Did a ghost just happen to whisper it into your ear?"

"Yes. Just like he's now telling me you are the one who summoned the demon." Blunt clearly believed in spirits, demons and the Otherworld so why not use that belief to frighten him?

"What?" he bellowed, his bravado rapidly fading behind his facial hair.

"Spirits know everything, Mr. Blunt. They know what you had for breakfast today, what you do in your office when the door's closed and what you do at night in the girl's dormitory."

The big man rocked back on his heels and his face turned the same sickly color as his eyes.

"So tell us, where is the demon now?"

He stared at me, shaking his head over and over, all the while backing away but not towards the door. Jacob stalked him, taking a step forward for every one Blunt took back. His presence felt strong to me, real, and I wondered if either Blunt or George could feel it too.

"Tell us," I said.

Blunt, still shaking his head, said, "No. No, I...I won't. You can't hurt me. Your ghost can't hurt me."

It was my turn to shake my head. "What makes you think that?"

"Spirits travel right through solid things." He was blustering, his eyes wide, his hand gestures wild. It was almost as if he was trying to convince himself. "They don't have any form. They can't grasp objects." He spun round and lunged for the fire tools. He grabbed the iron poker and brandished it like a sword.

George whipped the coat off his arm to reveal the pistol. He pointed it at Blunt. His hand shook. "Put it down."

"You wouldn't," Blunt said, more self-assured than he had been when discussing ghosts.

"He's right," Jacob said to me. "George won't use it." There was no accusation in his tone. Neither he nor I would blame George if he couldn't fire the weapon.

But George, surprising us both, stretched his arm out. "I

will use it. To save her." He nodded at me.

Jacob's gaze slid to mine. He grunted and crossed his arms then turned his attention back to the others just as Blunt lunged at George.

George jumped back and pulled the trigger.

Nothing happened. He cocked the pistol again but Blunt was on him, bringing the heavy iron poker down onto George's head.

George ducked and put an arm up in defense. The poker kept coming. A scream tore from my throat and I closed my eyes, a reaction I later chided myself for.

But instead of the crack of bone, the only sound was a grunt and it came from Blunt. I opened my eyes. Jacob had both hands on the poker, inches from George's head. He and Blunt battled each other for control, the older man's startled expression mingling with an angry one.

With a roar and a burst of strength, Jacob pushed up hard, causing Blunt to lose his balance and stumble. Using the momentum, Jacob thrust his opponent against the wall beside the fireplace. The force must have loosened his grip because Jacob was able to snatch the poker out of his hand. He swung it at Blunt's stomach. The impact made a sickening thud.

Blunt let out a *whoosh* of breath and bent over double, his face bright red. Jacob pressed the poker under Blunt's chin, sending his head snapping back. It hit the wall and his eyes rolled up into his head.

"Ask him about the demon again," Jacob said. He aimed the poker at Blunt's chest.

"Where's the demon being kept?" I asked, trying to keep my voice level. I did not want the men to see how squeamish the fighting made me. My insides might be wobbling like jelly but I would do everything in my power to ensure that's where the jelly stayed.

Blunt grinned a warped, nasty grin. "Get. Out. Of. My. School."

"Please, let's not have any more violence," I said. "I don't want my ghost to hurt you, Mr. Blunt. As you can see, he can wield weapons as easily as any of us. So please just tell us where the demon is and we'll let you go unharmed."

"It won't hurt me." He seemed to believe it too.

"Why do you say that?" It was George. He stood to one side, well away from Blunt and Jacob, the gun still in his hand but pointed harmlessly at the floor.

"Because I must be the only link you have to the demon or you wouldn't be here at all. And I think you want to find it before tonight." His beard and moustache lifted at one corner and the fleshy lips between them twisted into a sneer. "Am I right?"

Jacob, his face distorted with rage, shoved Blunt hard into the wall then pressed the length of the poker against the bigger man's throat. Blunt scrabbled at Jacob's hands, grasping nothing but cool, empty air since he couldn't see Jacob. His eyes widened with fear and perhaps the realization that he'd been wrong—Jacob might kill him. His cheeks and nose became a changing palette of colors—red to mauve to purple—and the veins on his forehead formed thick, bluish ridges. He tried to talk but only squeaks came out.

"He's going to kill him!" George took one step forward but hesitated. "Should we let him?"

"No!" I said. "Jacob, no! Stop this. Let him go."

"He deserves it," Jacob growled. His eyes frightened me. They were cold and dark, two voids of swirling anger.

Blunt jerked about trying to free himself, but it didn't dislodge Jacob. He held the poker against Blunt's throat as if his own life depended on it.

Oh God, I had to do something. "You can't do this, Jacob. Think about it. Think about what you're doing!" If only I could get through to the rational side of him, the side not blinded by fury. "Do you want another death on your conscience?"

George turned to me, his spectacles halfway down his nose. "*Another* death?"

I ignored him. My plea seemed to be working. With a roar of frustration, Jacob eased back. The schoolmaster slid down the wall like a splotch of mud and sat on the floor. He was still very pink and he held his throat with both hands as if he was holding it together. He heaved in great lungfuls of air and glanced feverishly around the room.

The maid entered carrying a tray of tea things. She gasped when she saw Blunt's state and the tray tilted dangerously to one side. "Mr. Blunt! Everything all right, sir?"

"He, uh, had a coughing fit," I said, trying to catch George's eye but to no avail. He held the gun in plain sight, seemingly unaware of the uproar he would cause if the maid saw it. I grabbed his spare jacket and threw it at him.

He placed it over his hand and the gun. "He's not going to talk now" he muttered, grabbing my hand and pulling me toward the door.

With my heart rampaging like an advancing army of soldiers, we left. I glanced over my shoulder to see if Jacob would stay or go. Fortunately he was right behind us, his gaze fixed on George's hand holding mine. I thought he'd still be angry, wanting to fight, but he looked worried. No, not worried. Haunted. The irony of the word wasn't lost on me.

We reached the carriage and George opened the door for me. I checked for Jacob but he stayed back near the school's porch. "Are you coming?" I asked.

He shook his head.

I wanted *him* with me, holding my hand, telling me everything would be all right. I wanted him away from Blunt. I wasn't entirely sure he could be trusted not to return and... "Please, Jacob, come home with me."

He stalked across the space between us and slammed his hand against the side of the carriage, right near my head. George looked around as if he couldn't detect where the sound had come from.

I swallowed my squeal of fright and blinked at Jacob.

He stood close to me, his palm flat on the carriage, his

forearm skimming the brim of my hat. He leaned down until our faces were level. "I told you last night," he said in that quiet, malevolent voice of his. "I'm dangerous. You should stay away from me."

And then he was gone and all that was left was the pounding of my heart and the background noise of George's voice as he spoke words that I couldn't quite hear.

"I can't," I whispered to the emptiness. "I can't stay away."

***

All I wanted to do when I got home was climb into bed and reflect on everything Jacob had told me that day. Unfortunately Celia bombarded me with questions over a dinner of roast pork in the dining room instead.

"Well? How did it go today?" she asked, popping a single pea into her mouth. Why did she always have to eat them one at a time? She couldn't be trying to impress anyone with her delicate eating habits since I was the only one there.

"Leviticus Price wasn't much help," I said. "He couldn't recall when he spoke to Blunt precisely."

"Oh. Yes of course."

I eyed my sister, a pile of peas balanced precariously on my fork near my mouth. "That is what you meant, isn't it?"

"Well...partly."

I frowned as I chewed my peas. Celia was being coy about something and she was not usually a coy person. Except on one subject. "Ah. You mean did I have a nice outing with George Culvert?"

"Now that you mention it, how are you faring with him?"

Faring? "We get on well enough."

"I see," Celia said as she cut off a small slice of pork. I put my knife down with a clank on the plate. She looked up from her dinner. "Is something wrong, Em? You're not finished. Aren't you hungry?"

I leaned over my plate to get closer to her, even though the large dining table kept us well apart. "I know what you're doing," I said.

"I am eating my food like a lady. You would do well to follow my example if you want to secure a gentleman for yourself."

"A gentleman like George Culvert you mean?"

She shrugged and anyone who didn't know her as well as I did would have thought her dismissive of the suggestion. I was not so easy to fool.

"I am not interested in George Culvert and he's—." I was about to say not interested in me, but that was clearly incorrect. "He can do far better than the likes of me."

It was my sister's turn to lower her cutlery with a clank onto her plate. "What has he been saying about you?" She'd raised her voice, a sure sign she was deadly serious.

"Nothing. He's the perfect gentleman."

She made a miffed sound through her nose. "I'd challenge him to find another girl more interesting than you." She stabbed a pea with her fork rather more viciously than necessary. "Or more suited to a demonologist. Does he expect a Society miss to merely overlook his peculiar interests?"

"Not George." His mother, however, probably would hope such a girl existed.

This time she stabbed two peas. It would have been amusing to watch if I wasn't a little disconcerted by her matchmaking. And if my mind weren't preoccupied with Jacob's behavior. Then there was our conversation in the carriage about his murder...

"Celia, can I tell you what else happened today?"

"Something else happened?" She seemed relieved to leave the subject of George behind.

"Yes. Quite a bit actually." I told her about our visit to Blunt first. I left out the part about the pistol, the fire iron and how close I came to a fight between Blunt and Jacob. There wasn't much more to that part of the story except to say, "We're quite certain Blunt is involved in some way with the demon and the thefts. We just need to prove it."

Celia's jaw dropped further and her eyes grew wider as I

spoke. Despite my omission of the grimmer facts, she appeared to comprehend the danger perfectly. "I forbid you to return to the school, Emily. Do you understand? Mr. Blunt does not seem like the sort of person we want to associate with. We certainly won't be performing a séance for him now."

I tried not to smile. "No, we won't." I didn't say anything about not intending to visit the school again though. No need to lie unless absolutely necessary. "There's more I need to tell you, Sis. I...I need some advice."

"Oh?"

"It's about Jacob."

She sighed dramatically. "Not again," she muttered.

"What does that mean?"

Lucy arrived and collected our plates. Celia waited until she'd left before she answered. "I know you see him more than you let on. I know you...like him."

"What of it?"

"He's a ghost, Em. You cannot think of him..." She lowered her voice. "...in that way."

"I think of him as a friend." I folded my hands on the tablecloth to stop them shaking. It was a lie of course, but I didn't think my sister was prepared for the truth—that I loved a spirit. I would always love him.

"I'm not a fool. I know you care for him as more than a friend." She too placed her hands on the table, steepling them as if in prayer. "I recognize a girl who thinks she's in love when I see one. And while I sympathize—."

"Sympathize!" I shot to my feet, bumping my chair and sending it tumbling backwards to the floor. "How would you know how I feel? You've never cared romantically for any man. That part of your heart shriveled up long ago, if it ever existed at all."

Her lips flattened. Her nostrils flared and tears pooled in her eyes. My anger evaporated as suddenly as it had flared at the sight of her struggling not to shed them. "I'm going to my room," I said.

"Emily!"

If she was hoping for an apology she wouldn't get one. I regretted my outburst but not what I'd said. Celia had never been in love. How could she know what I felt for Jacob? "I'm going to my room and don't wish to be disturbed," I said, rounding the table.

"But you wanted to tell me something about him! I'll listen—."

"Forget it. It doesn't matter." I passed Lucy outside the dining room. The red and green jelly she carried on a platter wobbled when she stopped to let me pass.

"Don't you want jelly, miss?"

"No thank you, Lucy."

Her face fell. "But I made it 'specially. Mrs. White says my jellies are a marvel."

It did look rather delicious. "Very well. Bring me some to my room, please." I tried to smile because she looked upset. "Thank you, Lucy."

She bobbed a curtsey that sent the jelly sliding. Luckily she righted the platter and continued into the dining room without mishap.

I ran upstairs and changed into my nightgown then flopped on the bed, suddenly too tired to sit up and read like I usually would.

I was woken by Jacob in the deepest, darkest part of the night. I began to scold him but the look on his face stopped me. By the light of the candle he carried, I could just make out the dread imprinted on every exquisite feature.

I sat bolt upright. "What is it?"

"The demon has attacked Forbes."

The name sounded familiar but I couldn't place it. "Who's Forbes?"

"My parents' butler."

The full implication of his words took a moment to sink in to my sluggish brain. But when it did, I felt ill. "Is he...dead?"

Jacob nodded once and looked away but not before I saw

208

the shine in his eyes, reflected by the candlelight. "He'd been with us for years."

"Oh, Jacob, I'm so sorry."

He shook his head and once more turned to me. His eyes had hardened again, the moment's vulnerability completely obliterated. "I need your help, Emily."

"I'll get dressed." He looked away as I put on a black dress, gloves and a long black cloak. I didn't bother with a hat and left my hair down. Usually I tied it into a braid before bed but I'd been too tired to do anything with it.

Jacob and I didn't talk. My mind was fully awake now, my thoughts tumbling over themselves, until one became very clear. Lord and Lady Preston were about to be burgled—and we had our best chance of sending the demon back to the Otherworld.

We left quietly, me with my boots in one hand, Jacob carrying the single candle. I had him wave it at the face of the clock in the entrance hall—it was three o'clock. Before we left, I found the amulet that had originally summoned the demon and hung it around my neck. I tucked the six-pointed star inside my bodice and glanced back up the stairs. All was silent. Hopefully we'd be back by dawn—I didn't want another argument with Celia. I felt bad enough about our dinnertime squabble.

Outside I put on my boots and together we set off down Druids Way. Oddly for our street, there was no wind. Not even a puff. Without a breeze to blow it away, the fog congealed around us, its damp fingers caressing my face, tangling my hair. I hated to think what my curls must look like with all the moisture in the air.

"It's very late," I said to Jacob. My voice sounded strangely disembodied in the thick night, our footsteps equally so. The feeble glow of the street lamps barely lit up the tops of their poles let alone us far below them. It was a strange feeling walking along the empty, fog-shrouded streets with a ghost at my side. My sense for the dramatic thought it the right sort of night for the dead—ethereal, silent, lonely.

"When would your family usually arrive home after an evening out?"

"They're already home. I checked. That's why I woke you."

"To warn them," I finished for him. The cold dampness seeped through my clothing to my skin, all the way to the bone.

I started to run.

Jacob easily kept up but the candle extinguished. He tossed it away. I would have taken several wrong turns in the soupy miasma if it hadn't been for him guiding me. We half walked, half ran and reached Belgrave Square quickly.

At first I thought the house was silent, safe, but then I heard it.

A scream. High, nerve splitting, and filled with terror.

"Adelaide!" Jacob disappeared.

Lights came on inside the house. Adelaide screamed again. Another, higher scream joined hers—Lady Preston's?

Oh God oh God oh God. I raced down the stairs and banged on the servants' door, praying someone was in the service area, hoping they heard me.

"Open—!" A hand clamped over my mouth, stifling my shout. I was wrenched back up the stairs to street level, my attacker dragging me. My heels scraped against the stone steps as I tried to stand. Then I was shoved against the wall of the house. My head hit the stucco and a jolt of pain ripped through my skull. The night turned blacker for a moment but I fought against the fog trying to cloud my brain. Someone held me upright with an iron-clawed grip, stopping me from sliding to the ground.

My vision cleared. A face loomed over me like a moon in the murky night. I didn't recognize it but it was familiar nevertheless. He had the same drooping eyes and small mouth as Maree Finch.

Tommy.

"Let me go," I said. "Please."

Finch laughed, baring two rows of crooked teeth like old

headstones. "Who's gonna make me? You?" He leaned in, his wide, white face close to mine. His breath, hair and his very skin reeked of ale and cigar smoke, sweat and something worse. I retched. That only made him laugh harder. "This the girl who can see ghosts, eh?" Was he talking to me or someone else? I tried to look past him but he was too big and the night too dark. "Looks like a mad thing." He sniffed my hair. And he thought I was the mad one.

Suddenly the sound of glass shattering filled the air. Finch pulled back, glanced up. "Christ," he muttered.

I followed his gaze just in time to see Jacob and a man dressed in servant's livery of scarlet breeches and coat falling from a high window. They were locked in battle and they fell together amidst a shower of glass, hurtling towards the footpath.

My heart leapt into my throat. I screamed. More screams echoed mine from inside the house.

It took me a moment to remember Jacob could not be harmed by such a fall. But his companion would not be so lucky.

I was wrong. The two hit the ground as one. Their impact sent a shudder along the pavement and cracked it open like an eggshell. Jacob sprang up immediately and to my surprise, so did the other man. It was as if they'd not just fallen several stories onto stone.

That's when I noticed Finch muttering behind me. I couldn't quite hear what he was saying even though his mouth was right near my ear, but I didn't think he spoke English.

Before I had a chance to guess at the language, my attention was drawn back to Jacob. He and the other man hurled themselves at each other like two beasts in the ring, using their bodies as weapons. Their chests slammed, shoulders hunched and heaved. Fists smashed into flesh. Flesh that wasn't like any flesh I knew—it didn't smack like real skin and no bones crunched. No blood was spilled.

The servant dove at Jacob, forcing him to the ground. Together they rolled into the circle of light cast by a street lamp and that's when I saw his face.

No, not face...*faces*. It constantly changed, forming and reforming into people I recognized and some I didn't—Finch, Blunt, Jacob, Adelaide, Lady and Lord Preston...

It was the demon, shifting shape as it fought.

Oh God, no. How could Jacob defeat a demon? From my discussions with George, I knew they were strong and that killing them was almost impossible and required a special Otherworldly blade. I also knew that being a supernatural creature meant the demon could tear Jacob's soul from his body. It could destroy his essence, obliterate him from this world and every other.

It could turn him into nothing.

I tried to get closer but Finch jerked me back. He was still muttering under his breath, the strange, poetic words blending together, sliding off his tongue. He was directing the creature—the demon—controlling it as it fought Jacob.

I struggled against him but his grip was too strong. He hissed in between his strange mutterings then looked over his other shoulder into the murkiness of the nearby alley. Something moved in the shadows. The sound of retreating footsteps echoed through the dense fog and I saw the flap of a coat before it was swallowed up by the night.

Finch grunted and bunched his fist into my cloak. He stopped chanting long enough to utter, "Soft-bellied toff." Did he mean me, or the person from the alley? Had someone been there or was it just a trick of light or my imagination?

Finch jerked me forward only to shove me back against the iron railing separating the pavement from the servants' stairs. Pain spiked down my spine as I almost toppled over the waist-high barrier onto the steps below. He stood in front of me now, his fist still bunching my cloak at my throat, but he was watching the fight. I followed his gaze and cringed as the demon's fist smashed into Jacob's mouth. On an ordinary human it would have knocked out teeth but it had little effect on Jacob.

Even so, I felt sick to my stomach. My heart had stopped beating the moment I saw him falling from the window and it felt like it had not restarted. If his soul was taken tonight by the demon, I didn't think it would ever beat again.

The demon punched Jacob once more and he reeled back from the force. Steadying himself, he ran at the creature as if he was still fresh and his fist connected with the demon's chin. How long could this go on? Would either of them tire?

I had to do something. Had to. Before the demon destroyed Jacob.

The amulet! With all the action, I'd almost forgotten about it. But Finch's big paw at my throat cut off access. I tried to pull away but my movement drew his attention and his fist tightened in my cloak. He snarled, baring teeth, and his mouth twisted into a gruesome smile.

With his focus on me and not the fight, the demon slowed, allowing Jacob to get in three quick, hard punches on the demon's chin, sending it reeling back into the shadows. He glanced at me for the first time since he'd fallen from the window. His eyes widened. His features seemed to collapse in on themselves.

"Emily!" His shout split the air.

Finch spun round and spoke in the strange language again. The demon flew out of the shadows and shoved Jacob back into the lamp post. The iron pole bent from the force.

"Jacob!" I struggled against Finch but it was useless. I was so weak by comparison, so *useless*. I couldn't get to the amulet. Couldn't get away. Couldn't *do* anything.

"Emily?" It was Adelaide. She and her father had emerged from the house, wrapped in thick coats with fur collars. Lord Preston's attention focused on the demon and what he thought of that I couldn't make out in the darkness. It must seem terribly peculiar, the creature with its changing faces fighting an invisible foe.

Two footmen joined them on the landing, pistols cocked.

Lord Preston also held a long sword, its blade gleaming even in the dull light cast by the lamp Adelaide held. She seemed not to know where to look, first at me, then at the demon, then at her father.

One of the servants aimed his pistol at the demon.

"That won't do anything," I said.

"Shut up!" Finch slapped me across the face. It stung. I bit down against the pain and shook off the dizziness.

"Father, do something!" shouted Adelaide.

Lord Preston turned to me, his face like thunder. But there was a hint of confusion there too. He said nothing, gave no orders, and I decided he must be attempting to make sense of what he saw or he'd have taken charge already. His fingers flexed around the sword hilt. It was the sort of weapon found on library walls or behind glass cabinets, all gold and shiny metal with a tassel hanging from the hilt. It had probably never been used.

"Call the police!" I shouted and kicked out at Finch's shins.

He slapped me again. My head buzzed like a hive full of angry bees. I blinked away tears and battled to stay upright as Finch moved. Suddenly he was behind me, his arm around my waist. Something cold and sharp bit into my throat.

A knife.

"Emily!" Adelaide screamed again.

Onlookers emerged up and down the street, their lamps and candles glowing like faint stars. In the distance I heard a constable's whistle but it was far away. Too far.

"Unhand her!" Lord Preston bellowed. Thank God he'd regained his sense of command although I doubted it would do any good.

Finch certainly didn't cower. The knife pierced my skin. His breath came hot and moist in my ear as he chanted. I could feel his heart beating at my back, as rapid and erratic as my own. But his hand didn't shake. His life depended on keeping control of the weapon.

Off to our right, everyone either watched the strange

spectacle of the demon or had their gazes on me. Adelaide, unaware that her brother's ghost was barely keeping a shape-shifting demon at bay, grew frantic. "Father! He's going to hurt her!"

"Stay," Finch commanded them in between muttering the lyrical chant.

The servants waited for their master to give an order. But any order to attack Finch would only bring about my death.

I closed my eyes.

An almighty roar from Jacob had me opening them again, just in time to see him throw himself at the demon. They toppled together. Finch gave a frustrated grunt and, miraculously, his grip on my coat loosened. It was enough. Just. I delved down inside my cloak and pulled the amulet up from beneath my gown.

I began the curse that Celia had taught me to send the demon back.

"Bitch!" Finch snarled. He snatched the amulet out of my hand, ripping the leather strip from my neck. "What d'you think you're doin', eh?"

The *whack* of the demon's head hitting the gutter forced us both to turn back to the fight. The creature, still in human form but with shadows swirling where there should have been a face, lay on the ground. It groaned and didn't get up. Jacob had used Finch's break in concentration when he took the amulet to deliver a knockout blow.

Finch growled low in his throat then began his chants again in earnest. The demon groaned but failed to rise. Finch swore and tried again. Still nothing.

Jacob glanced at me. He neither breathed hard nor sweated like a live person would after a fight but his hair was disheveled and his shirt torn. He stood there, fists pumping at his sides, and watched me with an expression I couldn't make out in the dimness.

Just watched.

"Jacob?" He could be at my side in seconds. With invisibility on his side, he could surprise Finch and snatch the knife away.

But he did not.

He didn't move in my direction at all. He just looked at me. And then he let out a low, primal wail like he was in pain. But he could not feel physical pain so—.

The demon stood up.

"Jacob, look out!"

He swung round and engaged the demon again. They tumbled together in the smudged edge of the lamp's light, limbs tangled, the *smack* of fists and the grunts of exertion the only sounds.

Behind me, Finch chuckled. "Your ghost lover wants you to join 'im, eh?" he said between chants.

I stared straight ahead, not quite at Jacob, not at anything. My heart had skidded to a stop in my chest. I felt hollow, empty.

Alone.

The notion that Finch might be right...that Jacob had not tried to save me...it was too much to take in. I couldn't even cry even though I was full of tears.

"You better come wiv me," Finch muttered. His arm squeezed my waist so hard I thought he'd snap me in two.

I gasped and scrabbled at his hands, tried to dig in my heels and plant myself on the spot.

But he was too strong. My attempts didn't even make him pause.

On the main landing, Adelaide also gasped but smothered most of it with a hand over her mouth.

Before I could turn and follow her wide-eyed gaze, a loud *whump* echoed through the night. Finch's grip slackened, he dropped the knife then slipped to the ground with as much grace as a rag doll. Behind him stood Lady Preston, a brass candelabra in her hand and angry triumph on her face.

I kicked the knife away and stepped out of Finch's reach. A footmen descended on him and stood guard. It all happened so fast. Adelaide ran down the stairs and wrapped her arm around my shoulders. Her mother calmly handed the candelabra to a maid and went to her husband. He folded her against his chest and rested his chin on her head, the sword loose at his side. His gaze returned to where Jacob and the demon fought.

But the demon suddenly spun round and fled. With a roar of frustration, Jacob chased it. I went to follow but Adelaide held me back.

"No," she said. "It's much too dangerous."

Behind me, the footman gave a short grunt. I spun round, just in time to see him stumbling backwards and Finch fleeing in the opposite direction to the demon and Jacob. The thick fog enveloped him before I could react with anything more than a gasp.

"Fool!" Lord Preston shouted at the hapless footman.

The servant rubbed his knee where Finch must have kicked him and shrugged an apology to me. I tried to reassure him but it was impossible to feel anything but a terrible fear pressing down on my chest.

The pressure eased slightly when Jacob returned. "Gone," he said. "It was too fast." He frowned. "Where's Finch?"

"Also gone," I said. "And he has the amulet."

Jacob paused then crouched down, the fingers of one hand on the pavement to balance himself. He wiped his brow with the back of his hand. As I watched, his shirt mended itself as did the small cuts on his lip and cheek. The skin simply re-covered them. There had been no blood of course and the skin was neither new nor pink. If his hair hadn't remained messy there would have been no evidence of the fight at all.

"Are you all right?" I asked.

"Don't come near me." He rubbed a hand through his hair and studied the ground near his feet. "Damn it!" He slammed his fist onto the pavement and a guttural growl tore from his throat. It was full of desperation, anger, hurt and so many more emotions I couldn't identify. It ripped through the blanket of night, shot through my heart.

I pulled away from Adelaide and went to him but he got

to his feet and moved to the edge of the light where I couldn't quite make out his features. "Don't," he said again. His voice sounded raw, not his own.

Adelaide came up beside me and held up her lamp. "My brother...he's here?"

I nodded. I couldn't speak. I wanted to go to Jacob, wanted to hold him. But he didn't want me near.

"Where?" Lady Preston joined her daughter and together they looked at the bent lamp post as if Jacob's ghost was there. "Where's my son?"

I waved in his direction.

"Can we speak to him?"

"I don't want to talk," Jacob said. He moved even further into the shadows so that only his silhouette was visible to me.

"Another time," I said through a tight, full throat.

Lady Preston's face crumpled, tears filled her eyes. Adelaide hugged her.

"He and I have Otherworld business to finish," I said quickly. "We'll return another day." It was the best I could manage when my thoughts were so jumbled together I could barely think let alone speak.

"Leave us!" It was Lord Preston, stomping down the stairs. As he spoke, two constables rushed up and took in the scene, truncheons poised to strike. "Move her on," he said, pointing at me. "She's not wanted here."

"But Father, she——."

"She's not wanted!" His bellow would have been heard up and down the street, despite the dense fog deadening it. The lights from the neighbors' lamps disappeared back inside their homes. I could only imagine what they must think of the events of this night and how it would be recounted in the clubs and coffee houses tomorrow. How would they explain what they'd seen? How much could they see? Certainly not the demon's changing faces.

"Jacob is here," Lady Preston said in a quiet voice, so steady compared to the first time we met but still small and thin like a child's. "He's busy now but he'll return soon."

Lord Preston took his wife's hand, looped it through his arm and patted it. "Go inside, my dear. Both of you. I'll sort this out and join you soon."

Adelaide didn't move as the constables approached me. "No, Father," she said, tossing her long braid over her shoulder. "You'll not treat her like a criminal. She's done nothing wrong."

"She can see Jacob," Lady Preston said, still staring off in the direction of her son. Jacob remained in the darkness but I could feel his presence as strongly as ever. It was troubled. And so very angry.

"It's all right," I said to Adelaide. "We have to go anyway."

"We." Lord Preston snorted. "You're very good, Miss Chambers. A genius at theatre."

"Theatre!" Adelaide cried, fists clenched at her sides. "Father—."

"Silence! Inside, both of you."

Lady Preston meekly climbed the stairs but kept looking over her shoulder into the shadows. Adelaide sighed and touched my arm. I nodded at her to go. It wasn't her battle and I didn't want her to be punished on my account.

"This is not theatre, Lord Preston," I said when they were gone. It was difficult to inject any real enthusiasm into the words. I just wanted to leave, with Jacob.

"You made all this up," the viscount said, nodding at the bent lamp post. "You're probably in league with that boy, the one who held the knife to you. And Forbes."

"Your butler? Of course not. He was a victim—."

"I saw his face!" he shouted. Even in the poor light I knew his cheeks were turning a mottled red. "There." He nodded at the spot where Jacob and the demon had fought. "Doing just as good a job of pretending as both of you degenerates. I don't know why he'd want to hurt my family like this after so many years of good service..."

"Forbes is dead," I spat as I shook off the constable who

reached for me. I'd had enough. Enough of being doubted, enough of being ridiculed, enough of being treated differently to everyone else. "A demon killed him and took on his form. That's how it got into your house. Didn't you see it just now? It was fighting your son's ghost. Jacob saved us by keeping it occupied. All of us."

"Forget it!" Jacob hurtled out of the shadows and snatched at my hand. Despite all his exertion, it was still cool. It always would be. "You're wasting your breath speaking to him."

"Miss," one of the constables said. "Don't make this hard for yourself, miss."

Lord Preston turned to go. I wasn't prepared to give up so easily but I had to back away from the constables. "Didn't you see its face change? You must have."

"I saw no such thing," Lord Preston said, his voice dripping with disdain. "It was much too dark to make out anything clearly. You are a liar, Miss Chambers, and a thief and perhaps worse. If I were you I'd leave before the police arrest you. I think we can safely assume a judge would have you committed to a mad asylum whether you were found guilty of these crimes or not, don't you?"

I should have stopped. I should have chalked Lord Preston up as a disbeliever and left it at that. But I couldn't. I was angry now too and there was nowhere for that anger to go except out. One of the constables grabbed my arm but I barely noticed. Jacob still held my other hand, strong and reassuring. "Finch is not my accomplice! He tried to kill me. He's been controlling the demon all along."

As had someone else. The person who'd left during the fight. My anger reduced to a simmer as quickly as it had boiled over. I jerked myself free of the constable's grip. "I'm going," I assured him then turned to Jacob. "We have to go to the school. I think Blunt was here."

The constable looked at me as if he thought I really should be in an insane asylum. I ignored him. I didn't have time to worry about what he thought of me.

"In a moment," Jacob said. He let go of my hand and picked up Finch's knife. He stepped up behind his father then tapped him on the shoulder with the blade. Lord Preston turned around, gasped then glared at me as if I'd somehow caused the knife to be there even though I wasn't close enough. For one heart-pounding moment I thought Jacob would stab him, but he simply drew the point down his father's cheek. Lord Preston yelped and jerked away. He snarled at me—me!—and smoothed down his moustache with his thumb and finger.

Jacob sidled up close to his father and blew in his ear. Lord Preston glanced around. "Next time you call her names I won't hold back," Jacob whispered barely loud enough for me to hear. Despite the quietness of his voice, the malice in it was unmistakable. I swallowed.

For the first time since we'd met, I believed what Jacob had been telling me all along. He was dangerous.

CHAPTER 14

The policemen took me as far as the corner of Belgrave Square and warned me not to return to Lord Preston's house or they'd arrest me. I thanked them and followed Jacob into the night.

"We need to go now, before Blunt escapes," he said.

Perhaps he already had.

But it would take time to get to the school, time we couldn't afford to waste. "You go ahead," I said, pulling my cloak tighter at my throat. It brought back the memory of when Finch had clasped it, right before he'd stolen the amulet. Without it, we had no way of sending the demon back to the Otherworld. "Stop Blunt leaving if necessary. I'll catch up."

Jacob shook his head. He'd calmed down considerably since the confrontation with his father. He could look at me now at least, although his gaze didn't quite meet mine. "You're not walking alone at night."

"There's no other way." I gave him a reassuring smile. I wasn't angry with him. Concerned, yes because I could sense something was very wrong, but not angry.

He lifted a hand to my face and brushed his knuckles down my cheek in a gesture that sent my heart flipping in my chest and filled my eyes with tears once more. He gave me the saddest smile I'd ever seen and whispered my name, as if speaking it aloud would hurt.

It was amazing the sound of my heart cracking didn't fill the night.

"Jacob," I murmured. There was so much to say but I didn't know where to start or how.

He touched a finger to my lips. "Shhh, my sweet." His finger dipped down to my chin and he kissed me, a fleeting, feathery kiss that was over too soon. But despite the tenderness, tension continued to ripple through him. He was still fuming.

Was he furious at himself for hesitating?

I hadn't a clue. I blinked back the tears but one escaped anyway. He kissed it away, his mouth so soft I wanted to sink into it. He licked his lips, tasting my tear.

"Jacob," I tried again.

"Don't," he said, voice shuddering. He stepped back, all business again. I tried to be the same, to shut down my feelings, but it wasn't easy.

"I have another idea," he said. "Let's wake up George and ask to borrow his carriage. He won't want to miss the fun anyway."

I wasn't so sure about that but I smiled an agreement. It was a surface smile. Inside me everything ached.

Hand in hand we ran the short distance to Wilton Crescent. "I'll go in and wake him," Jacob said when we reached number fifty-two.

"But how will he know it's you and that you want him to come with us?"

"There should be pen and ink somewhere in the house." He was gone before I could say anything else.

Hardly five minutes passed before a sleepy footman holding a candelabra opened the front door, his green jacket unbuttoned, his hair unpowdered. "Mr. Culvert wishes you to wait inside, Miss Chambers." He yawned and waved me through to the drawing room with the candelabra.

I wasn't surprised to see Jacob already there. We didn't speak as the footman lit the candles on the mantelpiece then bowed out of the room, yawning.

"Culvert snores," Jacob said when we were alone.

"What did he say when you woke him?"

"Well, he didn't scream."

"You thought he might?"

"I thought it likely." He gave me his devilishly crooked smile but there was no humor in it. Sadness still invaded everything—his words, his face, even the way he stood with his shoulders slightly stooped. He stared into the cold ashes of the fireplace and said nothing further.

I sat and waited in the awkward silence, trying to decide if I wanted to broach the subject of his hesitation in Belgrave Square. George saved me when he appeared, tugging on his crisp white cuffs. He was fully dressed right down to a black overcoat but his hair was in desperate need of taming. It stuck out on one side and was entirely flat on the other.

"My coach and driver will be around shortly," he said, holding out his hands to me. I clasped them and he squeezed gently. "Are you all right, Emily?"

Jacob frowned at our linked hands. I let go. "Well enough," I said. "Sorry to wake you, George, but we do so need your carriage."

"Of course. Think nothing of it. Glad I can be of service. Is Beaufort still here?"

I nodded and waved towards the fireplace where Jacob stood watching us beneath his lowered lids, an unreadable expression on his icy face.

"I'll go on ahead," he said, coming towards me. "I'll unlock the school's front door for you." The ice seemed to melt before my eyes, the tension slip away from his mouth, his brow. The pale candlelight barely illuminated the blue of his eyes but I didn't need to see their color to recognize the worry in them as they searched my face. He lifted a hand to my cloak's collar and straightened it. His thumb brushed along the underside of my jaw. "Will you be all right?"

I nodded. I couldn't speak. I just wanted to hold him, kiss him, but I was no longer entirely sure if that's what he wanted. He might be behaving tenderly towards me now, but what about later? I desperately wanted to ask him what he was thinking, and why he'd hesitated back at his parents' house, but I couldn't, not with George around.

Besides, I had a feeling I wouldn't like the answer.

He disappeared and I watched the space where he'd been for a long time until George's polite cough drew my attention.

He held out his arm. "Shall we wait outside?"

***

During the carriage ride to Clerkenwell, I told George everything that had transpired that night. From the light cast by the lamps mounted outside the windows I could just see the grave set of his face and the frown settling above his spectacles.

"So now we must speak to Blunt to find out once and for all how he is involved," I said. "And to find out where Finch lives."

He reached under the seat and removed a box. I recognized it as the one he'd brought with him the last time we visited Blunt. The one with the pistol inside.

We arrived at the school shortly after that. George took one of the carriage lamps and left the other for the driver. Together we tried the front door. It was unlocked, as Jacob had promised. I hesitated and glanced at George. He looked pale in the gaslight, a trickle of sweat trailing down his temple despite the coolness of the air. "I think it best if Jacob deals with Blunt first," I said. "If his methods fail then you should use that." We both looked down at the pistol. He tucked it beneath his cloak and nodded. A slight color returned to his cheeks. Whatever he was, he was not a coward. Fear did not make someone cowardly; allowing that fear to stop them taking appropriate action, did.

He followed me into the school, down the corridor, towards a sliver of light peeping out from underneath the door next to Blunt's office. Noises came from the other side—wood splintering, glass shattering, objects landing with thuds. Blunt's voice over them all, pleading.

"Stop! Please, stop. Don't hurt me. Please."

Jacob had started without us.

I ran to the door but George overtook me. "Wait," I hissed. "Wait out here." He looked like he wanted to disagree. "Just give me a moment," I said. "I'll try to calm Jacob first. You wait here to—."

"But Emily—."

"I'll be fine, George. Jacob will protect me and we need you as our surprise. If Blunt doesn't confess then you can come in and use whatever means at your disposal. I couldn't bear it if that pistol went off by accident."

I didn't wait for his answer but entered the room and was surprised to see it wasn't another office but a bedroom. Two candles flickering on the mantelpiece provided a little light, illuminating a mess. Someone sat in the big bed, the covers pulled over their head. Blunt. Jacob stood near the window, the broken leg of a stool in his hand. The rest of the stool lay on the floor in pieces along with torn sheets, clumps of wool from a pillow, shards of a mirror and various other oddments.

"Careful of your step," Jacob said to me.

Slowly, the bedcovers lowered to reveal the disheveled head of Blunt. "Thank God you're here," he said. "Tell it to stop. I haven't gone to the girls dormitory, I haven't! Not since that first haunting. Tell it, tell it!"

"The spirit knows," I said. "But he's still not happy." I nodded at Jacob. He nodded back. "He's here because of the deaths you caused, Mr. Blunt. You and Tommy Finch."

"I, I..." He swallowed so hard I could hear his throat working from across the room. "I had nothing to do with that, I already told you."

"Don't lie to me," I said with a sigh. "I'm tired. I want to go home. The sooner you confess and give us Finch's address, the sooner Jacob will leave you be."

Blunt's gaze shifted to the door as if he knew someone was out there even though no sounds came from the corridor. "Why do you want me to confess? What good will it do?"

"It'll bring peace to the souls of the dead." It wasn't exactly a lie. I felt as if the spirits of the demon's victims were listening, waiting.

Blunt's lips pinched tightly together. "You won't hurt me."

"We are out of patience, Mr. Blunt. If we need to hurt you to extract information then we'll do it. Come now, give in," I said when he didn't answer. "Your little scheme to rob the houses of your victims has been exposed."

"What? What are you talking about?"

"We know everything, Mr. Blunt, and so do the police." It was a lie but a necessary one. Jacob nodded his approval. "I wouldn't be surprised if Finch lets you take all the blame either."

Why didn't Blunt already know about our encounter with Tommy? He may not have stayed to witness the end of events at Lord Preston's house but surely he saw enough to not be entirely surprised. He certainly seemed shocked by the information. His mouth slackened. He hesitated.

It was too much for Jacob. "This has gone on long enough." He picked up a knife from among the litter scattered on the bare floor.

Blunt scampered back against the bed's headboard. He tried to bat the blade away but Jacob was fast and dodged every move.

"Call George in," Jacob said to me. "I want him to witness Blunt's death so that it's known you're not to blame."

"Jacob, no!" I shouted.

He ignored me and stabbed the knife into Blunt's nightshirt, right over the heart.

Blunt screamed as the blade tore through the gray linen and pierced his skin. Blood stained his nightshirt and the sight of it only made him scream harder. He tried to scramble away but Jacob knelt on Blunt's feet and shoved him back up against the headboard. "All right!" Blunt shouted. "I did it. Now get it away from me!" His breathing came in ragged gasps, fluttering the wisps of his moustache. "Call your ghost off!"

Jacob kept the knife at Blunt's chest. George rushed in, pistol poised, but I held up a hand to stay him. His eyes widened at the sight of the blood.

"What did you do?" I asked Blunt. "Did you order those people killed?"

"No!" Blunt shook his head very fast, sending his beard into a frenzy. "I helped Finch summon the demon, that's all. I told Maree to steal the book from your friend Culvert there, then I gave it to Tommy Finch. He's the one directing the demon. Not me, him! I swear, it's the truth."

"But you knew about the murders and burglaries."

Blunt hesitated and Jacob shifted his weight onto the knife. Blunt ground his teeth together and nodded.

"I think his role was more than he's admitting to," Jacob said.

"You helped Finch decide who to attack next, didn't you?" I asked Blunt. "*You* chose the victims. They all worked in grand houses where *you* had recently placed a servant." As soon as I said it, I knew it must be true. It made sense. Blunt knew which upper servant to attack because he'd questioned the lower servant he'd placed in the household. They'd been his spies—perhaps reluctant ones—informing him of the potential victim's movements.

Again Blunt hesitated and again Jacob pressed on the knife. The bloodstain on Blunt's nightshirt bloomed.

"Yes!" Blunt said, squeezing his eyes shut. "Satisfied?"

Jacob eased back just as Mrs. White entered the room carrying a candle. She clutched a shawl over her nightgown and looked, well, white. "Oh my," she muttered. "Oh my, oh my, Mr. Blunt..." Her gaze fixed on the knife that Jacob still held and she promptly keeled over in a dead faint. I managed to catch her and lower her gently to the floor. The candle fared worse but extinguished itself on impact.

Jacob dropped the knife. George steadied his pistol and aimed it at Blunt's head. "Now what?"

"Now we find out where Finch is keeping the demon," Jacob said without taking his eyes off Blunt.

"Where can we find Tommy Finch?" I asked.

Blunt swallowed. George cocked the gun. The *click* sounded terribly loud. "There'll be records here somewhere," George said. "Records with Maree's last known address. I suspect we'll find her brother there or if we can't, we'll find someone who can tell us for the price of a few coins."

Well done, George! I raised an eyebrow at Blunt. He swallowed again then groaned. He fell back against the pillows, deflated. "Very well. You can find him in the eastern shadows of St. Mary's in Dwindling Lane." He started to laugh, a thin, high-pitched laugh that sent a shiver down my spine. "You'll need more than one of those in Dwindling Lane, Miss Chambers," he said, nodding at George's pistol. "And more than your pet ghost too."

Jacob picked up a broken chair leg and Blunt threw his hands over his head. He slunk down into the covers. "Call him off!" he shouted.

Jacob waved the piece of wood at Blunt's head. "Tell him he'd better leave London before sunrise or I'll haunt him until he does."

I repeated the order to Blunt adding, "And don't think you can intimidate or harm any of your charges again. I have contact with every ghost up there and they don't like people like you. They'll find you wherever you are, I can promise you that."

Blunt nodded quickly.

"Well done," Jacob said.

George pulled me aside. "Aren't we going to call the police?" he whispered. "We can't just leave him here, unpunished."

"No," I whispered back. "It's likely *I'll* be arrested, not him. Besides, I think the warning is punishment enough for his involvement, don't you? I doubt he'll try anything like this again."

George, his gaze on Blunt cowering on the bed, nodded.

Mrs. White moaned at our feet. Her eyelids fluttered and opened. George and I helped her into the kitchen where we explained everything. All of it. She needed a cup of tea before she could make a coherent sentence but she appeared to understand what we were saying, and, more importantly, accept it.

Jacob hadn't joined us. I had no idea if he was still at the school, in the Waiting Area or if he'd gone to find Finch. I prayed he hadn't. I didn't want to think about what could happen if the demon attacked him again. He might have held it off in Belgrave Square but could he do so again? The thought of the demon removing his soul...it made my bones cold and my heart sore.

When I finished telling Mrs. White all I could, I asked her the question I needed to ask. "Did you have anything to do with this business?"

She lowered her cup. It tilted too far and tea spilled over the side. She didn't seem to notice. She was too busy looking offended. "No, I did not. Miss Chambers, I've been here for five years now, longer than Blunt, longer than most of the children. I came here after my husband died and I've not regretted a day since. I have no children of my own, no family that need me. This school has been my life, my sanctuary those five years." Her eyes filled with unshed tears and she carefully put the cup down in the saucer. "I'm never idle here and I've always been valued, by the children as well as the other staff. I'd never risk what I've found at this school, not for anything."

I breathed a sigh. "I'm very glad to hear it, Mrs. White. I'm sorry but I had to ask." The woman who'd sold Celia the amulet remained a mystery. Perhaps I would never learn her identity.

George cleared his throat and jerked his head toward the door. I didn't need to be told twice. With Mrs. White settled and promising to call the police if Mr. Blunt hadn't gone by the morning, George and I left.

Outside, he hopped up beside the driver. "Get in," he said to me. "I'm going to ride up here, keep watch." A glint of steel shone in the wan light. The pistol. It was our protection from whatever we might come up against in Whitechapel, both human and demonic.

I clamped down on my fear and climbed inside only to find Jacob seated on the far side, his arms crossed over his chest, his face in shadow. It wasn't a pose to invite me to sit close so I sat opposite. The separation didn't make me want him any less. He could have the most forbidding expression and I'd still want to be near him.

"Where did you go?" I asked, jolting as the carriage rolled forward.

"To Dwindling Lane to see if Finch is still there."

"And is he?"

He nodded.

"Good," I said. "We'll sort—."

"There's no 'we'. *You're* going home."

Jacob certainly had a lot more to learn about me if he thought I'd leave he and George to go on alone. "It would seem the carriage is heading towards Whitechapel, not Chelsea."

"Tell George to take you home."

I crossed my arms. "No. I know you think it's the best thing for me—."

"It *is* the best thing for you, Emily, I don't even need to think about it. Go home. It's too dangerous for you."

"It's just as dangerous for you, Jacob," I said quietly.

He leaned forward and stared at my mouth as if he wanted to kiss it, or bite it. It was hard to tell what mood he was in. "I'm already dead." His words hummed across my skin like a caress. If he was trying to addle my wits in an attempt to gain some sort of control then it was working. Almost.

"But you still have a soul worth losing," I said.

He made a sound of disgust in the back of his throat. "Are you sure about that?"

I switched sides to sit next to him. I felt rather than saw him stiffen. "Jacob, what happened tonight? At your parents' place? Tell me what was going through your mind."

He tilted his head back and blinked rapidly up at the padded ceiling. "I can't," he choked out. "God, Emily, stop being so stubborn for once and *listen* to me. Go home. Stay away."

"From you or from Finch?" I snapped.

"Both of us! Damn it, don't you see?" He rubbed both his hands through his hair then drew them together at his chest, as if he were praying, or pleading. "What happened at my parents' house should have warned you that you need to stay away. It was dangerous for you there and Whitechapel will be ten times worse. Finch will be expecting us now and I...." He swallowed hard. It was dim in the cabin but the shadows around his eyes were darker than they should have been on a ghost. "I can't...be sure how I'll react."

I felt the heaviness of his words on my shoulders, my limbs, my heart. They dragged me down until I thought I'd fall through the floor onto the road below. "I'm going with you, Jacob," I said through my tight throat.

His body shuddered and he wrapped his arms around himself. "Please, Emily," he whispered, "I need you to stay away. Don't put me through that again."

"Through what?" I slipped closer along the seat and reached for him but he shrank back as if my touch would burn. I clasped my hands together to stop them shaking and tried to look as if his rejection hadn't shattered me. "I have to come, Jacob." The steadiness of my voice surprised me. I thought it would be as broken as I felt inside. "I'm the only one who knows the curse to send the demon back. You'll be too busy fighting the demon to snatch the amulet from Finch and George...well, I'm afraid George may not be all that helpful when the crucial moment arrives."

He turned to the window and stared out to the darkness

beyond. He seemed calm, still, his shoulders relaxed, his profile smooth.

But then he let out a loud roar. The muscles in his cheek and jaw knotted, his hands clenched and he slammed a fist into the cushioned seat between us. If it had been made of wood or glass, he would have shattered it. I jumped and shrank back.

And then he disappeared.

I pressed a hand to my racing heart and sank into the seat. At least he'd given up trying to make me go home.

I was still thinking about Jacob's outburst when the carriage rolled to a stop. It tilted as George jumped down and opened the door for me. He juggled the pistol and lamp in one hand and helped me out with the other.

"All right, Weston?" he said to the driver.

Weston nodded grimly from his position on the box. Metal gleamed on his lap. Another pistol.

George lifted the lamp high. The opening to a narrow lane yawned between two crumbling brick buildings nearby. Of course it would have to be a *narrow* lane. A thief with a demon at his disposal would hardly live anywhere else, like a well-lit, broad street for example.

"Perhaps you should remain here with the carriage," George said. He let go of me so he could hold the lamp in one hand and the pistol in the other.

"I'm not sure the carriage is any safer," I said, glancing around. It was too foggy to see very far ahead but I had the feeling we were being watched by dozens of pairs of eyes. "Let's go."

Just as I said it, a loud crash came from the lane. Someone shouted, another scream followed it, and four small people ran out of the lane. They were children, barefoot and dressed in little more than rags that hung from their thin bodies. They took one look at George and his pistol, screamed again, and ran off.

"I think the demon's still here," George said without moving.

"And Jacob has already found it. Come on." I wanted to run but the lack of light meant I had to keep near George and his lamp. But he was so slow, and Jacob could be...

The stench at the mouth of the lane made me recoil. The stink of urine, excrement and degradation cloyed at my throat. I coughed into my hand. George retched and buried the lower half of his face in his arm.

"God," he said, "how can anyone live here?"

Another crash had me moving again. The fog hung in misty tendrils but through the veil I could just make out the shape of two people fighting. "Jacob," I said to George. "Come on."

But he caught my arm and pulled me back. "Where's Finch?"

I squinted into the farthest shadows and could just make out the figure of someone sitting on a crate, his back against one of the high brick walls looming up on either side of the lane. "There. Chanting probably."

"Giving the demon the advantage in the fight," he murmured. "Fascinating."

"This is not the time to be scholarly, George."

"Right. Of course. So..."

I took the lamp off him and turned down the gas. "Follow me."

I counted on the fog and darkness covering us, and Finch having his attention on the fight and not the entrance to the lane so that we could sneak up and knock him out. I didn't want to use the pistol. Taking a life was not something I ever wanted to do. Although I knew the dead still existed elsewhere, I'd spoken to enough souls troubled by their death to know I didn't want to send one to the Waiting Area. The pistol would be a last resort.

My plan of stealth would have worked if the demon hadn't landed a punch to Jacob's stomach, sending him careening into the brick wall. I gasped. Finch spun round, spotted us, but didn't stop his mutterings, merely intensified them. The demon responded. It leapt onto Jacob while he was still down and slammed its big fist against his chest. Jacob grunted in pain.

"Get him, George!" I shouted. "Stop Finch!"

George didn't move. Jacob roared again and I could just make out his hands clutching the demon's fist, trying to push it away from him. But the demon was so much bigger, a giant in comparison, and Jacob was in an awkward position to defend himself from such an attack. Oh God, no! *No!*

I turned to George. Even in the darkness I could see he'd turned white. A light sheen of sweat slicked his forehead. He pointed the pistol at Finch but his hand shook so violently the bullet could have gone anywhere.

"Forget the gun," I urged him. My voice sounded shrill. "Good Lord, George, attack Finch with your fists."

"My...um..."

There was no time to convince him to be manly and fight. I ran at Finch myself, the lamp raised to use as a weapon to knock him out. If I could only get him to stop chanting, Jacob might be in with a chance against the demon. A scream tore from him and I dared not look lest I see my worst fears realized—Jacob gone, his existence extinguished forever.

I no longer cared how I was going to stop Finch, I only knew I had to do it NOW. "Stop!" I shouted at him. I raised the lamp.

He suddenly stood and thrust something at me. The glint of steel was visible in the small circle of light cast by my lamp. A knife. "Back," he said. It was all he said. His chant came fast, the strange words tumbling out of his mouth. He glanced between the fight and me.

But it wasn't a fight anymore. Jacob was still holding the demon's human hand, stopping it from digging into his chest but only just. Now that I was closer I could see his face distorted with pain and exertion, his teeth bared as he used all his strength.

He couldn't last.

"No closer," Finch said to me.

I backed back to George. He still held the pistol but it wasn't even pointed at Finch anymore, but down at the ground.

"Give up," I shouted at Finch. "It's over. Blunt told us everything and the police have him now." It was an outright lie but if it was enough to get him wondering, pausing in his chants, it was worth it.

The news seemed to have little effect on him. "Blunt?" he said, barely breaking his rhythm. "You think he...?" He never finished the sentence but laughed as he continued controlling the demon.

There was only one option left. "Fire!" I yelled at George.

"I can't," he whispered. "It's murder."

"The demon's going to take Jacob's soul if we don't."

George swiped at his sweaty brow and pushed his glasses back up his nose. "He's already dead."

I stared at him in horror. "He may not be alive but he exists. He has thoughts and feelings just as if he were alive. If the demon extracts his soul he'll be nothing."

He shook his head. "There must be another way."

Jacob shouted again. Then he became silent. His mouth fell open in an empty scream and even in the darkness I could see him writhing on the ground, the demon's hand buried inside his chest. Everything around me went still. My mind cleared. I felt like I was floating in a bubble, not quite part of the world anymore but still able to see it, feel it. I had the most startling, amazing clarity all of a sudden.

I knew what I had to do.

I grabbed the pistol, aimed and fired. Finch fell down. Dead.

"Jesus," George muttered. He crossed himself.

The demon sat back on its haunches and looked around, its hand still buried in Jacob's chest. Jacob kicked out, toppling the demon. He got to his feet but his shoulders sagged. He rubbed his chest.

"The amulet," he rasped as the demon righted itself. "Hurry."

I ran to Finch's body and rummaged through his pockets, trying to concentrate on my task and not look at the blood pooling around him. I pulled out a few coins but nothing else. I rolled the body over and tucked my hand inside his shirt. My fingers touched sticky, warm blood and the cool metal of the amulet. The brass felt heavy and solid, reassuring.

"Anytime soon," Jacob said then grunted as the demon slammed its fist into his stomach. He doubled over, clutching his middle.

I pulled the amulet out but didn't remove it from Finch's neck. There was no time. I began to chant the curse Celia had taught me. As if I'd struck it, the demon stopped fighting. A strangled growl bubbled up from its throat. Then it ran towards me.

I paused.

"Don't stop!" Jacob shouted.

The demon kept running, straight at me. I could just make out the dark swirls of shadow where it should have had a face. It still wore the servant's livery but the clothes were ripped, the torn fabric flapping uselessly. I kept chanting.

The demon ran right past me and I groaned in frustration. If it got away the curse wouldn't work. It needed to be close. How close, I didn't know.

Jacob swore and began to run but he was either in pain or exhausted and couldn't catch it.

The demon passed George and I just hoped he would shout a warning to his driver to get out of the beast's way. He didn't. He dove at the creature and together they tumbled to the ground. George grunted a loud *oomph* as his shoulder connected with the stones.

I uttered the rest of the curse and prayed I had it right, prayed the demon was near enough for it to be effective.

A strong breeze whipped at my skirts and monetarily separated the thin curtain of fog only for it to re-settle around us when the wind died. George sat up, blinked. His glasses had come off and his eyes were huge. He was alone.

"Is it gone?" I asked.

Jacob came up beside me. "Yes." He looked worse than the last time he'd fought the demon but again his clothing quickly returned to the way it had been before and his skin healed, erasing all evidence of the fight. He grasped my shoulders and turned me to face him. "Are you all right, Emily?" He looked down at me with an intensity I was now used to.

I nodded. "You?"

"Of course." He let me go and strolled over to George, still sitting on the ground. He looked dazed, the poor thing. I suppose reading about demons is quite different to encountering one.

Jacob searched the immediate vicinity then found what he was looking for—George's hat and glasses. He held them out. George stared for a moment then accepted them.

"Thank you," he said. He stood and brushed himself off then slapped his hat on his head. "Shall we go?"

"Gladly." I glanced back at Finch's body. "What shall we do about him?" I didn't want to leave him there for the rats to eat. *Ugh.*

"I'll have my butler contact the police when I get home," George said. "They'll take care of it."

"Good idea but have him do it anonymously," I said. "None of this is your fault and there's no need for you to become involved any more than you are."

"You'll get no argument from me," he said on a heavy sigh.

The three of us made our way back down the lane to the carriage. The driver still sat on the box, the pistol in his hand. He looked immensely relieved that his master was alive. No doubt Mrs. Culvert would have dismissed him if George had wound up dead from this adventure. He hopped lightly down to the ground and opened the door.

George took my hand to help me in but I removed it and turned to Jacob.

He wasn't there.

The most awful feeling of dread swamped me. The demon was banished which meant Jacob had finished his assignment. There was no need for him to see me anymore.

It might even have led to his finally being able to cross over.

No, Jacob, please. Not yet. Don't leave me.

Somehow I didn't cry as I climbed into the carriage. It was as if my body couldn't make any tears. It was too empty. It felt like I'd just lost a part of myself. A big part. The best part. The most vital part.

And I hadn't even said goodbye.

CHAPTER 15

I managed to sneak back into the house and return to bed without waking Celia or Lucy. Already the sky was turning gray as dawn crept up on London with its usual stealth. I lay in bed for what felt like an eternity before my room finally lightened. I spent every single one of those minutes thinking. Waiting. Hoping Jacob would do his old trick of suddenly appearing in my bedroom.

And then he did.

"Jacob! Thank goodness." I tumbled out of bed and threw myself at him, not caring how I looked or what he thought of my unladylike display. I was just so blissfully happy to see him.

He caught me and circled his arms around my waist, holding me tight as if he would never let me go. The hard muscles in his shoulders and chest shifted, flexed. Then loosened. He pushed me away and held me at arms' length.

"He was in bed."

It was not what I'd expected him to say. Not even close. "Who? Finch?"

His hands dropped to his sides, severing all touch entirely. "No, Blunt. When I arrived at the school last night he was asleep."

My chest clenched. My mind reeled. This was not the conversation I wanted to have with him. I wanted to find out what happened now, would he leave, and what was troubling him. I wanted to know what was in store for us. Did we have a future?

But those questions would have to wait. Jacob seemed keen to tell me something about Blunt so it must be important.

"I, uh..." I gave my head a little shake to clear it. "It is a little strange now that you mention it. Surely he must have suspected we would be coming for him after what he witnessed at Belgrave Square. Unless he was very certain of Finch and the demon's victory."

"Nevertheless, if I was him I'd have left London immediately and destroyed all evidence linking me to the demon."

I twisted a strand of hair around my finger, thinking. It only made sense if... "What if it wasn't him at your parents' house?"

He nodded but said nothing. He didn't seem surprised by my conclusion.

"Who could it have been?" I asked.

"I don't know. Are you sure you saw someone?" He shrugged. "The light was poor, you were afraid... Could it have been a spirit?"

I sighed and brushed the end of my hair over my lips. Jacob's gaze followed it. "I suppose so. I don't know. Oh Jacob, what if we're wrong? What if Blunt wasn't to blame?"

He licked his lips and lifted his gaze to my eyes. "Don't think it, Emily. We were right. He confessed and all evidence points to his involvement. He's guilty. But..."

"But there might have been someone else," I finished for him. "Someone with a deeper involvement."

He nodded. "I think Blunt orchestrated the thefts, using Finch and the demon. He targeted the servants and the houses, gathered the information, but I don't think it was his idea. He doesn't seem cunning enough to me."

"He doesn't seem to want to get his hands dirty where the supernatural is concerned. That explains why he got Finch to control the demon. But if there was another involved, then who was it?"

He shrugged. "With Finch dead and Blunt gone, we won't learn the answer to that." He sighed and rubbed a hand over his chin. "And I've been wondering about one other thing."

"What?"

"My family was home when the demon entered the house. For the first theft, the house was almost empty. If I was organizing a burglary, I would ensure no one was home first, especially the family themselves."

"Maybe Blunt or Finch made a mistake."

He suddenly looked ill. If his face was capable of turning white it probably would have. "Or maybe the purpose was for my family to be home at the time of the break-in."

"Wh-what? But why?"

He shook his head. "I don't know. I really don't."

"No." I shook my head firmly. "No, that's ridiculous. Don't think it. It was a simple burglary." Even as I said it, a small doubt formed in my mind where I couldn't dislodge it. But if he was right and someone wanted to harm his family...why? Why go to so much trouble? It didn't make sense. "At least the demon has been returned," I said, trying to reassure him.

"But how long will it be before another is summoned?" His jaw hardened and he grunted in frustration. "I should have questioned Blunt more. Or Finch."

"You were fighting a demon! Besides, at the time neither of us thought anyone else was involved." I stepped closer and touched his arm to reassure him. He tensed, his muscles knotting, and I rubbed to alleviate some of the anger simmering inside him.

"Don't," he whispered and stepped back, out of my reach.

"No, *you* don't. Don't leave. Not yet." If he blinked

himself off to the Waiting Area without resolving any of the tension between us I was going to scream until the Administrators made him return. "We have something we need to discuss."

To my surprise he nodded.

I waited but he said nothing. The tension seemed to have vanished from him, but he certainly didn't appear relaxed. He shifted from foot to foot and looked everywhere except at me.

Finally, when neither of us spoke to fill the growing silence, his gaze met mine. Shock rippled through me. There was a shine in his eyes that wasn't usually there and a tightness to his lips as if he was pressing them together on purpose.

"Jacob? Say something." *Tell me you won't go, tell me you'll stay forever, tell me you love me.*

He took my hand in his and drew little circles over my knuckles with his thumb. "I want you to know what happened back there, in Belgrave Square."

Finally. Finally! But now that the time had come I was afraid. Absolutely terrified. A lump clogged my throat and my mouth went dry. I wanted to know the reason—of course I did!—but a feeling of dread swamped me. I was drowning in it. Against every instinct screaming for him not to speak, I nodded at him to go on.

"I warned you," he said. His voice sounded thick and hoarse. "I tried telling you I was dangerous, that you shouldn't develop feelings for me."

"I can't help it! Jacob, I love you—."

He smothered the rest of my words with a light, airy kiss. "Let me finish," he chided gently. "I'm dangerous to you because...because I love you too."

My heart swelled. I think I saw stars. Those beautiful words were exactly what I'd wanted to hear. Nothing, *nothing* could ever be wrong again now that he'd admitted it.

Then the bubble burst. The stars vanished and my heart collapsed in on itself. "What do you mean? Why does that make you dangerous?" But I knew. I knew.

"Do you remember that day Maree Finch tried to stab you at Culvert's house?" I nodded. "I knew before then that I loved you," he went on. "From the moment we met in fact. It was like...your breath filled my lungs, *your* heart beat for mine. But it wasn't until the incident at Culvert's that I realized how much I loved you." He watched me with a kind of ferocity, as if he could persuade me of his feelings by a single look. "When Maree ran at you with the knife it was like I was dying all over again. I hated watching you in pain, the fear in your eyes...it was horrible. I was consumed by you in those few terrible minutes...by everything about you. I knew then that I wanted to be with you. Forever." His thumb circled faster. "Do you understand what I'm saying?"

"Forever," I repeated dully. It was difficult to think straight. Impossible to breathe. "In the Otherworld."

He nodded and tilted his face to the ceiling rose. He blinked rapidly then looked back at me. "When I thought you could have died...I was...glad." He whispered, as if he was afraid to say it out loud because it would somehow make it more real. "I *wanted* Maree to stab you."

He removed his hand from mine but I caught it. I pressed his palm to my lips and kissed the cool flesh. His fingers uncurled against my cheek, his head bent closer to mine. "Ah, Emily, I'm so sorry."

I heaved in a breath. It was difficult with my chest feeling so tight but I did it. "I won't accept your apology, Jacob. You wouldn't have hurt me. I know that like I know I can see the dead. You worried about my health when I got wet and you even warned me to stay away from Whitechapel. That's not the actions of a man who wanted me to die."

He shook his head and pulled his hand free. "I didn't want to hurt you and I didn't want to see you get hurt. The thought of you being ill or in pain...I couldn't bear it. I wanted the end result without you feeling even a moment's discomfort. Until..." His eyes shuttered closed.

"Tonight."

His nod was slight and I would have missed it if I hadn't been watching him so intently. "I can't explain how I felt," he went on, opening his eyes again. "Perhaps I was drunk from fighting the demon, or frustrated from spending so much time with you and not being able to claim you as I wanted to, or perhaps I was all too aware that our time together was limited."

I let his words settle before I spoke what had been on my mind for some time. "So the other night when you left my room abruptly, it wasn't because you realized I would grow old and ugly while you stayed young and handsome?"

He suddenly laughed. "Oh Emily, I do adore you."

I frowned. It had been a perfectly serious question. "Your exact words were: 'What if I grow weary watching you wait?'." I could never forget them. They were branded on my memory.

He reached up and touched my hair, curling it around his finger as I had done earlier. His laughter vanished just as rapidly as it had erupted. "I was afraid I would...do something terrible to you if the waiting became unbearable for either of us. It had nothing to do with you aging while I didn't. That's why I left that night, not because I didn't want to stay with you forever but because I didn't want to encourage your affections any more than I already had. I didn't want you to love me, you see. Knowing how you felt about me only made it harder not to think about you joining me in the Waiting Area, and in the Otherworld when I'm able to cross. I began to justify your death to myself after that." He turned away and buried his head in his hands. "Oh God, Emily, don't you see?"

I saw. And I should have been afraid of his admission, of him, but I was not. "You're a good person, Jacob. What you're feeling is perfectly natural." I pressed myself into his back and put my arms around his waist, holding him close. I kissed him through his shirt near his shoulder blade. "You're a wonderful, caring, brave soul and nothing you say will stop me loving you."

A shudder rippled through him and I held him tighter. But only for a few beats of my trembling heart because he shrugged me off and moved away to stand near the door.

"You were right when we first met," he said, his voice raw with emotion. "Do you remember? You said I'd forgotten how a gentleman should behave when I insulted your sister." I began to protest but he put up his hand and I stopped. "I am starting to lose a little bit of my humanity each day. I can feel it. I'm slowly losing myself, Emily. I don't want to, just like I don't want to hurt you, but I can't help it."

"Don't talk like that. You're still very much a gentleman."

He shook his head. "I can't come to you anymore," he rasped.

"But I'm going to help you find your killer, your body." It was the only thing I could think of to hold onto, the one thing tying Jacob to this world, to me.

"I'll do it on my own."

"But Jacob—."

"No. I can't risk another hesitation like tonight. Ever. Or I won't be the person you love anymore. Do you understand? Having you despise me for that would be...worse than anything I could bear."

I understood. And I hated myself for it. The tears poured down my face but I didn't care. I let them flow unchecked as I watched him. His nostrils flared and the muscles high in his cheek throbbed.

"Goodbye," he whispered.

And then he was gone.

I sat down on the rug on my bedroom floor, lowered my head to my knees and cried until Celia came in and guided me back to bed.

***

I spent the day in bed. I slept fitfully. Celia and Lucy both came and went on occasion, fussing and trying to get me to eat, but I barely heard anything they said. My sister didn't ask me why I was so upset and I was grateful for that.

But her sympathy ended the following day and the questions began almost as soon as she hauled me out of bed. She helped me dress then marched me downstairs to the small parlor behind the front drawing room. Lucy set a breakfast of eggs and toast in front of each of us. I pushed mine away.

"Tell me what happened," Celia said when Lucy left.

I did. Everything.

Afterwards, she watched me for a long time over the rim of her teacup. There were no recriminations for leaving in the middle of the night, no lectures, but no gentle or wise words to make me feel better either. I was grateful. I didn't want them. Nothing would make me feel better ever again. I had a hole in my heart the size of England and it was sucking everything out of me, even the tears.

"So that's that then," Celia announced. I wasn't sure if she was referring to the demon being returned or Jacob leaving. I didn't care.

Later that morning George visited. We talked over the events of the night. I left out the part where Jacob had said goodbye.

Celia, however, did not. "The ghost is gone." She smiled at George and handed him a large slice of sponge cake. It was his second. "More tea?"

He held out his cup and returned her smile. While he was studying his cake, no doubt deciding how best to attack the mountain with his fork, my sister winked at me.

With a huff of breath, I got up and left. She could flirt with George on my behalf without me.

That afternoon she knocked on my bedroom door and said we were going to visit Mrs. Wiggam.

"Can't you go alone? I'm very tired." I'd just woken from a nap but I felt like I needed more sleep. I couldn't imagine ever feeling completely awake again. Jacob was gone. What was there to be awake for?

"No. She sent me a note, pleading our help, blaming us for her husband haunting her. Can you believe it! The nerve of the woman when it was her demands for money that made him so angry."

"Let them sort out their own problems," I said and rolled over in bed.

She sat down on the mattress behind my back and placed a hand on my shoulder. "You can't remain in here forever. He's gone and you're needed."

"I don't care."

She hugged me, her face close to mine. Her hair smelled like lavender. "You have a gift, Emily. With that gift comes the responsibility to use it properly. If the events with the demon have taught me something, it's that. We summoned Mr. Wiggam, admittedly on his wife's behalf, but we now must end her suffering. At least we have to try. I...I'm worried about what he might do to her if we don't intervene."

I sighed and rolled over. Why did she have to be sensible all the time? "Let's go," I muttered.

She smiled sympathetically and hugged me tighter.

***

I expected the Wiggam household to be in turmoil but it was quiet. Messy but calm. Shreds of newspaper littered the hallway and drawing room floor, muddy footprints spoiled the rugs, and what appeared to be flour was strewn over every piece of furniture. Most of the figurines, candelabras and other objects that had decorated the mantelpiece, walls and tables were either broken or missing although a few had been spared. An oil painting of a lighthouse by the sea, a small black statue of a rearing horse. They had probably been favorites of Barnaby Wiggam. It was truly a terrible scene and I could only imagine what it had been like for his widow living there while her dead husband made his presence known by destroying her house.

Mrs. Wiggam calmly laid out a cloth on the flour-covered sofa for Celia and I to sit on. She offered no apology for the state of her house, or her person. It had only been a few days since the séance but she looked like she'd not eaten or slept in that time. Her waist seemed to have shrunk, sacks of skin hung loosely under her eyes, and her hair looked more tangled than mine had that morning after my night out. I felt sorry for her but didn't dare show it. Nothing about Mrs. Wiggam's countenance invited pity.

"I'd have tea brought up but the maids have all left," she said with not a hint of shame.

Barnaby Wiggam appeared in the vacant chair by the window. He seemed more translucent than the last time. Or perhaps I was used to seeing Jacob, solid and strong, not dim with fuzzy edges like Mr. Wiggam and the other ghosts. It made we wonder, again, why Jacob appeared so real to me. I would probably never find out now.

Mr. Wiggam crossed his arms and glared at his wife as she exchanged inane pleasantries with Celia. The entire scene struck me as absurd and a bubble of laughter escaped, despite my best intentions to smother it.

Mrs. Wiggam glanced at me the way her husband looked at her—as if everything was my fault.

"He's here isn't he?" she said, glaring at the chair in which her husband's ghost sat.

"Yes," I said.

She *humphed* and shrugged, accepting the ghost's presence.

"Good," Celia said, urging me to speak with a raise of both her eyebrows. "We're here to speak to him."

"Don't trouble yourselves," Mr. Wiggam said, heaving himself up from his chair. His face was still very red, the purple veins prominent on his cheeks and nose, as they would always be thanks to the manner of his death. "I'm leaving."

I almost choked on my surprise. "Why?"

"What's he saying?" Mrs. Wiggam asked. "What does that good-for-nothing lump want now? My life?" She stood and offered her wrists to him like a platter of biscuits. "Take it! Isn't that what you want to do? Fetch a knife from the kitchen and end it all here. Go on!"

He laughed, a grating, humorless laugh. "Tell her I don't want to take her with me. Eternity is a long time and I'd prefer to spend as much of it as I can without her."

"Is that why you're leaving?" I asked.

Mrs. Wiggam, sensing her blood would not be spilled by the ghost of her dead husband, lowered her arms. She sat back down in her chair, smoothed her skirt over her lap and gave my sister a polite smile as if nothing was untoward. Celia didn't return it.

"I'm leaving because I'm tired of haunting her," Barnaby Wiggam said. "No, actually I'm just tired of *her*. This is only fun for so long and I've realized something important these last few days." He picked his way across the messy floor and removed the painting of the lighthouse from the wall. The sea in the picture was calm and the sun shone on the red-brown rocks and the white sail of a ship in the distance. "As much as I wanted to hurt her, I couldn't bring myself to do it. It's not in my nature." He returned the painting to its hook on the wall and stood back to admire it. "It's strange, don't you think, Miss Chambers?"

"What is?" The painting? It looked lovely to me, peaceful.

"That the characteristics of who we were during life, our essence if you like, are carried with us to our death. Up there, in the Waiting Area, there are thousands of souls waiting to cross over, each one of them as unique as they were in life. Did you know the Otherworld is segmented?" I nodded. "The segment we're assigned to depends on how good we were when we were alive. A scale of worth if you like." He looked down at the flour-covered rug. "I don't know what the segment where the rotten ones go is like and I don't want to know." He thrust his triple chins at his widow. "I've never committed a mortal sin so I'm quite sure I won't end up in the worst section. However I'm not so good that I'll help *her* clean up."

I stared down at my folded hands in my lap. Jacob too had been a good person in his lifetime. Even George thought so and he hadn't been his friend. As Mr. Wiggam said, a good nature in life meant a good nature in death too. That didn't change. Jacob hadn't changed. Everyone told me he'd been kind when he was alive—a little unobservant of those around him, but never mean. He'd never harm anyone on purpose. It was the same in death. He wouldn't hurt me. Couldn't. I knew that to the depths of my soul.

Jacob Beaufort wasn't dangerous.

Mr. Wiggam gave me a short bow. "Good bye, Miss Chambers."

"Wait!" I sprang up from the chair. Mrs. Wiggam and Celia watched me, curiosity printed on their faces, but neither interrupted. "There's a spirit in the Waiting Area...I want you to give him a message from me if you see him."

"But you're a medium, you can summon any ghost you wish at any time. You just called my name and I came."

"You came when I called because you wanted to. Jacob...probably doesn't want to."

"Very well. How will I recognize your ghost? There are many souls up there."

"He's more solid than others. You can't see through him and—."

"What do you mean, *more* solid?" He held up his hands, twisting and turning them as he studied them. "I'm as solid as I ever was when I was alive." He patted his bulging stomach and laughed.

"Not to me you're not. But Jacob was."

Mr. Wiggam dismissed my description of Jacob's presence with a shrug. "What's his name?"

"Jacob Beaufort. Tell him I said he was wrong. Then tell him what you just told me."

"Very well. I'll see what I can do." He bowed again and winked out of existence.

I turned to Mrs. Wiggam. "He's gone."

Her eyes narrowed and her gaze flitted around the drawing room. "Is he coming back?"

"No. Celia?"

My sister rose. We said our farewells to Mrs. Wiggam and

she promised to employ our services again when the house was set to rights.

"That would be delightful," Celia said with an ingratiating smile. It wasn't until we were out of the street altogether that she said, "I sincerely hope we never return there."

I couldn't agree more.

We walked for a while without speaking until we turned into Druids Way. We held onto our bonnets and bent our heads into the breeze.

"You asked Mr. Wiggam's ghost to tell Jacob something up there." She nodded at the sky—it was cloudless for once, the constant haze turning it a faded blue—but neither of us knew where the Waiting Area was actually located. It was as good a place as any I suppose. "What was it?"

I told her about taking our good and bad characteristics with us when we die. We'd arrived at the steps to our house by the time I finished. I looked up, half hoping to see Jacob lounging against the door as he had been on our first meeting. He wasn't.

Celia did something entirely unexpected then. She sat on the top step and patted the spot next to her. "Tell me how he died."

I did, or as much of it as I knew. I held nothing back. By the end of it I was shaking. Celia put her arm around me and rocked me gently. After a while, she said, "This Frederick boy is at the heart of it all."

I nodded. "The person who killed Jacob is most likely connected to him in some way."

"No, I mean he's at the heart of Jacob's guilt and for all we know, that guilt is what's stopping him crossing over. You need to prove to him he's not a bad person. Remind him Frederick's death was accidental and help lift the guilt from his shoulders."

"How do I do that when he won't even speak to me?"

She sighed and squeezed me. "I don't know that part. But I do know you're a clever girl and that we don't yet have all the answers. Find them and then decide what to do."

Sometimes my sister astounds me. She appears so disinterested in deeper matters, matters of the mind and the heart, and yet she can say something so insightful. I tilted my head to rest it against her shoulder.

I only wished she knew what to say to make Jacob come back.

LOOK OUT FOR

Possession

The second EMILY CHAMBERS SPIRIT MEDIUM novel.

Other books by C.J. Archer:

The Medium (Emily Chambers Spirit Medium #1)

Possession (Emily Chambers Spirit Medium #2)

Evermore (Emily Chambers Spirit Medium #3)

Her Secret Desire (Lord Hawkesbury's Players #1)

Scandal's Mistress (Lord Hawkesbury's Players #2)

To Tempt The Devil (Lord Hawkesbury's Players #3)

Honor Bound (The Witchblade Chronicles #1)

Kiss Of Ash (The Witchblade Chronicles #2)

Redemption

Surrender

The Mercenary's Price

ABOUT THE AUTHOR

C.J. Archer has loved history and books for as long as she can remember and feels fortunate that she found a way to combine the two by making up stories. She has at various times worked as a librarian, IT support person and technical writer but in her heart has always been a fiction writer. C.J. spent her early childhood in the dramatic beauty of outback Queensland, Australia, but now lives in suburban Melbourne with her husband and two children.

She has written numerous historical romances for adults. Visit her website www.cjarcher.com for a complete list.

She loves to hear from readers. You can contact her in one of these ways:
Email: cjarcher.writes@gmail.com
Twitter: www.twitter.com/cj_archer
Facebook: www.facebook.com/cjarcher.writes

Made in the USA
Lexington, KY
12 September 2015